THIS
DARK
EARTH

JOHN HORNOR JACOBS

G

GALLERY BOOKS

New York   London   Toronto   Sydney   New Delhi

Gallery Books
A Division of Simon & Schuster, Inc.
1230 Avenue of the Americas
New York, NY 10020

First Gallery Books trade paperback edition July 2012

GALLERY BOOKS and colophon are registered trademarks of Simon & Schuster, Inc.

For information about special discounts for bulk purchases, please contact Simon & Schuster Special Sales at 1-866-506-1949 or business@simonandschuster.com.

The Simon & Schuster Speakers Bureau can bring authors to your live event. For more information or to book an event contact the Simon & Schuster Speakers Bureau at 1-866-248-3049 or visit our website at www.simonspeakers.com.

Designed by Renata Di Biase

Manufactured in the United States of America

10 9 8 7 6 5 4 3 2 1

Library of Congress Cataloging-in-Publication Data

Jacobs, John Hornor.
　This dark earth / John Hornor Jacobs.—1st Gallery Books trade paperback ed.
　　p. cm.
　I. Title.
　PS3610.A356434T45 2012
　813'.6—dc23
                                                              2011050655

ISBN 978-1-4516-6666-3
ISBN 978-1-4516-6667-0 (ebook)

For my whole fam-damily,
especially Kendall, Lily, Helen, and Cookie

The race of man, while sheep in credulity,
are wolves for conformity.

—*Carl van Doren*

I know not with what weapons World War III will be fought,
but World War IV will be fought with sticks and stones.

—*Albert Einstein*

THIS
DARK
EARTH

1

GENESIS

It was a family, once, Lucy saw. And maybe they fit together like puzzle pieces when whole, mother and father pressed together, the boy nestled between them. But now they were broken, a thin gibbering wail coming from the child thrashing on the hospital floor, the mother frantic and pawing at his narrow chest, choking up sobs in great heaves, grappling for his flailing arms, while the father stood helplessly, opening and closing his hands into fists as if wishing for something to fight.

"Help me." It wasn't a scream, but more alarming because of the lowered tone and urgency of the woman. The man dropped to his knees and took the boy's wrists in his big, raw-boned hands. He was a laborer, that was clear, black haired and thick of waist. The boy shared his looks, dark hair, and sturdy build from what Lucy could see beyond the wreckage of the young face.

Lucy stepped closer. The child had swallowed his own lips and was now trying to gnaw off his fingers. She paused to set down her coffee on the nurses' station and then moved toward the grisly trio.

"Cathy!" Lucy bellowed, using her most commanding voice to be heard over the boy's gibbers. She'd been walking past the admittance ward, headed back to the microscope for her morning slides, when she heard the commotion.

"Hold on, damn it," a voice came from behind a partition.

The father grunted, cords standing out on his arms as he gripped the boy's wrists tight to try to keep them away from the lipless, snapping jaws.

Cathy prairie-dogged up, spied Lucy, and ducked back down. Then she appeared around the corner carrying a first-aid kit, a packaged syringe, and a bottle.

The boy's heart hammered away inside his rib cage, pushing tachycardia, and Lucy could feel the heat of his fever even before she touched him. She checked his pulse: 120 bpm or thereabouts. Hard to tell with him jittering in her grasp. He looked to be seven or eight years old, judging by size, strength, and muscle tone.

"I hope that's a sedative you're holding. This kid is out of control, Cath."

Cathy frowned at her, then glanced at the mother and father.

Lucy winced.

The boy whipped his head around, slinging fine blood droplets, and sank his teeth into his father's wrist. The man bellowed like an ox and tried to yank his arm away but only succeeded in pulling the child up from the floor.

Lucy struggled to prize the child's jaws open, but he was latched on like a pit bull.

She turned and ripped the purse from the mother's shoulder.

"What are you doing?" The woman's eyes were wide.

Lucy put one hand on the boy's forehead and shoved his

head down onto the tiles. At the sharp *crack* of impact, his mouth opened, releasing the man's mangled wrist. Lucy stuffed the purse straps into the child's mouth and reflexively he clamped down hard and groaned. Cathy, falling to her knees, sank a needle into his arm. He arched his back, bowing up and off the floor, slobbered and growled through the bit, and then relaxed.

The father slumped to the side, cradling his injured arm. The mother sobbed. Cathy reached out to the child's mother, making comforting sounds.

Lucy stood and looked around. Another mother and child and an elderly couple were staring at her as if she had attacked the boy. As if she was some kind of monster.

This is why I don't do wet work, she thought. *My bedside manner sucks.*

Lucy felt an overwhelming need to leave. She forced herself to wait until Cathy had bandaged the child's hands and done triage on what was left of his lips. Reconstructive surgery was going to work middling at best.

On her way out, Lucy retrieved her coffee. It was still warm.

Lucy loved cancer.

She loved the problems, the puzzles, the mystery of the disease, its pure viciousness and its strange recursive paths and tactics. It was a formidable opponent, and she respected it, in all its myriad forms.

Brushing hair from her face, Lucy leaned over the microscope and placed her eye to the ocular.

Purple foam of dotted circles: renal carcinoma. Black sky strewn with spider-shaped stars: probable sarcoma. A surf of sea-blue histocytes: classic chronic myeloproliferative leukemia—CML for short.

The zebra of the bunch showed bloody aspirate with no bony spicules, looking for all the world like the Cassiopeia constellation. Lucy took her time. She rechecked the chart. Twenty-seven, female, pregnant. The woman had smiled nervously at Lucy during the biopsy despite Lucy's scowl and the needle burrowing into her flesh. She had brown eyes, Lucy remembered, and a little crook to her smile pulling her lip down. Her stomach was just beginning to pooch. She looked nice and maybe in a different world, if Lucy had been a different person, the two of them would have been friends.

But Lucy didn't really have friends. She had a husband, Fred, and a child, Gus. And an electron microscope.

Look at the human body. Break it down into component parts. Skull, mandible, vertebrae snaking down between scapula and clavicle to the pelvis. Wreath that structure in a rich integument of flesh, muscle and sinew, and connective tissue wrapped around delicate, intricate organs that moved vital fluids about the body. *Raise your hand and flex your fingers,* she thought, eye to ocular, *and a million little exchanges within the chemical machine of your body result.* She raised her hand and adjusted the magnification of the microscope. The zebra was puzzling.

The mystery of the body, she thought, and didn't know if she was referring to the human body or the humans themselves. Easier to focus on the puzzles that she could solve, rather than those she couldn't. *Focus*, she thought as she twisted a knob on the microscope, causing a spray of cells in her vision to blossom and calcify.

For an instant, she thought back to the boy from earlier in the morning, spasming on the floor, lips and fingertips eaten away. There was a terrible look on the mother's face, one Lucy didn't think she'd ever seen before in all her years of medicine, and it was a great blank wall to her, beyond her understanding. A family in wreckage . . . Easier to think on the boy's affliction. An ugly reality, to be sure, and puzzling too. What could've caused that behavior? What if that had been Gus?

She leaned back from the microscope's viewfinder and allowed herself a moment to let her eyes rest. To think upon the boy on the floor.

She checked the slide again. The spray of stars showed her things that no astrologer could perceive, and she felt, for just an instant, an intense moment of joy as she discerned the nature of their arrangement, the problem solved. No doubt about it, mature B cell neoplasm. Packed marrow. *Cancer, you old devil, come to visit here again.* Then the realization that always followed, like guilt after masturbation, that the cancerous cells didn't exist solely on a microscope slide. They had been part of a greater whole, once. She'd removed them from a woman. A woman with nice hair, a wedding band, a crooked smile, and a maternity clothing catalogue peeking from her purse.

How do you tell a patient that her child will never be born? Due to her cancer, she'll miscarry far before term?

Delicately.

Which presented a problem for Lucy. For delicacy, she

relied on residents. She was the brain. Let the hands give comfort. Let the mouths speak platitudes, impart the bad news, and soften the blow.

Lucy leaned back and rubbed her eyes.

As she made her notations on the chart of the woman with Burkitt lymphoma, Dr. Robbins poked his head into her office.

"I need you to help us, Lucy. It's all hands on deck," he said, blinking. She winced at the sailing reference. "The waiting room's going mad, just packed to the gills."

Lucy tucked a wild strand of hair behind her ear and said, "So, what else is new?"

"Right. It's always a madhouse. But this is different, Luce. Something strange is going on." He bit his lip, and she thought of the boy again.

"Okay." The rack of samples could wait.

In the hall, Robbins walked with his hands in his pockets, his head bowed.

"So what's up?" Lucy asked. She wasn't used to having to prod Robbins. A pediatrician, he had florid cheeks and, usually, a jovial disposition.

"There's something going on and I think—"

Robbins looked up and Lucy saw concern etched into his face. His clothes were disheveled and his face showed two days' growth of beard. This was SOP, but he usually smiled.

"The stockpile—"

"What about it?"

"Why are we here?" he asked. His voice stayed soft, but she could still hear the stress rippling through him. "We're here because this town grew up around the chemical stockpile.

And the adjacent military base. We're in the poorest county in America, maybe—definitely one of the poorest in Arkansas. With most of its population either in the military or feeding off of it."

Lucy shrugged. "I don't understand what you're talking about, Robby. You're not making sense."

He frowned and squared his shoulders.

"Let's go to the waiting room and I'll show you."

He turned and walked away, shoes clacking on the virulent green tiles, into the wash of light from the window. She jogged to catch up.

She had almost rejoined him when they neared the double doors that served as a barrier between reception, atrium, the waiting room, and the rest of the clinic. Through the metal and plastic of the doors sounded the screaming of adults, the cries of children.

Robbins popped the circular metal button on the wall and the double doors swung open with a hiss.

The noise was deafening. Lucy's step faltered.

People lay strewn everywhere. Mothers huddled in plastic chairs and clutched squalling babes. Old men cursed and scowled. Women cried and children screamed in pain. At least two elderly lay upon the cheap, gum-spotted carpet.

The waiting room was a menagerie of neurological errata and dysfunction. When Lucy was younger, interning in the psychiatric ward of the state hospital, the chief resident had sung "Dysfunction Junction" to the tune of the old Saturday morning cartoon "Conjunction Junction." He would've been howling now.

The receptionists had shut the receiving windows and were hiding in the office, as far as Lucy could tell. Two orderlies grappled with an older man whose arms shook and rippled with muscle tremors as he bellowed curses. Cathy and Melissa, a high-school volunteer, walked through the room, handing out forms to those able to hold them.

Closer to Lucy, a male barked, then grunted. She turned to look.

An elderly man on the floor contorted his back into a painful half-moon, only his head and heels touching the floor. His fists were balled and pressed into his thighs. *Opisthotonus.* Lucy had seen this in textbooks but never in person. Tetanus could bring on such dramatic contortions.

A gray-haired woman sat near the man, looking away from his horrible position. She spoke in a low, urgent voice.

"Shit on me. Crap in my hair. Dogshit. Sucking cock. Cumgargling. Assfuck. Christfuck. Virginwhore. Godquim—"

A boy stood stock still in the center of the room. Every muscle of his body was contracted, locking him into an almost farcical position: one arm out, halfway extended, hand closed and palm up, the other grasping his side. He looked as though he might begin fencing.

A black girl no more than ten thrashed on the floor, spasming and foaming at the mouth. Her hands bled, leaving red curlicues on the carpet. Her mother stood above her, wringing her hands, as the father pressed himself against her in a feeble attempt to smother the spasms. The girl brought red-tipped fingers to her mouth and began to bite.

Whatever that boy had this morning, it's catching.

8

"Please, Doctor. Help my baby, she won't stop crying."

Someone tugged on Lucy's sleeve. She turned to look. A woman with a swaddled babe in her arms. Robbins approached.

"Jesus Christ, Robby." Lucy felt at her pockets, helplessly, as if something there might help her. "Self-ingestion. Self-violence. Spasms and seizures. It's like all of the big weird neurological baddies have manifested themselves in our waiting room."

"Doctor?" The woman's voice was desperate, lost and urgent. "Please help my baby."

She looked at Lucy with wide, clear eyes. The child screamed, a high-pitched ululation, and then stuffed its hand into its mouth.

"Come with me," Lucy said.

With mother and child in tow, Lucy pushed her way through the crowd. As Lucy passed, a tottering old lady flopped to the floor, and each limb began to twitch independently of the others, as if the woman's body had suffered a schizophrenic break.

Choreoathetosis, Lucy noted. *Another one.*

They ducked into a waiting room. Robbins locked the door and led the woman to a cushioned examination table. She set her child down and removed the blanket.

"What's her name?" Robbins asked softly.

"Deborah. We call her Deb."

"Age?"

"Six months."

"What's wrong with her? Fever? Crying?"

The woman nodded.

Robby said, "What made you bring her in?"

"She was shaking. She started crying and her legs and arms just started to . . . I don't know . . . vibrate."

"She cough or choke?"

"Coughed, maybe. I think." She was a short woman, heavyset like most of the folk around White Hall, with originally brown hair done up into a confectioner's mess, bleached and highlighted. She had French nails with designs applied to them and cheap jewelry, two rings, a necklace, and large, tacky earrings. Tears welled at the corners of her eyes and she wiped them away, smearing mascara. "I don't know. She spat up her milk." Her hands shook and she rubbed her face. Not much sleep recently. "What is going on? Why is everyone out there?"

"I don't know," Lucy said. "But I intend to find out what's wrong with your baby."

The mother showed her teeth to Lucy. Lucy realized it was the woman's attempt at a smile.

She peeled away the child's clothes and diaper.

With the baby nude, pink, and splayed upon the paper-wrapped examination table, Lucy felt a twinge of nostalgia for Gus at that age. When he was just a baby, she felt such love suffusing her, she found herself speechless when she held him. And she was content to stay in that speechless state beyond thought or reason. Just pure emotion. But as he grew and took his first steps, his first stabs at speech and then abstract ideas, she had such problems with his ignorance that, to her shame, she let Fred commandeer the child's upbringing. After all, she was the breadwinner. Why not have Fred raise Gus?

Without Fred, she'd have been lost. He guided both her and Gus through those rough waters.

This child was wonderfully plump and apparently healthy, despite being flushed with fever. She had a thick head of amber hair and blue eyes, now narrowed in pain. Her tiny fists waved in the air, angry.

Lucy pulled the diaper tabs to examine the child's genitalia and take her temperature.

"Hold the phone." She held up the diaper, heavy and wet. "Robby. You see this?"

"What is it?"

Turning, Lucy moved the diaper into the light.

"Her urine looks orange."

Robbins washed his hands in the examination room sink, rubbed them with antibacterial foam, and then listened to the baby's heart and took her pulse.

"Tachycardia. One hundred and thirty beats per minute. And rising. She's a hummingbird."

Lucy turned to the mother—her hand covering her mouth in disbelief or pure horror, Lucy couldn't tell.

"Robby, you going be okay here? I've got to take this to the lab. No infant gets gout."

Robbins nodded absentmindedly and continued examining the infant.

A crash rattled the frosted-glass window. Booming male voices sounded from the waiting room. Then screams.

"Robby, lock the door behind me, okay?"

"Will do." He didn't look up from the child.

Lucy removed the white doctor's coat and unpinned her long brown hair. She wrapped the diaper into a ball and reconnected the tabs, saying, "I hope you have another one." Immediately afterward she realized how that must sound and hoped the mother knew she meant another diaper, not another child.

Maybe that's just the way my fucked-up mind works.

The woman gave a pained nod.

Lucy opened the door as quickly as she could and stepped out into bedlam.

"Oh, shit," she whispered to no one.

The older man who'd suffered the spine-cracking episode of opisthotonus lay unbowed. But the boy still stood in the fencing position, and it looked as if the girl who'd been thrashing about on the floor had chewed off her lips. Cathy mopped at the child's face with cotton, a bottle of antiseptic clutched in the opposite fist. Dr. Patel leaned over her, injecting something—most likely benzodiazepine—into the girl's arm.

Lucy moved across the room to the contortionist. The woman sitting near him continued to curse, staring unblinking at the plastic ficus tree in the corner.

Lucy knelt and searched for a pulse. The loose skin of his neck made it hard to find. It was weak and fluttery. She opened his eyelids.

Pupils nonresponsive.

Turning his head, she noticed an orange smear on the man's earlobe. Without anything to take a sample with, she reached into her pocket and found her house keys. She dug into the man's ear, scraping away some of the orange substance.

"What're you doing, *bitch*?" A deep voice, close, behind her.

Lucy turned. Another elderly man stood over her. Liver spots ran up his arms and disappeared into the sleeves of a plaid shirt. He had the look of a withered eagle chick, bulbous head with wispy white hair perched precariously atop a thin, wattled neck. He was rangy and lean, if doddering, with oversized joints due either to arthritis or to unfortunate genetics. His lips drew back from dentures; his hands were balled into knobby, furious fists.

This isn't going to go well.

Still crouching, Lucy lurched forward, putting her shoulder into the man's groin. Knocked off balance, he howled and fell down hard on his ass. His hands jittered.

"Cunt! Rip your tits off!" His body shuddered and then he emitted a strange sound. *"Eurppp!"*

She rose, leaping forward, and dashed to the pneumatic doors.

She swiped her key card across the sensor plate, waited breathlessly while the doors swung open, and sprinted through.

In her office, she locked the door and felt intense relief that there were no glass windows, frosted or otherwise, in her workspace. Just a solid-core door with the placard Pathology to its right.

She set the diaper and her keys down next to the microscope. Hastily, she popped open a case of slides and, taking a swab from a glass container, began preparing them. No time to formalin fix the specimens.

She slipped the infant's specimen into the scope, centered it in the viewfinder, and adjusted the ocular and focus.

Bright orange crystals filled her vision, like an airburst over a crowd on the Fourth of July. An explosion of light and color.

Hyperuricemia. Too much urea for the body to handle. She's sloughing off the excess through her urine.

She prepared another slide, this time from the old man's sample on her keys.

Another bright explosion of color against her retina. A field of orange crystals.

Urea coming from his ears? That's bizarre.

She turned to the computer, to the diagnostic database, and placed her cursor in the search form field.

She thought for a moment, then began to type.

Hyperuricemia, for the uric residue in the diaper and around the ears. *Coprolalia*, for the involuntary cursing. *Choreoathetosis*, for the spastic movements. *Opisthotonus*, for the spine-cracker. *Dystonia*, for the boy in the fencing position.

She jabbed at the return key. The search results filtered onto her screen.

Three hits: progressive supranuclear palsy, drug-induced acute dystonia reaction, or Lesch-Nyhan syndrome.

What the hell is Lesch-Nyhan syndrome? I've never heard of it.

She clicked through, and, as she read, her stomach began to twist and ball into a painful knot. She turned, dug through her purse, and found a flat package of Marlboro Lights. A secret shame, smoking. She knew if her colleagues found out, she'd be ridden about it for months. She fished out a cigarette and lit it with a match from a book tucked into the pack's cellophane.

Lucy took her time, drawing the hot cigarette smoke into her lungs and expelling it toward the ceiling in a blue cloud as she reread everything. The nicotine calmed her. She'd be good for the next few hours or so. And now, knowing what she did, it might be a long time before she'd get another smoke.

When she was through, she dropped the cigarette to the tile floor and ground it out.

She wiped off her house keys and pushed them deep into her pocket.

Then she turned to the cabinets and rifled through them. She withdrew swabs, ethyl alcohol. She found gauze and tape and cotton and swept them all into her purse. She considered trying to break into the drug storage but realized she'd need a chainsaw to get through the door. No drugs. She'd have to make do.

With her purse full, she slung it over her shoulder and then opened the drawer holding her needle gun. The big one for aspirating tissue. She took the package of extra needles, placed them in her purse, and held the gun by the handle, form fitted to her hand. She held a five-inch sliver of steel in her fist that could easily be used in self-defense.

She turned and headed back to Robbins.

The waiting room was quieter now, which made Lucy nervous.

The woman had stopped cursing and the belligerent old

coot who'd called her a cunt was nowhere to be seen. Cathy and Melissa handed out bottles of water. A woman nursed her baby, frowning.

The man who'd suffered from opisthotonus was still on the floor.

Lucy went to him and knelt. His lips were gone, along with his fingertips. He must've come to while she'd been in Pathology and begun eating himself. She shivered.

Okay. Today is officially fucked up.

She felt for a pulse. None. His eyes stared unblinking at the buzzing fluorescent tube above.

"Cathy!" The nurse looked up and trotted over on white, cushy shoes. She knelt beside Lucy, smelling of Mentholatum.

"This man is dead, Cath."

Cathy covered her mouth with a trembling hand. "Oh, no. This is—"

"Listen to me, will you? Just listen." She cleared her throat. "I'm not exactly sure, but I've analyzed some samples from this man and an infant, and I think they both have the same thing. There's no way for me to be absolutely positive without a genetic test, but that isn't going to happen in the next couple of hours. I need you to lock the entrance doors—now. Send someone to check the other exits."

"What? Lock the doors?"

"Yes. Lock them. This might get worse; it looks infectious, and we've got to take care of the people here. If I'm right—"

"Right about what?"

Lucy wanted another cigarette. "I don't know yet," she said. "But clearly, it's infectious, and those that—" She thought about the withered geezer who called her a cunt. "Those that contract it are dangerous. We've got to go on lockdown."

Cathy put her hand to her mouth again, as if to stifle some exclamation. She had soft white palms and each plump finger ended in a pink, shiny nail. Kind hands. A healer's hands.

"Just do it, will you? Lock the doors." She stopped. Tried to smile. Failed, maybe. Maybe not.

The nurse nodded. "Okay."

Lucy stood and walked to the examination room. As she entered, she saw the mother huddled in the corner, crying. Robbins sat in a plastic chair with an unfocused look. He stared up at the fluorescent lights, pushing his lips in and out while rubbing his chin. The baby lay on the table, unmoving, tinged blue gray.

"Oh no."

The mother drew her knees to her chin and moaned.

"My baby. My baby . . ."

Lucy set down the tissue-aspirating needle and seated herself on the physician's stool in front of Robbins.

"Robby," she said in a low voice. "Whatever this is . . . It's totally bizarre. I analyzed the orange crystals from . . ." Lucy glanced at the mother.

He wasn't listening. Lucy touched his knee; he blinked and looked at her.

"This is not a good situation, Luce." He tilted his head at the woman grieving for her child.

"What these people have could be Lesch-Nyhan syndrome. It's very rare and triggers on the Y chromosome."

"Lesch-Nyhan? I've . . . that sounds familiar. But it's almost unheard of. And . . . let's see . . ." His eyes unfocused as he looked at the wall, his gaze moving back and forth between two invisible points, searching. "It only occurs prenatally."

"Yes. Caused by a deficiency of hypoxanthine-guanine phosphoribosyltransferase activity. An inborn error of purine metabolism associated with uric acid overproduction and a continuum spectrum of neurological manifestations depending on the degree of the enzymatic deficiency." Almost like being in med school again, the recitation of symptoms. She'd always been strong in school.

She took a long breath, opened her eyes, and looked at Robby, ticking off symptoms on her fingers. "Lithiasis and gout. Neurological manifestations, including severe action dystonia, choreoathetosis, ballismus, cognitive and attention deficit, and self-injurious behavior—everything we've witnessed. All you've got to do is peek out in the waiting room to see it all. But what I can't figure out is *why*. Or how." She balled her hand into a fist and ground it into her thigh. Lucy felt infected by the mystery of the thing. It was a puzzle, and it needed to be solved.

"Wait. Did you say Y chromosome? Then . . . then how could this child have had it? She was female."

Hearing the past-tense usage, the mother wailed again and began pulling her hair and shaking her head. Robbins winced at the sound. Lucy found it hard to concentrate, and for a moment, despite full knowledge of the woman's terrible loss, Lucy just wished she'd shut up so she could think. So she could figure out the problem. Followed swiftly by an intense flush of shame for feeling that way.

"Do you have anything for her, Robby? The mother?"

Sedatives.

"No. These examination rooms are bare. And it can't be Lesch-Nyhan. That only occurs in boys."

Lucy shook her head, irritated. She threw up her hands and said, "Shit. I don't know."

"I've read about knockout gene therapy where you can take a viral vector, like adenovirus, and carry a 'suicide gene' to a target, render it inert, and induce a disease."

"You're talking biological warfare." She looked around for a moment, helpless, and stuck her hands into her pockets. "How could this have happened? There's got to be a more rational explanation for this."

"You're right. It's too much. It's science fiction. And the government wouldn't ever be that careless—"

Lucy snorted. "I never would've pegged you for a romantic, but sure as shit . . ." She felt horrible about saying it the second it came out of her mouth. In a constant state of abrasion, chapping asses, and rubbing people the wrong way. For a moment, Lucy recalled her exit interview at Baptist Hospital in Little Rock. The head pathologist, neatly ensconced behind his massive desk, had raised his meaty hands like a priest at benediction, looked at her sadly, and simply stated, *We'd like you to start pursuing other opportunities. You're just not a good fit here, Lucy. We need someone who plays well with others.* She had stood and kicked away her chair, slamming a fist down onto his desk. He had jumped and leaned away from her. *I'm a scientist, Jerry. Not a goddamned kindergartener. You can fuck right off.* She regretted the last bit, for truth, but very little else about her stint there.

She sighed, at her past failures or for the looming mystery

of whatever this disease was, she couldn't say. "We can't know its origin. The fact we're right next to a chemical stockpile just clouds the issue. It could be from anywhere and already moving into pandemic stage. No way to tell. But what does it matter? It's happening. And we have to find out what it is and how to treat it."

"Lucy. Luce. Hold on a second. Listen to what you've just said. There's a biological agent loose. We've got to go. This place is going to get very ugly, very soon."

"Leave? We have to treat these people. We have to solve this—"

"Shoot 'em full of sedatives. Then we run. The children with Lesch-Nyhan need restraints all their life. Most of these folks are adults. It's quiet now, but it's about to be a psychopath's wet dream out there." He moved to the door. She was actually startled when he put his ear to the glass to listen. "And I need to get home to Rachel. To my girls."

From the corner of her eye, Lucy noticed a motion on the table. She turned and gaped. The infant moved sluggishly.

"Robby. The baby."

The mother pushed herself into a standing position, using the wall as a brace.

"Deb!" She lunged forward and huddled over the infant, tears falling on blue skin.

"Mrs. . . ." Lucy realized she didn't know the woman's name. "Please let me examine your baby."

The baby waved her arms, opening and closing her mouth. In death, or what had seemed to be death, her eyes had glazed over, but they focused on the woman now.

"My baby isn't dead. But so cold—"

"Ma'am, please."

Robby whispered, "You witnessed the tachycardia. Her heart gave out. I watched it happen. This child was dead."

The infant squirmed and the mother gave her her hand in comfort. The baby grabbed the proffered finger and stuffed it into her mouth.

The mother said, "She's teething. It's really been hurting her lately. Rubbing her gums helps."

"What's your name, honey?" Lucy asked, remembering Cathy with the mother this morning.

For a moment she looked as if she didn't know herself. "Martha."

"Martha, make room. Please. I need to examine Deb."

Lucy turned, began to snatch for Robbins's stethoscope, then stopped herself and pointed at the device hanging from his neck. He blinked, then gave it to her. Lucy pressed it to the infant's chest and listened for a heartbeat. Nothing. She pulled back the blankets covering the infant's legs, grabbed the thermometer, and took the child's temperature anally. The baby didn't flinch.

Eighty-five degrees Fahrenheit. And dropping. Like a cooling corpse.

Yet the infant moved.

Martha winced and pulled her hand from the child's mouth. Blood crowned the tip of her finger and beaded down the side in a long rivulet. It made a soft *pat-pat* sound as it dripped to paper on the table. The baby half screamed, half moaned.

Lucy turned to Robbins. "What is going on here, Robby? This goes way beyond biological warfare."

He shook his head. "I have no fucking clue."

"This child is dead."

Martha frowned at Lucy but remained silent. She glanced at the blood-smeared mouth of her child.

A thump sounded as something heavy hit the door. The frosted-glass window cracked.

Robby said, "It's time to get out of here, Luce."

"Hold on a moment. I want to take some blood and another crystal sample. See here? She's got it in her ears as well as her diaper, which means—"

Something slammed into the door again, and the window went white with small fractures. Another blow and it would be gone.

Lucy removed a Vacutainer for drawing blood from its wrapper and moved to the examination room's cabinets to get alcohol and a swab.

"Luce. This is absurd."

She ignored him. *It's an infant, so I should use a finger stick, but . . . Christ, the thing has no pulse! I have to use the Vacutainer.*

"Lucy."

The child seemed even cooler when she swabbed the crook of her arm with the alcohol-soaked cotton. As she placed the needle close to the child's skin, Robby said, "Goddamn it, Lucy. Wake up!"

He grabbed her shoulder and spun her around.

"Martha, get your child," Robby said, shifting his gaze

away from Lucy for just an instant and then turning back to her. "Enough, Luce. It's time to start thinking bigger."

Martha moved to the table and gently reswaddled her girl. Hands trembling, she kissed the baby's gray head.

"Bigger?"

"It's contagious, that much is certain, whatever this is. We've got to think about our families."

"Call Rachel."

Robby dug a cell phone from his pocket and dialed. Lucy watched him as he listened. Eventually, he shook his head and his expression grew even more grim. "'Network busy,'" he said.

"So we still don't know anything."

A scream came from outside the door, a scream beyond anything she'd ever heard. The sound was half rage, half pain, like some pig sent to the slaughter, still alive before having the skin stripped from it. It was a sound that defied education, went beyond learning, and affected her on a physiological level. Her skin prickled, her muscles tensed. She was watching Robby when the sound came. Lucy noted his pupils dilating, marked his increase in breathing and the flushed quality of his skin. Heart rate up, increased blood flow. His body was preparing to fight. Or flee. Once again, it struck her as strange how her mind could still switch to the analytical, even in the worst situations.

She looked down at her hands, the Vacutainer and cotton-swab now looking so helpless and feeble against the mounting tide of mysteries, of questions she'd never be able answer, puzzles she'd never be able to solve.

"Okay." She shook her head, half to clear it, half to come to grips with what was going to come next. She took a deep breath and said, "You're right. We have to go."

Robby gave a little manic laugh. The stress was visible in his posture, his expression. "I realize how hard that is for you to admit, Luce. So I won't rub it in. How do you want to do this?"

Lucy grabbed her needle gun. She raised an eyebrow at Robby. "I say we go out the back way near the employee parking lot."

Robbins checked his pockets. He pulled out his keys.

From the waiting room, a sound of shattering glass reverberated through the building. The door rattled in its frame. Martha whimpered and pressed Deb close to her chest.

"Okay." Lucy held up the big needle for aspirating tissue and looked at her companions. "Quickly, right? You ready?" At Robby's nod and Martha's terrified blinking, Lucy jerked open the door and stepped into the waiting room.

The contortionist stood, swaying, in front of her. Blood dripped from his lower lip, and he turned dull, milky eyes toward Lucy. He took a step forward, raising his arms.

"Go! Go!" she yelled. Robbins and Martha dashed behind her, moving toward the automatic doors.

Attention fixed on Lucy, the contortionist let the others pass. Lurching forward, he grabbed her arms, opened his mouth, and tilted his head as if to bite her face.

This is not *happening.*

She twisted in his grasp, but the man drew her closer with astonishingly strong hands. His mouth gaped.

Oh no, you don't.

She was surprised at her own strength. She wrenched herself away and stepped back to get more space. Then, as if she was throwing a punch, she dipped her knees, flexed, and shot her fist outward, toward his face. He didn't flinch or dodge.

It's as if he's lost all reflex . . . All his autonomic functions are suppressed. Nonexistent, maybe.

The needle went through his eye, into the brain, more easily than she thought possible. The haft popped the sclera and crushed the vitreous fluid from the eyeball. The needle jutted from the ocular cavity. The contortionist fell backward, pawing at the handle of the needle. He flopped to the floor, squirmed, then stilled.

How horrible, to die twice in a single day.

Looking beyond him, Lucy saw the waiting room had turned bloody during her palaver with Robbins and Martha. The foul-mouthed old lady with the religious bent shuffled slowly past the fake ficus and turned toward Lucy. Again, milky eyes glared at her. Lucy couldn't pin it down exactly, but there didn't seem to be any awareness in those eyes. It was as if some deep-sea creature felt eddies and currents spun off a passing fish and moved to attack, working on pure instinct.

She can smell, maybe. Hear sound or feel the vibrations of air. The eyes don't move in the sockets, they don't track. But she knows I'm here. The glassiness would occlude sight somewhat. If she can see me, I'm very blurry.

The woman lurched forward. Her legs and arms seemed to tremor still.

For a moment, Lucy stood paralyzed. The sight of the woman, half of her face missing and the entirety of her front covered in blood, locked her in place.

"Lucy!" Robbins's voice came from her left. "The doors are open. Come on."

Everything happened at once. The clinic's front door exploded inward, billowing smoke. The explosion knocked Lucy sideways, toward Robbins and Martha. Her head smacked against the wall and the world went white and then tilted horribly as she fell.

When she sat up, men in black military garb poured through the husk of doorway, wearing masks that obscured their faces, their weapons raised. Lucy made herself move. Pushing at the floor with her hands, she scrambled to her feet, head spinning, and threw herself after Robbins. The back doors began to close just as she passed through.

Behind her, a cacophony of gunfire ripped through the smoke, and she felt more than sensed the hard motes of bullets filling the air around her. Something spun off Lucy's skull, and she pitched forward onto the tile floor.

The doors behind her closed seconds after she saw the soldiers begin shooting people in the waiting room, but not before she saw one of the patients lurch toward a figure in black, knock his gun aside, and drag him to the floor. Bullets ripped through the bloody old woman, yet she didn't fall. She lurched and turned toward her attacker.

It wasn't until bullets began ripping through the door that Lucy forced herself up again. The screams grew louder, the gunfire wilder and more frantic.

Tracers swam in the corners of her vision, and she found her body responding sluggishly to her own commands.

Robbins and Martha had already disappeared down the hall, and Lucy nearly bowled over Martha as she rounded the corner. The woman, shell-shocked and stunned, stared down at the floor. Robbins lay on his side, clutching his calf with both hands, trying to stem the flow of blood.

"They shot me." He looked at Lucy, eyes wide and bulging, and then laughed. "They shot me! I'm a doctor, for chrissake!"

Lucy knelt and looked at him closer, puzzled by the crimson that spotted his shirt.

"Are you hit in the chest?"

"No." He nodded at her hair. "Looks like they got you too."

She touched her scalp. A long, wet furrow traced the left side of her skull. It throbbed, and suddenly, Lucy became aware of the pain.

She reached for his belt.

"Hey!"

She laughed, maybe a little too wildly.

"Robby, I'm not gonna rape you right here." She unbuckled the belt and ripped it from his pants. "I'll wait till later."

After tying off his calf, she helped him up. Down the hall, the gunfire continued in spurts.

"We've got to get out of here. There's an emergency exit at the end of this hall. We'll have to cross the picnic area to get to our cars. You still have your keys, Robby?"

He nodded, wide-eyed. Martha cradled the infant, cooing

softly. Lucy noticed the bundle jerked and shifted in the woman's grip.

Lucy wiped her hands on her skirt, suddenly glad of her running shoes.

"Good. Remote key ring. Keep pressing the unlock button. You still drive the Suburban? Big monster?"

He nodded.

"Great. Let's go."

The gunfire died and the clinic was silent except for the bright sound of falling glass. In the distance, beyond the walls, a high-pitched scream sounded, rising and falling. Sirens.

"Shit. Whatever has gone wrong, it's not just here." Lucy's mouth felt dry and she shivered. "I've got to get home. Gus, Fred. They'll need me."

Martha sobbed and shifted the bundle on her chest. Robbins tottered, and Lucy grabbed him and threw his arm over her shoulder.

They moved down the hall, Robbins's leg trailing a thin ribbon of blood, until they reached the emergency door. Looking through the window, Lucy couldn't see anybody—military or otherwise—so she pushed it open and waved them out.

They moved haltingly across the lawn, toward the parking lot. Air sirens shrieked, and Lucy heard the deep rumble of vehicles, though she couldn't determine their directions.

It was mid-July; sweat prickled her temples and spotted her shirt. She looked at Robbins, who seemed to be holding up well. She'd have to check his wound once they'd reached somewhere safe.

Martha walked away from Lucy and Robbins.

Lucy stopped. "Martha, where are you—"

"I've got family of my own. My little sister. Now that Deb is okay—"

"Martha. Look. We'll take you. You might need our help."

The woman holding the bundle swayed and passed her free hand across her forehead. Then she looked at Robbins and frowned. Her expression was clear—she didn't think he'd do much to improve the situation.

Lucy raised her voice. "Damn it, woman, we're both doctors. Come with us. It'll be safer. Everyone's going crazy! Do you want to be alone?"

As if to punctuate her words, a fusillade of gunfire came from inside the clinic. Then, a rumbling grew and grew until Martha winced and Lucy raised her hands to her ears. A gigantic low-flying plane appeared above the tree line, its massive props buzzing the air in near subsonic frequencies. It passed overhead, frighteningly close—so close Lucy could see the open side door of the plane, the men there with headphones on, and more behind them in shadow, pointing and yelling silently, their voices blanketed by the noise of the props cutting the air. Dull gunmetal glinted in the sunlight and the open mouths of large-bore weapons swiveled, searching for a target.

The massive sound made Lucy stagger; it rattled her skeleton and vibrated her flesh. Robbins moaned. From beyond the clinic, two black specks rose into view and the sound buffeting them took on a rhythmic, percussive pulse. Helicopters, angular and heavy.

Martha looked around wildly.

"Come with us. We'll help you."

Martha nodded and shifted the swaddled infant in her arms.

Another DC-10 rumbled across the sky. Beyond it, two jets shrieked through the blue, leaving contrails.

"Holy shit."

Lucy jerked Robbins forward, nearly knocking him off his feet. "Press the goddamned button, Robby!"

A vehicle chirped. They scrambled across blacktop. At the SUV, Lucy yanked open the back door and shoved Robbins into the seat. Martha hobbled up behind.

"Gimme the keys." Lucy opened the driver's door. Robbins dangled the key ring over the seat. She snatched them out of his hand and tossed him her purse. "Get me my phone and then patch yourself up."

She cranked the ignition, and the Suburban roared to life. Lucy slammed it into gear and peeled away, turning the wheel hard.

The Suburban's chassis shuddered as a tire hit a curb. Through the roof, Lucy felt the vibration of helicopters passing overhead.

The Suburban barreled around the side of the clinic past the patient parking area, toward the front of the building, passing near a dull green army vehicle—Lucy didn't know what kind, but it looked armored and sat in front of the smoking front doors of the clinic.

Lucy slowed. Military men and patients milled on the pavement under the awning, some in the mulch beds to either side of it.

She stopped the car.

"Wait just a second, guys."

She opened the door and it dinged a tinny warning. She ran around the front of the Suburban, toward the clinic's entryway. The people looked disheveled. Dazed. Bloody.

Her feet crunched on glass. They turned to face her.

Lucy gasped and stepped backward.

One of the soldiers staggered forward, guts spooling out of his stomach and dragging on the ground. A girl, the one who'd bitten off her fingertips and lips, was now missing her pelvis and legs. The child pulled herself over the threshold of the clinic and onto the concrete walkway with raw, stripped fingers. An elderly man's head tilted over dramatically where a bullet had blown out his neck, exposing sinew and gristle.

A toddler stepped forward, apparently whole except for bite marks on his arms.

Lucy's stomach lurched. All were dead. Despite reason, despite her training, she knew this with certainty.

These people were dead.

More came from the building, slowly, onto the walkway and into the sunlight. Walking corpses.

Milky white eyes held her in an intense, unfocused gaze.

They came for her, moaning.

She turned and ran to the Suburban. The creatures followed.

A helicopter, wreathed in deafening sound, passed over again and swung its tail about, presenting the clinic with its profile. Lucy glimpsed a man behind a mass of gray metal. Despite the din of rotors, she heard a *brrrrrppp*, like a great

31

mechanical belch, and the awning and front of the clinic disappeared in a quickly expanding billow of smoke seeded with bits of cloth, spatters of blood, and small chunks of brick and cement.

Lucy threw herself into the SUV. Bullets chewed the walkway. One of the dead vanished in a mist of blood.

She blindly cranked the vehicle into gear and jammed her foot to the accelerator. They shot forward, careened around the median, and sideswiped a poorly parked sedan. The passenger window turned white with a web of cracks.

The wheels screeched as she accelerated onto the highway. The Suburban tilted sideways on the turn, and Lucy feared they would topple. But it rocked back down on its shocks. In front of her, the road was empty and the interstate overpass fast approached. Semis and automobiles whizzed along Highway 65. Some slowed, most likely to gape at the helicopters. She mashed the accelerator to the floor.

A myriad of tiny geysers, puffs of smoke, and asphalt ejecta traced a path toward the Suburban.

"They're shooting at us!" Robbins's voice pitched toward hysterical.

Holes appeared in the hood with a sharp *thunk*. Shafts of sunlight, like columns sprouting in a line down the roof, fell into the cabin of the vehicle. Robbins barked a garbled noise of surprise. Lucy looked down at the floorboard and saw, through a smoking half-inch hole, pavement whizzing by underneath in a blur. The engine coughed and began to whine.

Lucy craned her neck to look at Robbins and Martha and the child—the child! Martha clutched her bundle tight to her chest and peered behind them, out the back window, as smoking bullet craters streaked in a dotted, quick path away from the SUV. The thunder of helicopter rotor blades diminished, and Lucy turned back to the wheel.

The Suburban coughed again and slowed dramatically. Then sputtered. Something in the engine whined even louder, caught, then jerked forward with renewed acceleration. Lucy was at a loss to even begin to know what might be damaged.

She grimaced at the irony: she knew the most intimate functions of the human body, but a combustion engine was a mystery to her. She stomped the accelerator, and the vehicle jumped forward. The beast still had some life yet.

She spied a truck swerving into the oncoming lane. Again, the beat of rotors grew audible. The helicopter completed its turn and began another pass. The oncoming driver plunged his vehicle off the road and into the crusty bare lot adjacent to the interstate, the truck bottoming out with a shower of sparks, bouncing up and then flipping into the air, as graceful as a gymnast, before hitting the ground and smashing into a wretched pretzel of steel and smoke.

The SUV's engine sputtered again, tossing Lucy forward, and then caught once more, accelerating. The interstate was close now.

Gunfire exploded in front of the car and Lucy wrenched the wheel to the right, nearly bouncing them off the road.

The Suburban heeled the curb and then dashed into shadow underneath the overpass. They jumped the curb and bounced up the concrete slope where the interstate met its supporting struts. Lucy mashed the brakes, and the SUV slewed to a stop—but not before the roof hit an I-beam strut high up the slope, just beneath where cars passed overhead.

The roof crumpled.

Martha screamed.

Lucy had seen television shows in which people took refuge from tornadoes in this same space. It had to be better than open road against an armed warship.

"What the—" Robbins spluttered. "What the fuck is happening? It's just . . . it's absurd." He fumbled at his waist and withdrew a phone. He flipped it open and peered into its face.

Lucy reached between the seats and grabbed her purse. She turned to Martha.

"Get out! We've got to get out of the car! If they can, they'll blast this thing into vapor." She pointed to the other side of the overpass's belly, the shadowy area where the bridge began. There were spaces between the I-beams where they could hide and it was doubtful that even the helicopter fire could penetrate the three-inch steel of the struts supporting the overpass. "There. Go there!"

Martha sat still. Little tremors passed through her body and she looked at Lucy with wide, frightened eyes.

"Go now! We don't know how much time we have!"

Lucy jumped out of the Suburban and wrenched open the back door. Martha spilled out, nearly dropping the bundle at her chest. Lucy peered into the car. Robbins blinked owlishly with a dazed look, muttering to himself, trying to make a call.

"No signal. How can there not be a signal? This plan is nationwide—"

"Robbins! Forget the fucking advertisement! We've got to go!"

He looked around, eyes fastening on Lucy. He slumped, almost imperceptibly, as if having his own private apocalypse. Painfully working his ass out of the SUV, he flopped forward, and Lucy caught him as he fell from the vehicle.

Martha had already made it halfway to the other side. Lucy grabbed Robbins's hand and pulled him down the slope.

Unbearably loud now, the helicopters rumbled past, blowing hard gusts of wind under the bridge. Deafened by the helicopter, Lucy couldn't hear any more cars or semis buzzing above them on the interstate. The sound became an absolutely monstrous sheet over her. It was hard for Lucy to even form a thought under its onslaught.

Lucy grabbed Martha's arm to help her across the highway. She could feel the woman's muscles twitch and spasm under her grip. The swaddled blanket shifted in Martha's arms.

She glanced back and saw Robby slowly making his way down. Lucy released Martha and turned to help him but before she could move, an enormous wind hit her with the force of a hurricane, knocking her down and wreathing her in a deafening blankness. Within the din, she perceived another *bbrrrrppp* and the Suburban turned itself inside out, the twisting and screaming of metal piercing the thick, thunderous air. Robbins jittered and disappeared into a red mist that hung, particulate and thick, in the air.

Grabbing Martha's hand, Lucy turned and sprinted across the remaining highway and up the opposing slope, dragging the woman behind her, toward the shelter near the top. She heard another *bbrrrrpppp* and sensed the bullets howling through the air, but all she felt was a stinging sensation on the backs of her legs. Powdered concrete blew past her. She crouched in the dark recess of the overpass, where slope met supports.

"We'll be safe here," she said, almost to herself, as the machines' noise diminished gradually.

Martha grunted. Lucy turned to look at the woman.

Her face was pale, and her cheek, just below the eye, twitched. Her arms spasmed slightly. Lucy reached over to touch Martha's face, to test for fever, but the wild-eyed look the other woman gave her made Lucy pause and withdraw her hand.

Suddenly, the sound of the helicopter returned, overwhelming and vast. A hot wind blew through the space below I-40 and Lucy worried that the warship was now disgorging soldiers to root them out of their hiding spot. She peeked around the girder.

Hanging in air, fifteen or twenty feet above the ground, was the chopper. The black gunmetal of its carapace glinted evilly in the sunlight beyond the shelter of the overpass. The pilot, visible even through the tint and glare of the helicopter windshield, looked vaguely insectile in mirrored goggles, green helmet, and sound-suppressing headphones as he surveyed the space underneath the bridge. As the chopper rotated, presenting its side, the gun swept into view.

The pilot put a hand up to his ear, listening to something, and nodded. Suddenly the helicopter rose and the deafening roar of the rotors died away to a buzz and then faded completely.

"Holy shit," breathed Lucy. She sank back against the

concrete slope and for long moments just let her heart hammer away at her chest.

A thought struck her and she sat upright.

"Why did they leave?" She turned to Martha. "Why would they leave us here? They had us trapped. I've got . . . oh no. Robby."

Pushing herself to her feet, she dusted off her hands and walked swiftly down the slope toward the road, where the remains of the Suburban had blown.

Martha screamed.

The sound held no words, only garbled phrases. Martha flipped backward, tendons standing out on her neck, and her head hit the ground with a meaty *thunk*. She arched her back, balling her fists on her thighs. She continued to bend, and cracks sounded from her spine.

Opisthotonus.

Martha had it, whatever it was. Whatever turned the clinic into a slaughterhouse. Whatever brought the dead back from the grave.

The infant spilled to the ground and rolled down the slope, unwrapping. It stopped at Lucy's feet.

Lucy looked down. The baby's hue wasn't too different from the concrete's. With small, chubby hands, it pulled itself toward Lucy, looking at her with those same milky eyes. It emitted a sound a crushed kitten might make, mewling.

The sirens began screaming once she reached the blacktop of the interstate. The road had become as dead as the clinic, almost. It was long minutes before any vehicle appeared. She could see a rising forest of smoke plumes coming from the south where she knew there to be a small residential area.

The trucker who picked her up was a brawny, thick man, bristly and unkempt. The cab smelled of cigarettes, energy drink, and corn chips. But the fecund normalcy of the man almost made Lucy want to cry.

"Shit, you're bleeding." He nodded at her head.

She touched the wound with delicate fingers. It didn't hurt too much.

"There's a first-aid kit in there." He pointed at the cab's oversize glove box. She popped the clasp and withdrew a white and blue box with a red cross stenciled on the top. Opening the box, she took some gauze, twisted the top off the bottle of hydrogen peroxide, doused the soft white material, and wiped the side of her head. It streaked with brown.

"What's going on? There was a pileup back there, a couple of miles back. People stumbling around all bloody. After I passed through, looked like the cops were barricading the interstate." He shrugged and added, "CB and radio's out too."

She pointed to the roof.

"Hear that?"

He looked at her, puzzled. Then his eyes narrowed. "Yeah. Sirens."

"Something has happened."

"What?"

"An outbreak. A virus. It does strange stuff. It—" She shook her head. "How fast can this thing go? We've got to get out of the area."

"I guess I can get her up around ninety, maybe. Hundred going downhill. But she eats up too much gas that way."

"If you don't step on it, gas will be the last of our worries."

"Hold on, ma'am. I can't just start speeding 'cause you say so. I own this truck. She's all I got. Pay for the gas too. And filling her up is expensive."

He shook a cigarette out of a pack and lit it with a steel Zippo with a skull and crossbones raised on the side.

"Where are you from?"

"Alabama."

"You ever heard of CSEPP?"

"Uh, I think so. I've seen stuff on TV."

"It stands for Chemical Stockpile Evacuation Preparedness Program."

"Hold on. Hold *on*." He rubbed his nose with the hand holding the cigarette. For a second, Lucy thought he might catch his eyebrows on fire. "You telling me there's been a chemical spill?"

Lucy shook her head. She felt the ever-present pressure to take charge and answer his question, even though she didn't *have* an answer. It was part and parcel of being a doctor—you're trained, *conditioned* to answer questions in med school, specific, detailed questions. In every stage, questions: pre-med, med school, internist, resident, fellowship, and then to practicing physician and beyond up the great chain of medical being. Indeed, medicine was a codified way to answer questions. It was a landscape of queries and unknowns. And sometimes one of the innumerable small questions with their small answers led to bigger and bigger questions that became harder to answer. Questions that began with *why* instead of *how* and *what* and then the minutiae of medicine unraveled, unspooled, and you're left with concepts and hard realities better suited to a priest or philosopher than a physician. *Don't ask me* why *we get sick. Don't ask me why we have to die or why there is cancer. There is and we do. I focus on the HOW.*

But all she said was, "Maybe. I don't know, really. It could be some sort of chemical but looks more like a viral outbreak. And that means there's no telling its origin. It could be from . . ."

"Anywhere?"

She remained silent for a moment, thinking, rubbing her bottom lip and doing her best not to dash down her personal mental rabbit hole.

"Like the flu or something?"

At that Lucy laughed, and even she could hear how it sounded as though she were unraveling, coming unglued. *The questions will keep getting bigger.*

"Or something. But about two million times worse."

"And this thing got loose."

She passed her hand over her eyes, suddenly weary.

"Can I have one of those?" she said, nodding at his smoke. He handed her the pack and lighter.

She took a breath. "Look. I'm gonna be totally honest. You're gonna think I'm . . . Whatever got loose, it makes you go crazy first. Causes all sorts of . . . fucked-up neurological stuff. Like eating parts of yourself, seizures, spasms. Tourette's."

"Tourette's? Like yelling out *fuck* in a theater?"

She nodded. "But worse. Much worse. *Did you hear what I said about eating yourself?*"

He glanced at her, then looked back at the road.

"Then your heart races, tachycardia, until it can't take any more and practically explodes." She lit a cigarette, drew in the smoke, and exhaled.

"Then," she said, slowly, watching the man, "once you're dead, your body revivifies. It gets back up. Attacks whoever is nearest. Eats them. I witnessed it myself. It's as if all the weird neurological stuff is boiled down to its essence. Violence and consumption. But the body is dead. Or seemingly dead . . . I never had a chance to test at the cellular level."

The man's eyes went wide. "You got it?" He started to slow the truck. "Get out."

"No. I don't."

"Get out. I got a daughter."

"No. I don't have it. And I have a family too."

"How the fuck do you know? Huh? You're getting out right here."

"I know because I'm a doctor. All of the original patients lived in White Hall. It must've gotten into the water or something in the environment and then infected them. Once infected, it travels through bodily fluids. Bites." She didn't add, *I hope, because if it's airborne . . . say good-bye to the human race.*

She held out her arms. "I haven't been bitten."

He leaned back in his seat.

"You sure?"

"I'm sure. As I can be." She laughed. "You're having a hard

41

time believing I'm not going to go mad and revivify. But you believe it *can happen*. That's kind of fucking amazing."

His blunt face went through a series of expressions—outrage, anger, puzzlement, and then, surprisingly, amusement. He gave a pained smile. "Zombies."

"What?"

"You're talking zombies. The government do this?"

She stayed silent for a while, realizing the absurdity of what he'd just said. Zombies. The strangeness of the situation pressed in on her, and she shut her eyes tight to blot out all sensation and live, for the moment, in the weightless existence of pure thought. But she couldn't seem to regain the calmness needed for problem solving.

She laughed. He was correct. Zombies they were.

"I think so. I'm guessing it's a biological weapon they developed, realized it was too nasty for the world, and then tried to hide it away. Destroy it, maybe. Could've been stored at the stockpile here. Or somewhere else. There's just no telling without an investigation." The words were bitter to her. She should be in on that. She should be the one to pursue this rabbit all the way into its hole and beyond, if needed. *If I'm right, no one will ever investigate this mystery, God help us. Not this one or any other. Ever.*

He whistled and then leaned forward.

Lucy went on. "We've got to get out of here. Fast. I have a suspicion—"

"What?" He looked scared again.

"Okay. I'm just guessing. There was a leak at the stockpile or somewhere else. The virus got loose and affected people in the vicinity. But not farther out. A range, you know. Maybe it could only live for a little bit in the water. Or in the air, though I doubt it's airborne, because if it was, I would have it." She peered out the window, brow furrowing. "It's extremely virulent because human agents actively spread the disease through attack, through bites."

"Yeah. Zombies."

"If it came from here, we have no idea how far it's spread already. How many were infected and drove to Baptist Hospital in Little Rock? How many stayed in their homes? It could have made it to Memphis by now. Monroe. Shreveport."

"I hear you. But what are you saying?"

"They chased us with a gunship. Big helicopter with a machine gun. They killed . . . they shot my friend. A doctor." She couldn't believe it, but she was crying. Tears came from the corners of her eyes and a hot, uncontrollable sob burst from her chest.

"They had us trapped under the overpass. Then they just left. Took off, like they needed to get out of the area. I think they realized its potential but misjudged its virulence."

"What are you saying?"

"When you get a wound, you sterilize it. You . . ." She thought about her words, very carefully. "You cauterize it, maybe."

"I don't understand."

She was quiet for a long while, smoking her cigarette. She looked at the man, then crushed the cigarette out in the ashtray.

"Just drive as fast as you can. We have to put as much space between us and White Hall as possible. We might only have a few minutes."

Understanding crossed his face, and he put the semi into a lower gear and hit the accelerator. Soon the truck shuddered with speed.

They passed a pileup in the left lane. Mangled cars. People on the ground, some bleeding. Some contorting. Some spasming. Some were already upright. Revivified and shambling. Zombies.

"Holy fuck," he said. "Oh my sweet Jesus."

One of the zombies, missing an arm and part of his rib cage, stepped too close to the semi as they passed. They heard a thump.

The trucker dug under his seat and pulled out a revolver. He tucked it into his belt.

"This is a goddamned nightmare. My girlfriend's back in Alabama."

"You tried to call her? Check your phone."

He dug it out of his pocket and flipped it open and dialed. After a moment, he said, "'Network busy. Try back later.'"

"I don't think that's an accident. Things could be happening everywhere. People are . . ."

"Desperate. What could be happening . . .?"

"Other than zombies and gunships shooting civilians? No clue, but . . . believe it. Drive."

"Hey, you don't have to harsh on me. I picked you up, remember?"

Abrasive, they called her at Baptist Hospital when they let her go. *Arrogant and possessed of an intolerance unbecoming to a physician.* That one smarted some. Why the hell did it take zombies to get her to pull her head out of her ass long enough to try to get along with others?

Because social niceties are a survival mechanism, that's why.

She nodded. "I'm . . ." She hesitated. "I'm sorry. For everything." Lucy put her hand on his shoulder. "Thank you for saving me. My name is Lucy Ingersol."

He grinned, showing tobacco-stained teeth. "Hey, it's okay. You're just a little intense." He patted her knee. Normally she would have had something harsher to say about such familiarity, but she knew it was meant in good spirit.

"They call me Knock-Out. Jim Nickerson. But Knock-Out's what all my friends call me."

The semi jerked and the lights on the dashboard went dark. The tape deck went out. The truck slowed dramatically, as if the engine had completely malfunctioned.

"Oh no."

"What do you mean, 'oh no'?"

"Stop the truck!"

He jammed his foot on the brakes and the semi jumped and rattled. It rolled to rest on the shoulder.

"EMP!" Her voice sounded shrill. "Electromagnetic pulse! Knocks out all electronics. We've got to find cover!"

"What? I can't—"

Throwing open the door, Lucy dropped to the ground and sprinted along the highway. She heard Knock-Out clamber down from the cab and yell, "Wait! Lucy!"

Ahead, she spied a culvert and drainage pipe passing underneath the highway. She ran down the length of the shoulder and jumped into the concrete culvert. Knock-Out huffed behind her.

She turned back to see his progress and she heard a small boom in the distance, like someone slamming a door in a large house. She stopped. It was such a small sound, she allowed herself to hope. Her perception stilled into a series of snapshots, like a camera shutter sticking. The sky streaked with color, turning brilliantly white, like a new sun coalescing from stardust. Black upon white. Knock-Out's silhouette in midstride, the hulking shape of the big rig behind him, a wall of fire growing beyond the tree line, rising toward heaven. The once blue sky now striated with wispy thin clouds. Her hair swinging toward the light. Wind at her back.

White light.

She threw herself to the bottom of the culvert and Knock-Out landed next to her. The sound became massive: not a roar, not an explosion, but a sound that went lower than the human ear could perceive and stretched away into infinitely higher pitches. Her stomach and intestines felt liquefied. Only pure desperation and self-preservation kept her moving. She scrambled toward the drainage pipe's mouth, Knock-Out close behind.

She'd passed over the pipe's mouth and was pulling at Knock-Out's shirt when the shock wave ripped past them like the mother of all tornadoes, carrying rocks, trees, debris. It passed over the lip of the concrete gully, tearing away their breath and making their clothes ripple as though they were in free fall.

Lucy screamed, the sound lost in the din, clawing herself

backward, further into the pipe. Knock-Out pulled himself over the mouth and flopped onto his side.

The world became a furnace, and it was Knock-Out's turn to scream. Again Lucy witnessed him silhouetted by light. Outside, beyond the pipe, air turned to fire.

Their hair, their clothes, ignited.

Knock-Out threw himself on top of her. He gripped her like an overamorous date and rolled up one side of the pipe and then down again, dousing their backs in the half inch of water standing stagnant at the bottom. Lucy's head bashed into the pipe wall and the world spun.

She felt something akin to relief as the darkness at the edges of her vision crowded in and everything became black.

When she awoke, Knock-Out sat on the lip of the pipe, looking up at the sky. Half his hair was gone and horrendous blisters covered the back of his neck and ears, the exposed backs of his arms.

He smoked, looking at the ruins of the sky. He smoked, just like everything around them. The whole earth was aflame.

She pushed herself up and out, making him move to the side.

He shook a cigarette out of his pack, lit it with the Zippo, and handed it to her. The bright snick of the lighter came through even above the crackle of fire. The woods beyond the interstate's shoulder tilted crazily to the left and burned.

Lucy raised the cigarette, drew the smoke deep inside her.

She felt hollow, like an empty husk, dry from too long in the sun. She stood and looked up.

A billow of black smoke, streaked with orange and red, rose away from the earth, so massive it covered half the sky. The head of a mushroom cloud.

She took Knock-Out's hand, pulled him up, and walked up the shoulder to the interstate to survey the remains of the old world they once knew.

2

EVERYTHING THAT RISES MUST CONVERGE

Everything is everything.

Meemaw used to say that, and I never understood what she meant.

I came to her house with a fractured jaw, a splint on my arm, and a broken heart. Pa went to jail and I never saw him again. At night, I cried in my bed and Meemaw cradled me, smoothed my hair.

"Why'd he do it?"

"Shhh."

"Why was he so *mean*?"

She stayed silent, thinking. "He must've been born that way."

"Maybe his parents were mean."

"Maybe. Never met them." She said this as if she really didn't care. "It don't matter, Jimbo. He is. You can't fight against what is."

"But Momma's gone. Everything's gone—"

"Shhh, baby. Everything is everything. It can't be gone."

My heart was broken, and the world ended when my mother died.

* * *

The doctor is beautiful, and I'm glad she's with me. She's beautiful despite the soot, despite the bloody gouge crossing her skull and the fact that half her hair has burned away. I've known her for just moments, but she's beautiful and I can't imagine how I'd deal without her.

Maybe because I'm scared.

It all happens so fast. Everything. I pull over. She hops in. I thought she was a lunatic at first, claiming to be a doctor, but . . . really you just can't fake it. Only doctors act like doctors. And like all doctors, she came before the bad news. Cancer. Tumors. Zombies. Nuclear explosions.

She talks to me and then everything catches fire in a hot wind. Without the wind, we'd choke in smoke, but the smoke is whisked away behind us, making my eyes tear and itch.

We walk the interstate for what seems like hours, baked by the heat of the infernos to either side of us. The pine forests crackle and howl and stink of creosote.

Behind us, the cloud rises.

Amazing how long a cloud like that can hang in the air. It's like some gigantic, radioactive pastry rising in an oven.

It's so big, looking at it gives me the same feeling I had when we drove to the Grand Canyon. Seventy-nine, I think it was. I was just a boy. We drove across America, my grandfather, my grandmother, and me. Meemaw reading magazines and smoking. Peepaw humming with the radio. I always loved the road because of them, the way they were content in the cocoon of car and sound. I miss them.

We came to dry country and drove for days. The sky

became brittle and cracked at the horizon. It took hours to park, the lot full of cars releasing a horde of tourists with bulky cameras and picnic baskets, and when we did, the chasm was only yards away. I stood on the edge in Buster Browns, nervous at the brink, and tried to grasp the vastness of the abyss.

The cloud we walk underneath is the same. It's hideous and beautiful by turns. The mushroom rises behind us in the east. Before us, the setting sun smears the sky with color. The interstate is a long thread through burning piney-woods. We're higher up than the rest of the land, a little. A delta. Without the world being set afire, it'd be muggy and we'd be swarmed with mosquitoes. Chalk up one point in favor of nuclear annihilation. No more skeeters.

She looks at it too. The cloud. I can see her cringe.

"We've got to get inside," she tells me, face intense. She's the most focused person I've ever met. When she looks at me, I feel flayed, bare.

"Why?"

"Fallout. Radiation. Every minute we stay outside, the more we risk sickness. Cancer."

Walking is hard. My body's become used to the soft seat of the semi. My feet are like rotten pieces of wood. The flesh of my neck bubbles and bursts. I feel my own fluids leaking down the back of my neck.

Ahead is an off-ramp. A charred figure stumbles toward us. One of them.

"Still hard to get my head around it," I say. "Zombies."

I have the pistol tucked into my belt. I guess I should get it out. I've never shot it, but I'm ashamed to admit that to Lucy. She is probably the better shot—she looks as if anything she tries is easy for her. Though growing hair might be troublesome from here out.

"Here. Take it."

"What? The gun?"

"I'm not much of a shot," I say.

She takes it, pops it open, checks the rounds. Little brass circles in a larger gray circle.

The charred figure has come close enough for me to smell it. Burned hair. Melted plastic. Underneath all the char, it has the smell of pork, fatty with drippings. My stomach rumbles. I wish I was nauseated.

"Holy Christ, forgive me. I'm drooling like a goddamned dog."

She gives me a sharp glance. Beautiful. And razor-sharp.

"It's normal to start salivating in autopsies. Okay. Not normal in everyone. But in a percentage of people. It's old, animal memories. Don't worry about it. You're fine."

I nod. Hope she's right.

She cocks the hammer of the pistol. The zombie is only ten or fifteen feet away. Lucy walks calmly forward, closing the distance. The thing—it is impossible to tell its sex, and anyway I don't think you can even think of them as male or female anymore—raises its arms and totters at Lucy, trying to meet her.

She shoves the pistol into its face and pulls the trigger. There's no blood. No fancy explosion of brain or skull. No screaming. It drops. That's all. The lack of drama or fanfare makes me pause, scared. It feels so much like murder. It's too easy.

Lucy looks at me and I can tell she's thinking the same thing.

"Knock-Out, we've got to get inside."

She's said this before. But I nod. We walk up the rise, up the off-ramp. This area didn't get hit as hard by the blast. There's another overpass crossing the interstate. We're not very far from Little Rock, maybe five or six miles out, and I recall, because this is my route now, that there's a Shell Git-N-Go filling station off to the right. They've got a fry-station serving gizzards and livers. Cold beer. Pretty young thing behind the counter, a little thick around the middle but with bright eyes and the nice smile. Not anymore, I imagine. We go that way.

There's quite a few of the shamblers milling about. Some of them are burned, but others seem whole, if you can call walking around after you're dead whole. The smell of charred meat is overpowering.

The station is burning. The air stinks of burning tires and plastic and an oily smoke pours off the husk of the building and is whisked up and away into the already smoke-filled sky. My eyes tear, and there's a cough building in my chest. Thank God for the wind at our backs.

The gas tanks have exploded and the vehicles around the building are black husks, much like the zombies. They turn in a group, like fish or birds. Creatures of the same instinct. To eat. To destroy, maybe. I should ask Lucy. She could make it understandable.

Ash begins to fall like snow.

She pops the chamber on the revolver and counts the remaining rounds.

"Too many. Can you run?"

"As opposed to what? Getting eaten?" I laugh. "Hell, yeah, I can run."

This doctor, she takes off, her long legs devouring the pavement. I run too, behind her. She's slender, swift, and deadly, pumping her arms with a pistol in her hand. With each stride, my feet sting and pain shoots up my legs. Boots aren't suited for the mile sprint. They're made for walking, as the old song goes.

The dead bank to follow, coming around the twisted columns of the gas pumps like a school of particularly vicious fish swimming around black coral.

We leave them behind, but they keep following.

It's the moaning that gets me. It sounds like an angry mob of deaf-mutes. Unintelligible and urgent.

Lucy slows, looking to the left and right. To the left, trailers. To the right, a little pillbox house with frill around the eaves and reflective globes in the front yard. Nestled in pine trees. A gravel drive. The fires haven't touched it.

She peels off the highway, her shoes crunching on the gravel. She dashes across the lawn, dodging the potted plants in whitewashed tires, up the porch steps, and stops.

My chest feels like the inside of a charcoal grill, crusty and black. My wind comes in great sooty heaves. After a moment, I climb the steps and stand beside her.

She looks at the porch. A smear of blood marks a trail inside the house. The door is open and the lights are out.

Lucy looks at me and raises the gun, pointing inside the dark of the house.

"First thing you do, Knock-Out, is lock the door. Bar it with furniture. Someone's in here. Dead. Or dying. We stay together."

I nod.

"After that, find tools so we can barricade the windows, the doors. Then we'll figure out what to do next. I have to get to—" She looks distracted for a moment, and I know what she's thinking. Her child. His name is Gus; she told me in the cab.

"We'll find him." I want her to concentrate. It scares me when she loses her focus.

She blinks and gives me a sharp look. I toss my head at the open door.

"Right," she says, squaring her shoulders. "Let's go."

Inside, I'm blind, nearly. I can see the bright shapes of windows but no details of the interior. But something moans. I hear a thump.

"Close the door!" Lucy whispers as loud as a scream. "I'll take care—"

I turn and shut the door. There's a dead bolt and a clasp. I fasten both then turn back to the house.

My eyes are adjusting to the dark. We're in a narrow hall. Lucy's moved down it a bit, gun out.

My legs are watery and weak, but I force myself forward, behind her. A spill of light from a window shows us a kitchen. In it, a shape moves. One of the shamblers. It turns and steps into the light.

It used to be a woman, older, blue haired. Frumpy and heavy breasted. Still wearing slippers. She looks up with milk-white eyes. Her skin is bluish green, but her mouth drips with red. She's holding an arm in her hands. The arm is small and showing bone. I'm scared that the arm is so small.

The shambler drops the piece of flesh and its face becomes enraged. It seems the zombies still have one emotion left to them: anger. A garbled sound comes from its throat, half like a scream of rage, half like the bleat of a goat. It comes forward in a brisk limp.

Granny is spry.

Lucy's arm pops up, gun out, and she fires, lighting up the dark hall with the muzzle-flash. The boom of the gun makes it hard to think. I'm blind again, but I feel Lucy falling back against me.

I crab walk backward, toward the door we just entered through. I'm ashamed of my terror. I force myself to my feet.

"Can you get this bitch off me?"

I lurch forward, grab a cold, flabby arm, and hoist. It's like lifting a wet, carnivorous sack of flour.

Dead weight.

Puns are the lowest form of wit, my Meemaw used to say. She was right.

Once I pull the shambler off Lucy, she stands.

"Knock-Out," she says, a little hitch in her voice. "This has got to be the longest workday I've had in . . . well, forever."

She looks around. My eyes have become used to the dim light. Night is coming.

A thump sounds from the front door. The shamblers from the Git-N-Go have arrived.

Lucy, eyes wide, holds a finger to her mouth, indicating I should be silent. She steps over the Granny-shambler on the floor and goes through the door, into the kitchen. I follow.

I hear her breath catch, and suddenly she turns and throws her arms around me and buries her face in my chest. She smells like baby powder and burned hair, but I don't want to let her go. When I look over her shoulder, I see.

It's fresh and bloody. A child. Age? Your best guess. A boy, judging by the shoes. Chuck Taylors. Shreds of a T-shirt and jeans.

There's crimson handprints, small things, on the back door, on the handle and at the dead bolt. The whole incident plays out like a bloody diorama. He comes home, or down the stairs right off the kitchen, finds Granny, maybe spasming, maybe already blue gray. Asks her what's wrong. Granny moans. Grabs the child. Bites him, maybe on the neck, or arm, or hands, as he tries to fight her off, already bleeding. The instinct to survive is so strong.

There's a smear of blood on a drawer. Another small hand-print. He died trying to get something to fight her off. To fight it off.

I disengage from Lucy. "Go check the windows. The shamblers are at the front door."

"We've got to be quiet." Lucy averts her eyes from the mess on the floor. "They can't see, their eyes are too cloudy. If they can see, it's only a little, like swimming in murky water."

"But they hear and smell like the dickens, don't they?"

Whispering is hard. My throat is already raw from the smoke and dry heat coming off the nuclear forest fires.

"We have to build a safe room. Against the radiation. If we can seal a room with plastic, it'll protect us from fallout and keep them from smelling us. If we don't take shelter from the fallout, we'll be dead from cancer by the end of the year. If *they* don't kill us."

I nod, try to show her I understand. I've been x-rayed before. The techs wore big bulky protective vests. Like booze, or smoke, crank or blow, too much of it will kill you. Why should radiation be any different?

"More than likely, they'll go away if they hear another noise or smell something else."

"Okay," I say. My voice sounds steadier than I feel. "I'll take the kitchen. Find trash bags to seal windows. Something to eat. Whatever looks useful. I'll take care of the—" I don't know how to finish that statement.

But she nods, squeezes my bicep, and smiles at me gratefully. I feel warm. It's been a long time since someone has touched me.

"Water. Whatever else happens, we'll need water."

She turns and pads up the stairs. I turn back to the kitchen. To the boy.

I can hear thumps from the front of the house. It's hard to know how smart the shamblers are. Can they work out locks? They're dead, right? Can they figure out how to break windows? Climb over a sill?

I go straight to the sink and open the cabinet doors. It's where I put the garbage bags at home, so it makes sense

Granny-shambler would put hers there. She's got sense. A large pack of Glad trash bags. Apple cider vinegar. Pine-Sol.

A yellow flashlight.

I take out a bag, open the mouth, and scoop air, popping the bag open. It makes a sound like a sail catching wind, more volume than you'd imagine.

The noises from the front door get louder—thick wet sounds that hit my ears like the sound of someone gargling with meat by-products or trying to talk around a mouthful of Vienna sausages, angry and confused and vocal—I can hear the thumps and even the scratches too. It's weird how the mind conjures images. I imagine horribly maimed hands, black and textured like pork cracklins.

The problem with the way the shamblers sound is the same problem I had with my daughter when she was a toddler learning to talk: I want to correct the shamblers. It's like words are just beyond the soggy, mush-mouthed pronunciation. If only they focused just a little more.

I could concentrate on survival if they'd just pronounce their moans right.

I go to the drawer that has the bloody stain. The boy was reaching for something. Granny-shambler stopped him.

Inside is a hammer with an oversize head and bright orange handle. Nails. Duct tape. I snatch up the hammer and thread it through a loop in my jeans. The tape and nails go into the bag. There's some batteries in the far back of the drawer. I pop them into the bag.

The moans have died down. But there's still the sound of scratching, like some big rat, and I don't like it. I can hear the floorboards creak and shift as Lucy makes her way around upstairs. The house is old.

I catch a whiff of shambler char, that fatty plastic-barbecue smell. I don't know if their numbers are growing or they're just getting stinkier.

God, I hope it's just stink.

In the corner of the kitchen, underneath the stairs, is a narrow door. A pantry.

I twist the knob and step in. There's a string hanging in front of me and I pull it before I remember that the electricity is out. I dig through the Glad trash bag and, after a moment, find the flashlight and flick it on.

It doesn't work.

But I do have my Zippo. It's seen me through thick and thin.

I chink it open and hold it up high.

Cans. Jars. Bottles.

There are shelves with boxes and bags. I'm sure all of it is edible, but it's pretty dark, even with the light from the Zippo.

The cans, I dump a few into the bag. I grab a few of the jars, which have got to be pickles or jam.

I don't know what the bottles are, but I hope they're booze.

I dump some of the boxes into the bag.

It's too heavy in my hand now to carry easily. There's clomping overhead, and the shamblers at the front door have discovered that they do have the gumption to break glass. I dash around the corner and look down the hall. One of the shamblers has put his fist through the little window inset in the front door. I didn't even notice it when we came in, but now there's a blue-green hand groping around. I'd laugh at the cartooniness of the motion if it wasn't so goddamned scary.

I go back and throw open cabinet doors. Pans. No thank you. China. Fuck that. Lighter fluid and matches? This is good. There's a wick lantern and two jugs of kerosene. It all goes into my bag.

Next: a Ginsu knife. What the hell would I need that for? I'm never going to grow the balls to get close enough to one of the shamblers to use a fillet knife. It looks pretty, though.

I turn, and the trash bag clanks against a cabinet. I realize it's as heavy as I'll be able to carry before it rips. My looting day is done. I set it down on a table with a clank.

I hear more clomps and Lucy appears at the base of the stairs. She's got a bedsheet in a desperate fist and a wild look on her face.

"There's about twenty of them outside. Must've heard the gunshot."

She stops and looks at the remains of the boy. I should've taken care of that first. From my bag, I take the rectangular can of kerosene.

She understands immediately.

"New plan. We can't stay in this house."

The dead batter the door now. Their moans sound like demon-possessed seals, goofy and scary at the same time.

I look to the kitchen window. The daylight has totally died, but there is still ambient light—from the forest fires, maybe. Maybe reflected from the mushroom cloud. The sun might still be shining on it.

"I think I spotted another house. So—"

"We're gonna let 'em in here. Trap them."

She nods, cocking her head at me.

I can see it all in my mind's eye.

I say, "I'll douse the hall with the kerosene, open the door, and haul ass back here. We'll go out the back door, through the kitchen." After a moment of pure terror, I realize I haven't even peeked out the back. There could be an army out there, and we'd just run right into their welcoming arms. And mouths.

She has the same thought. Watching her, I can see the way she thinks, coming to the same conclusions I've come to. I can see the movement of decision on her face.

Lucy dashes to the back door, pulls aside the curtain. She sighs. Nothing bad.

"Okay, then." I raise the tin can of kerosene and twist off the top. "You better not burn my ass up. It's already a little charred."

I pull my Zippo from a pocket, kiss it, and hand it to Lucy. I douse the boy with liquid. I want to pray for him but can't imagine that a God who would let him die this way would give a shit about my prayers. When he's thoroughly sodden, I motion Lucy to the back door to stand ready, and I go to the front of the house.

The hall seems bigger now. But that's probably a trick of the light. There's a blue arm coming through the little window in the door, and a charred black one. The black one sloughs off dark ash. The blue one, nothing. Jagged edges of glass cut into it, but they don't draw blood.

I splash the walls with kerosene. I pour kerosene on the hallway floor. There's a runner carpet, and it soaks up quite a bit of the stuff. The can is empty quicker than I'd like, but it lasts to the kitchen and I squirt the last of it into a small puddle on the floor. I drop the can and, crouching, go to the front door.

It's bizarre, but they know I'm there. They moan and howl louder the closer I get. They can smell me. Or hear my breath. That's almost too frightening for me to bear.

Lucy barks from down the hall, "Knock-Out, come on! You've got to do it." I turn to look at her and see she's got the lighter ready.

I open the door and run.

I don't look back, but in my mind's eye, the door opens just a bit before the shamblers realize they can enter. Thinking this makes the itch on my neck and the rippling goose bumps on my skin subside a little.

I feel the wounds on my arms and neck and back open with my dash toward the back of the house. Hot fluid leaks into my clothes. The burns have given me extra senses—I can feel the shamblers knocking the door aside and lurching into the house. But I'm long gone.

I pass Lucy and snatch the garbage bag from the kitchen table. She flicks the lighter and throws it onto the floor, into a puddle of kerosene. I'm already out the back door, waiting, when she barrels through the opening and jumps the three steps down to the turf of singed lawn, her bedsheet bundle in hand.

I shut the back door. I pull the hammer from my belt,

drop the garbage bag full of loot for a moment, pull a nail from my pocket, and drive it through the wood of the door into the frame. I'm not a good shot, but I'm hell at construction. I drive in a second nail.

One of the plates of glass in the door cracks.

The flames rise and flicker in the house. Shapes, like ungainly devils, move through the blaze into the kitchen.

"Come on, Knock-Out!"

A shambler appears in the door's window, hair aflame, and slams a fist through the glass, grabbing for me.

I turn, snatch the trash bag, and perform the same jump into the yard that Lucy made. I land heavily and fall to my knees, dropping the hammer, but the turf is springy and she's there to help me up. I pick up the hammer from the ground.

We run through the pines in the dark. All the light has gone from the sky, and it's nearly pitch dark now. It's hard running and carrying the trash bag. I'm cradling it to my chest, trying to support the bottom so all the goods don't fall out.

I feel like a robber running from the cops. Except these cops will eat me and the world has changed.

I sense more than see the mass of a building rising in front of us. Lucy runs ahead of me, and I know where she is by her breath and footfalls and an occasional glint from her watch reflecting the far-off yellow light of the flames. We stumble and grope in the dark. I look back and see the house behind us burning. It casts a faint orange glow on the building in front of us.

We find a door and it's unlocked. We duck inside the house. She fumbles at the dead bolt, and I hear the metallic click of the mechanism locking. For the second time today, I hear a muffled boom, and then there's yellow light filtering through the window. The first house just exploded. I hope it's taken apart the shamblers at the seams. I know I shouldn't feel that way about fellow human beings, but there it is. I hate them.

There's a moment of fumbling in the dark, and Lucy grabs my hand and pulls me up some stairs, down a narrow hall, into a bathroom. How she knows where to go baffles me.

I slump to the floor and let the trash bag full of stuff clank on the tile floor.

"Get up, man," she says, low. "We've got to cover the windows and doors. You brought the trash bags?"

I nod, slowly standing back up, and then realize she can't see me nod. "Yep. Hold on. Shit."

I rifle through the trash bag by feel. My fingers land on a hollow cardboard box that rattles. Matches. I hand them to her. She strikes one, and I find the bags.

The lantern is intact. I set it aside. I fill it from the other tin of kerosene and light it.

"We're not going to be able to use that in here."

"What? Why?"

"We're going to seal the room as best we can. I don't want to die from carbon monoxide poisoning and stupidity after surviving zombies and a nuclear explosion."

"Oh. Shit."

"We'll have to use matches. You got the bags?"

I hand one to her.

She opens up her makeshift linen sack. She's like a very

prim and proper hobo. She pulls out a roll of duct tape and fastens the bag to the door. The adhesive makes *brrrpt* sounds as she tears it from the roll.

I hand her another bag. It takes three to secure the door.

Once the lantern is out, she tapes the window but leaves a corner free, so we can lift it and look out. I'm having trouble standing. My feet are swollen and painful.

She plugs the sink and turns on the water. It's surprising how loud it is. I can hear her clothes whisk and whisper. I can feel her stirring the air in the dark with her movement.

"I don't want to do this, but while that house is burning, we've got to get as much water in the sink and tub as we can. After we wash. We need to stay inside for the next twenty-four hours, until the cloud has dissipated. We should stay inside for longer, but—"

"Your family."

"Yes. Take off your clothes." I can hear rustling in the confines of the bathroom and what sounds like keys hit the floor.

"What?"

"Take off your clothes and get in the shower." Her bare feet slap on the porcelain of the tub. She draws the shower curtain inside the tub; it's loud and sticky. The whole room echoes like a cave. The plastic is thunderous in the dark. Who knew plastic could be this loud?

"I . . ." I don't know what to do. This day has been a doozy, as Meemaw might say. First zombies, then nuclear explosions, then fire consuming the whole world, then running and shooting and more fire. Now I'm supposed to shower with a beautiful woman.

I think she's grinning but know there's nothing sexual in it. "I know it sounds crazy. But we have to do it, and the more noise, the more likely the . . . the revenants . . . will come sniffing for us. There's radioactive particles all over you. We have to wash them off. And clean your burns as best we can. I'm sorry I didn't get my—" She stops. She's thinking about what's happened. "My purse. I had some medical supplies. But I raided the last house's medicine cabinet in the dark and haven't checked this one. Let's just get clean as fast as we can."

I shrug and pull my shirt over my head. I drop my pants. And even though it's still summer—as if seasons have any meaning anymore with that cloud hanging overhead—I have goose bumps. I know she's in the shower, naked. I'm ashamed, but my body responds.

She cranks on the water and it is very loud, louder than the sink. But the water is hot and it burns on my wounds. I yelp.

"Shhh." She puts a hand on my arm and then removes it quickly. I crowd at the far end of the shower, away from the spigot, hands over my erection. I can't see anything. But I can smell her. The handles squeak as she adjusts the water flow.

I don't know if it's that we're both naked, in a shower to-gether, but she says in a lower, almost husky voice, "It hurts bad, huh? The burns?"

"Yeah. But . . . we've been so busy, this is the first time I've really felt it."

It's a strange moment. Pitch black, naked, in a shower with a beautiful woman. A woman I've just met. A doctor. She's like some kind of superhero. My back is on fire again.

She's quiet for a long time. The water is loud.

She squirts something from a plastic bottle into her hand—a little bleat of shampoo—and the smell of kiwis fills the shower. It's such a sweet smell, I realize how much I stink of ashes and dust and char.

I can hear her working up a lather, the sloppy sounds of soap in body crevices. I hear her gasp once, and I remember the gouge on her scalp. Then she's rinsing.

"Okay, let's switch." I turn sideways, my front toward the wall. I don't understand why she doesn't get out. She brushes past me, and the tips of her breasts trace lines on my back, burning more than my wounds. She sticks the bottle in my ribs, and it's cold and jars me from my arousal. I soap up and rinse. It feels wonderful.

When I'm done and it's obvious that the shower is over, I'm relieved but disappointed too. When will I have another shower like this? When will I have another shower?

I turn off the water. Sudden silence except for dripping. I can understand how blind folks' hearing is heightened to compensate for lack of sight.

"We forgot towels."

"There's a closet. Behind where you sat when we got here."

"I'll get them. If we're gonna be sittin' here, no need to get the floor totally soaked. Stay there."

I step out of the shower. I'm glad for the darkness and that she can't see me, find the door, and blindly fumble my way through the closet. When I feel soft fluffy fabric, I grab and tug. Towels. I dry myself off and get Lucy a fresh one. She steps out and dries off too. I drop my towel to the floor and try to mop up the runoff, then wrap a new towel around my waist.

"We need a little light," I say.

"Wait till I get this towel around me."

I wait.

"Okay."

I move to the sink and take the matches from the ledge. I light one.

Lucy, sitting cross-legged on the tile floor, hair frizzy from the shower, begins to look through her loot.

"Once the tub is empty, rinse it again and then fill it, please. If we get—"

"Trapped?"

"Yeah. If we're trapped, we'll need it."

I sit down, facing her. We rummage through our bags.

I have the kerosene and the useless lantern. She has bottles of pills, ibuprofen, Pepcid Complete, expired amoxicillin, Lasix, Neosporin, and a bottle with five Cialis. I have a box of spaghetti. She has two shirts and a pair of pants that might be big enough for me. I have a cheap bottle of white wine; the twist-off cap is a blessing. She has very old tampons, circa 1983 it looks like. I have a can of Rotel brand tomatoes. She has a bottle of witch hazel. I have prunes. She has a jar of ancient Vaseline. I have a box of votive candles.

From what I can tell, the people of Granny-shambler's house all share the traits of being old, liking spicy food, and getting constipated. Someone might be having sex, maybe poor Chuck T's mother. I can't imagine who the Cialis might be for.

It's a toss-up if the candles are a bigger score than the shitty wine.

"Light a candle and turn around," she says, voice pitched low. "I'm going to look at your burns."

I do what she says, and I'm struck that it seems so natural for me to follow her lead. I always rankled when Angelyne bossed me around. But with Lucy . . . it's different. Is it because she's a doctor? Because she's more beautiful? Or because she's both?

I rotate myself, using my hands, but remain cross-legged.

She scoots the loot aside—not before twisting the cap off of the wine and taking a swig—then crawls forward. She hands me the bottle, and I drink.

"Wait." She pops open a bottle of pills and puts four little brown ones into my hand. I can hear her rattle some into her own palm.

"Ibuprofen. Take them."

I pop them in my mouth and wash them down with the wine. The wine makes my mouth pucker, too tart and too sweet all at once. But when it has gone down the pipe, my stomach burns a little more and my neck, my ears, and my arms burn a little less.

I hear the crackling of paper and realize she's unwrapping a tampon. She squirts witch hazel on the tampon and begins to swab my neck with it. It stings. It hurts. More than you can imagine. I suck air through clenched teeth.

I don't crack jokes about the tampon.

She chuckles.

I ask, "What?"

"Just this morning—was it this morning? it seems so long ago—I told myself I don't do wet work."

"Wet work?"

"Dealing with patients. Hands-on doctor stuff."

"You can't say that anymore."

"No. I can't."

I wince. Whatever she's doing back there really stings. When I have a moment, I ask, "What exactly is witch hazel?"

She stops wiping my burns. I look back and see she's trying to read the label.

"You know . . ." she murmurs, "I have no idea. A plant maybe. I know it has lots of alcohol in it, and that's why I'm putting it on your neck. To clean it."

Her legs go to either side of mine. She starts working on my ears.

Her fingers feel cool on my skin, and I can smell the kiwi scent of her hair.

"Well, you'll never grow another mullet."

I stifle the laugh.

"We won't suffocate, will we? You know, from the candle?" I ask, and my voice sounds loud in the small space. "Since we've taped everything up?" She's a doctor and knows these things. Except about witch hazel.

"It's either carbon monoxide poisoning or anoxia, using up all of the oxygen in an environment. I think we need to extinguish it at some point. It could kill us . . . maybe. But only if we've created an airtight seal, which I doubt. Cracks in the walls, gaps in the windows, spaces in the tiles . . . I don't know. But sound travels through air. Radioactive particles travel through air. So we're killing two birds with one stone by taping the windows. But we need light right now for a few minutes. And I've got the corner of the window still untaped. I hope that'll be enough. I haven't heard anything downstairs."

She falls silent. Maybe realizing she was talking, well, too much.

Lucy finishes my ears, takes out another tampon, squirts more witch hazel, and rubs the backs of my arms.

"Would you have really dumped me on the interstate?"

"Not just yes but hell yes. You'd convinced me the crazy virus existed. Why wouldn't I think you had it too?"

She stops wiping my arms.

"I'm worried that everyone has it."

Silence.

"But you didn't. Dump me."

"You were convincing. I've never—" I don't know how to say it. "I've never met . . . never met someone like you. You're . . . intense. And honest. And a little scary."

I can't see, but she might be blushing. She's quiet for a long while.

I take another swig from the bottle and hand it back to her.

She takes a swallow and says, "Do you have any more cigarettes? We shouldn't, but—"

"Yeah. The world is ending. Wait a sec." I pull a rumpled flat pack out of my pocket. I ferret open the lining and inspect what's left. Three cigarettes, butts smashed narrow. I draw one out. It's bent halfway through.

"Put your finger on the rip and it'll be just fine."

I take out one for myself. She lights hers from the votive and then hands the candle to me. I spill translucent wax onto my hand and it burns, but by now I've become used to the sensation. It's been a long day. This morning, I woke up in the back of my cab in a parking lot, ready to drive another thousand miles.

The smoke fills the space and doesn't dissipate. We look at each other and smoke, each of us lost in our own thoughts. I can't help but notice her athletic legs, her long, willowy neck. She's slim and delicate as steel and I feel awkward that I'm not. That I'm bulky and hairy and weak.

"Why do they call you Knock-Out?"

"Jim Nickerson. My name."

"That doesn't figure. You do look like a Knock-Out, though."

I stay quiet for a minute.

"I got the name because I was so good looking when I was a teen. I modeled." Her expression doesn't change. "Really."

"Fat chance."

I snort. Her shoulders rise in alarm and I look around, as if that could help.

No sound from downstairs or outside. The light from Granny-shambler's house has died, and the zombies have dispersed or died in the blaze and explosion.

"A middle-weight fighter in the navy. Won some fights. Don't know how to shoot very well, but I'm handy in a bar."

She squints her eyes at me.

"Give me your hands."

I give her my paws. I didn't realize it until my hands were in hers, but she is nut brown. I'm pasty white.

"You've got an old boxer's break and heavy scar tissue on

your knuckles. That doesn't mean you were a fighter, though. And you've already told me a lie once."

I duck my head.

"Someday," I say, "I'll tell you."

She nods and rubs her face.

"You don't talk like a trucker."

"I went to college for a while. Okay, junior college. I listen to a lot of audiobooks." When she stays quiet, I feel compelled to go on. "Truckers aren't idiots."

"I didn't mean—"

"No, it's okay. I guess there are a lot of idiot truckers, come to think of it. But most of us are just folk trying to get by, to survive."

She looks at me a long while with those big liquid blue eyes, and maybe something in her softens. She nods.

I take another swig, then stretch. I'm tired but wonder how we're going to sleep.

There's no way to stretch out unless we do it side by side, and suddenly, I'm so weary, I'm not even worried about asking permission.

I twist, smooth out the towels, and lie down, my leg pressing against hers, but my head at the other end of the narrow room.

It takes her a moment to force herself to get comfortable.

I'm asleep before I know it.

In the morning, I'm sore and stiff. I wake almost not knowing where I am—almost. My neck feels like the skin of a

Thanksgiving turkey, golden brown and oozing fluid. Nuclear explosions are not my favorite.

Gray light filters through the window. Lifting the untaped flap, we look out onto a snowy morning. It's June.

"Ash," she says in a dead voice. "The easterly wind must've crapped out on us. This is not good."

"Look, tracks." Two lines of footsteps in the ash lawn wander off around the corner of the house. The tracks are long and messy. They look like the tracks of dead people. Someone—a couple of someones—shambling.

Lucy stands and shakes blood into her legs. She touches her toes. She looks older today than she did yesterday, but I imagine I do too. She hands me a shirt. I put my pants on under the towel. She's already dressed in clothes she took from the other house.

"I want to check out the house now that we have light."

I nod. "What about the ash?"

"It's highly radioactive, and we don't want to breathe it or get it on our skin."

We slowly untape the door, and I heft my hammer. Lucy has kept track of the pistol, so we creep out of the bathroom and down the hall, opening doors slowly.

Bedrooms on the left and right. We inch down the stairs, pausing to listen. I'm in front with the hammer raised. I glance back at Lucy and she's got both hands on the gun, one hand cradling the other, weapon pointed at the ceiling. A shooter's grip.

"You look like a cop," I whisper.

"Shhh."

Something thumps and then slides.

Running in the dark from the other house, we never even looked around enough to know if another door was open.

At the bottom of the stairs, I inch around the end of the cheap-looking bannister and turn the corner into what I believe is the main hall. Kitchen to my left, unknown rooms to my right. Front door in a line before me.

The front door is open.

Brown stains are on the floor, leading toward the room to my right. Directly under the upstairs bathroom we slept in.

I peek at Lucy. She nods at me to go ahead. She takes a hand off the pistol, points at it and mouths "too loud," and then points at my hammer.

I'm not real happy about what she's saying; my knees are knocking and watery. But she squints at me and I'll be goddamned if I'm going to have her think me a coward. Even though I am.

I turn the corner. The room is a dining room and lounge with a TV set and couch.

There's two of them. One stands in the corner looking at the ceiling—where we'd been sleeping—and the other sprawls out on the floor. It's shaking a little and missing a leg at the knee. The standing zombie is a scrawny young man in his twenties with baggy britches and dagger tattoos on his arms that probably look uglier on bluish-gray flesh than they did on live skin. But they're really shitty. He should've gotten his money back.

He turns, senses me, and immediately lurches forward, arms reaching out.

Like Granny, he is pretty spry. Untracking eyes. Horrible

breath, like rotten pork. I swipe him with the hammer, and he lets out a gargling yelp that sounds way, way too loud in the purposeful quiet of the house. I'm fending with my left hand, stupidly, and the shambler grabs my wrist and brings my hand toward his mouth. I wonder if his teeth were this nasty before he died or if they've become black zombie-teeth overnight. I'm betting, in life, he didn't brush.

Down South, we say "buck wild." I go there, to Buckwilds-ville, with the hammer, beating the shambler's head back and away from my hand. It doesn't let go, which is bizarre. Normal folks, you give them a good whack, and they're out cold or at least dropping everything. Not that I've ever actually given anyone a whack with a hammer. Scrappy-Doo here is my first. This guy hangs on with determination. He's giving it 110 percent.

I rear back and put everything into the swing. The hammer-head pops the shambler directly on his crown and I feel this satisfying crunch, like a gigantic soft-boiled egg being cracked with a spoon, and the dead guy's head takes on a new, flatter and looser shape, like a flesh-bag of broken glass. He falls on top of the floor creeper, who'd been crawling toward me. Missing a leg, the crawler looks like a giant, human-shaped charcoal briquette. If Egghead hadn't dropped when he did, he'd probably be chewing on my calf right now.

I crack the crawler's head too, and he stops moving. I rise up and Lucy is staring at me with big eyes, her pistol pointing at the zombie on the floor.

"God, I came so close to shooting that one." She looks at the charred dead guy on the floor. Doubly dead.

"Thank God you didn't. They'd probably be swarming us."
I smile at her. "Lemme go shut the front door."

No one is on the lawn when I shut and lock the front door.
There's a small spill of ash on the stoop and a bit inside the
house. Silly, but I hold my breath and try to avoid it.

We walk through the house, checking doors and windows.
I find a garage through a door off the kitchen. There's a
Honda Accord hybrid in there. An empty space for another
car or truck. The stuff stored in the room—hunting boots
and camouflage coats, weed-eaters and lawn-care utensils, gas
cans, a gun case—makes me think a truck. In the corner is a
bulky, tarp-covered object. Lucy appears in the doorway to
the kitchen. In lighter times I might've joked about a truck
parked next to a hybrid, but the expression on Lucy's face
doesn't warrant jests.

"Go check the gun cabinet," she murmurs. "I'll see if I can
find the keys for the car."

I walk to the cabinet and open it. There are a variety of
hunting rifles and shotguns. Two scoped bolt-action rifles,
.270 and A-Bolt 30-06. A semiautomatic .22 rifle. The smell
of the cabinet reminds me of my Peepaw, the smell of WD-
40. A pump-action 12 gauge. In the cabinet below, I find a
variety of hunting knives, ammunition for the guns, and a
matte-black gun holster with a dull pistol in it. It's heavy, and
it feels dangerous even securely fastened in the holster.

I hear Lucy pad toward me.

"You find the keys?"

Raising her hand, she jingles a key ring.

"I hope you have a belt," I tell her.

"Why?"

"Because there's a new sheriff in town, and she needs a gun holster."

"Don't you want it?"

"No," I say, shaking my head. "I've always been a miserable shot. I'll take this." I heft the shotgun. "I might be some help with it. And I've got my trusty hammer."

She tries to smile and fails. She's jonesing for her family, and I'm no help. But she takes the pistol, draws it from the holster, and checks the magazine.

"Nine millimeter." Obviously, she has experience with guns. More than me, it looks like.

"Whatever happens, we're gonna need some bags," I say, watching her. She holds the pistol in her hand and stares at it like someone who's picked up an interesting rock and thinks it might be worth something but isn't sure. "You think you can find food or water or whatever we might need and bags we can pack it in?"

She turns again and goes back into the house. I'm a little worried about her. Yesterday she was like a superhero, but today she's a little lost. Maybe she's not a morning person.

There's a camo bandolier for shotgun shells in the ammunition compartment, and I take it out and load it up and sling it across my chest. I feed the shells into the shotgun, work the action to put one in the chamber, and then feed a last one in. My fingers haven't forgotten Peepaw's lessons. It's taken an atomic holocaust and zombies to make me start remembering my family. But I don't want to think about Emily.

I put the shotgun within reach and then go to the

plastic shroud in the corner. I've got a sneaking suspicion what might be under it.

Pulling off the tarp, I'm greeted by the sight of a Honda 4x4 ATV with front and rear racks for hunting and cargo. The bright red plastic fenders and cover plates still shine new, and there's only a bit of mud on the tires. The key is in the ignition.

I'm reminded of a tune, but I don't have a head for music and even less of one for lyrics, so I can't recall the song, but I start humming a happy little ditty anyway.

I check the gas tank, and it looks empty. I turn the key over one click. Nothing. Not even the whir of solenoid or sparks from the battery.

I'm shitty with guns, but I'm pretty good with things that scoot, so by the time Lucy returns with a duffel bag that looks stuffed with things, I've got the ignition plate off with a screwdriver from the toolbox I found and I'm ready to hot-wire the little red beast.

"Shouldn't we check the car first?"

I blush. "I guess so. What about the electric magnetic—"

"Hmm. Electromagnetic pulse. Comes before big hydrogen fusion bombs. Knocks out . . . overloads really . . . modern electronics. The higher the altitude, the wider the effect. I guess whoever made the call to nuke us didn't want to wipe out the nation's electrical grid."

"How do you know this stuff?"

"High school science nerd."

I don't even have to stretch my imagination to see it: Lucy, in glasses with an armful of books, making rockets and dissecting piglets and running track with skinny knees and awkward glances at boys and—

I can't get distracted thinking about a young Lucy, so I say, "Well, let's check out the car."

Lucy pulls the keys from her jeans and walks around to the driver's door. She opens it and sits in the seat, but her legs hang out the door still.

She puts the key in the ignition and turns it over, one click, like the ATV. Nothing. She turns it over all the way. Dead.

"I can hot-wire the ATV. Bypass all the complicated electronics that are dead anyway. No problem. I used to have one."

For once I can do something. She's the superhero and I'm just her sidekick now, but that's all right with me. As long as I'm breathing and not shambling.

A horrible thought strikes me.

"Do you become one of those things if you die of old age?"

Lucy blinks twice, thinking.

"Well, with luck we'll find out, many, many years from now."

I laugh, a weak sound.

"We've got to get dressed," she says.

"I'm dressed now."

"No. Here." She throws the bag to the floor. "There's a leather jacket in there that might fit you. Did you find any gloves or helmets?"

"No, but—"

"Armor. That zombie almost bit off your fingers." She

shakes her head disapprovingly. "We've got to protect ourselves. I know it's summer, but we'll hydrate and put on a bunch of layers. If one of them bites, it—"

"It's all over, isn't it?"

"No. I don't think so. I think we *all* might be carriers by now. Everyone's infected, and many patients had it without bite wounds. There's no way I couldn't have been infected at the clinic, I breathed the air, I drank from water-fountains. I touched people." She thought of the boy spasming on the floor, eating his own lips and fingers. "So . . . some folks suffer symptoms and die. Everybody else just turns at death. But yeah, if they get their hands on you, it's pretty much over."

"Except for the shambling."

We search the garage. In a drawer of the worktable, I find a pair of grease-stained leather gloves.

"Allergies, most likely." Lucy pulls a stack of white dust masks, for yard work, down from a peg on the wall. In an oversized drawer, I find a circular saw with a couple of sets of protective glasses.

I put on a pair and hand the other to Lucy. She hands me a white mask, like we were in Hong Kong for their monthly SARS epidemic. Actually, I wish I was in a SARS epidemic rather than this situation. Except for finding Lucy.

Watching her move, I think of Angelyne, my girl back in Alabama. But where Angie was blunt and busty and, if I'm being honest, somewhat brutish, like an unhewn block of wood, Lucy is lithe and graceful. Full of thought. I should probably feel bad about everything. But I don't. I don't want

Angelyne to shamble. But I don't want to go back to her, either, and maybe that's why I stayed a trucker and never settled down with her. I was always leaving, always finding somewhere else to go.

I put on the leather jacket. She rummages in the bag and pulls out something that looks like a child's version of an Indiana Jones jacket. She pulls it on. I hand her the gloves.

"You don't want them?"

"I need to be able to drive the ATV."

She nods.

"I'll get the four-wheeler in shape and ready to go if you'll pack the other stuff. We need to be running before opening the garage door. Should we take these other guns?"

She thinks for a moment and then says, "No. They'll just slow us down. If we had the car—"

"Right. Take what we need, nothing else."

She turns to the door and then turns back.

"When you were going to kick me out of your semi, you said you had a daughter. Were you going to kick me out to save yourself or to try and get home to save her?"

I don't know what to say. Everything that's happened swims in my head, and I get images of Lucy sitting in the passenger seat of the semi and images of my daughter—images rising like fish to the top of a pond, broaching the surface, then submerging.

"I don't—"

"Because I'm beginning to think I can't really ask you to go with me. You need to go back up to the bathroom, close the door, and wait. Days, even a week or more. The radiation—it's going to give me cancer, surely. And you too, if you spend much more time out there."

"My girlfriend is too far away for me to do any good. Back in Alabama. My daughter is eighteen and in the army reserve. She's in Iraq. A half a world away." I give a little half-hearted laugh. "You're the only person I have right now."

Lucy opens her mouth, and then a tear pearls and traces its way down her cheek.

"Oh."

"There's no way of knowing what's going on with the rest of the world," I say as calmly as I can, hoping the hitch in my voice goes unnoticed. "As far as I know, she's safer there than we are here. She's probably better armed and equipped."

Lucy looks at me, and then away to the ATV, and then at the wall. She's working up to something.

"You should stay. Stay in the safe room. You'll be better off there. Leave in a few days, and you'll have much better chances to survive the radiation."

"What's the fallout circle . . . uh . . . the circumference?"

"The radius. It depends. Many, many miles at the least."

"But the wind usually blows west to east, right?"

She nods, looking at me. I can't read her expression.

"So won't my chances be better if I go upwind, out of the fallout range?"

She shakes her head, but I can see she's thinking. "I don't know. Leaving with me, we're sure to get some fallout in our system." She puts her hand to her waist, resting her palm on the pistol's grip, truly like a sheriff. "But I'm going. I just wanted you to know the risks . . . I can't be . . . responsible if you—"

I stand and grab a red fuel tank nestled in the corner of the garage. It's half full, two gallons' worth of gas. A smaller can has the word *mixed* scrawled on it with what looks like a Sharpie. I can only assume what I've got is unmixed gas. I turn back to her as I'm filling the ATV. She's still looking at me, and I still can't read her expression.

I sigh. "How the hell are you going to get out of here without me, anyway? I'm a trucker. Being on the move's in my blood. Do you know how to drive one of these things?"

"No. But—"

"Yeah, I'm sure you could figure it out. Forget that. I'll drive. You navigate, and shoot."

She draws a lungful of air, holds it, and then releases. She kneels and puts her hands to her face.

"You don't—" She clenches her fists, opens them, then rubs them on her jeans and stands again. "You don't know how much . . . how glad I am you said that. Thank you, Knock-Out."

My cheeks burn, and I don't know what to do with my hands.

"Shit. I got to move, I said. And we make a good team."

She laughs, tossing back her head. Her neck is long and graceful, and I can see the pulse in the hollow of her throat.

"So let's get going."

I grab the shotgun and put it in the gun rack, strapping it down. I fasten the safety glasses to my face.

"Here." She hands me a bandana, bright red, and I tie it

around my neck, bandit style. She has a large blue napkin and ties it around her neck. She pulls a couple of baseball caps from the wall and throws me one.

We stand, look at each other; we resemble gaudy banditos who've shopped at Walmart.

"Well, it's not quite biohazard suits, but it'll have to do."

I pull the air filter over my nose and mouth and Lucy mirrors me. She slings the duffel bag onto the ATV's rack and uses a bungee cord to strap it down. I take the screwdriver I stripped the ignition cover with and use it to jump the positive and negative wires, hot-wiring the ATV. It coughs, sputters, and dies. I repeat, this time cranking the throttle.

It catches and suddenly the ATV is roaring in the close confines of the garage. Lucy goes to the door and lifts it, sliding it back on its rollers. I turn the vehicle, pointing out, and wait until Lucy comes and hops on the back. She wraps her arms around my waist. Her touch is hot and stings some, and it takes me a second to realize it's from the burns. For a moment, even through the mask and bandana, I can smell the kiwi scent of her. I'm flushed with her presence, and my heart begins to race.

"Get out your gun, Lucy. Here they come." I don't want to say it, but I have to. I'd rather she stay embracing me.

Three shamblers—a man, a woman, and a boy-toddler—are coming in from the road, down the gravel drive to the house. Weird, but they're like an undead family. The kid is straggling to the side, walking on a leg that's hideously crooked. The foot is twisted to the side, and the child is pushing off the stump. The father totters, a big spill of blood down the front of his shirt and half his neck gone and large hunks of his shoulders. Momma looks almost whole except for where they chewed off her arm, her face otherwise untouched.

I kick the ATV into gear, and we're moving, out of the garage and across the drive, toward this undead family. I angle for the kid, away from the parents.

Lucy lays her arm on my shoulder, gun out, and fires. Another atomic bomb explodes, this time right next to my face. I can't hear the ATV anymore. The mother shambler wheels, tilts, and face-plants. The father turns and lurches toward us, but we're already past.

When we hit the boy, he gets caught in the rack, one hand gripping painted metal. I crank the throttle, and there's a lurch, the hand disappears, and the ATV jumps, like going over a speed bump.

Out and away from the family of walkers, we buzz down the road we ran in the dark, past the still smoking rubble of the house we first hid in. Not much left there. The sound of the ATV is loud, and grating, more due to what it might attract than for sheer volume.

A few dead mill around the husk of the Git-N-Go. The forests are still smoking along with the building. I bank the ATV toward the interstate, tires buzzing on asphalt. After Lucy's over-the-shoulder gunshot, my hearing returns slowly. Lucy grips me around the middle, and even though the world is empty, I feel a great contentment suffusing me. For that short time, life doesn't get any better.

A few shamblers lurch and wheel at the sound of the

four-wheeler, but we're moving fast now, kicking up ash and leaving the undead behind. I take a right and roll down the on-ramp to the interstate.

The sun is having a hard time piercing the slate-gray skies, and I can't tell if the clouds are water vapor or something more poisonous, but it's still morning when we get to her neighborhood. Big houses are nestled in a forest here, overlooking downtown Little Rock. Edgehill Drive. I think of my rented house back in Alabama, pillbox small and shabby.

This is a rustic but rich exurb where people keep their doors locked because they have things everybody else wants: money, art, big expensive cars, fancy appliances, healthy children. Lucy's street teems with white shamblers in expensive clothing.

"Take this left!" she yells and then fires the pistol. The nearest zombie, a well-to-do lady in a business skirt, silky blouse, and what appears to be a scarf but is really the evidence of major trauma from a nasty neck wound, grows a bright carnation of blood in her forehead and pitches over.

I'm glad Lucy is a crack shot. She should've lived in the Old West. I'm convinced if she had, we'd have heard of Doc Ingersol. Maybe someone famous would've played her in a movie.

We've seen more shamblers and less fallout the farther away from White Hall we ride. No living walk the streets. I've seen some people peeking from behind quickly drawn curtains, but none of them tries to contact us. Except one guy. He shoots at us from the top of a building, shouting cuss words.

Even Little Rock has no electricity. No lights, few cars on the roads, and great plumes of smoke on the northern and southern horizons. Lucy had hoped the EMP hadn't affected the city, but either it has or something has gone screwy at the dam or at the nuclear plant in Russellville. I'm worried what those smoke plumes might mean.

Now Lucy yells again, "Turn left!" and I follow her directions into an alley—really a rear access road, with leaves and mulch pits lining the shady lane—and then she yells, "Stop!"

We're at the gate to a big stone house with a heavily fenced backyard. It looks like an urban fort, cypress timbers two inches thick, impermeable to termites and, I hope, zombies.

"I can see why you wanted to get home," I say, but she can't hear me through the mask.

She hops off the ATV and, pulling a key chain from her pocket, reaches through the hole cut in the fence door and fiddles with the other side.

The shamblers have followed us down the alley. They toddle and lurch, making garbled sounds. It's time to earn my keep and make my grandfather proud.

I pop the straps on the 12-gauge shotgun, snatch it up, and flip off the safety. There's already one in the chamber, so I raise the gun to my shoulder and take a target: a big shambling martini-and-steak-eating guy in a fitted suit. I wait.

"Lucy! Hurry the fuck up! They're coming!"

I can't hear her reply.

The undead dealmaker comes forward, arms out, his

mouth working. He's different from some of the other shamblers. He looks as though he really wants to talk. But all he can say is, "Aowurg." He's fresh. His eyes aren't milky.

"Fuck!" I hear that from Lucy. I turn to look, and she's furiously working her hands.

They're closer now, so I point the shotgun in the general direction of the suit, do my best to target the guy's head, hold my breath like my grandfather taught me, and pull the trigger.

He falls down but starts to get back up. A miss. But after he rises, I see that I've peeled the left side of his face. Birdshot is useless if you want to destroy the brain.

A dead teen in hip-hugger jeans and a baby tee takes the lead. She still has an iPhone in her hand, which makes me think that when she died she kept her most precious objects close to her. Once, I might've gawked at her figure, but now not so much. I'm more interested in Lucy and whether she's opened the door.

The iPhone shambler is showing copious cleavage, which I reluctantly target. I hate to mar a rack as pure as hers, but destroying the brain isn't possible at this distance. So I fire at her chest and knock her back a few feet. She sprawls on her ass, losing her iPhone. In John Wayne movies, this is what they call delaying tactics.

"Knock-Out! Come on!" I turn and see Lucy has the door open. Twisting back to the dead, I quickly target and shoot the dealmaker and the iPhone shambler again, knocking them back into the followers.

I run back to the ATV and jump on, shotgun in hand, intending to drive it inside the gate. But I've forgotten that it has to be hot-wired, so after I get on, I get back off, cursing. The shamblers keep coming, but with more brute strength than I've mustered in a while, I push the damned thing through the gate and Lucy slams it shut and padlocks the latch.

"Let's get inside," she says, breathing heavy.

The zombies reach the gate, and it begins to rattle and jump. I stick the bore of the shotgun in the hole Lucy used to unlock the gate door and pull the trigger three more times, kicking out shells and blasting back the zombies.

"Save your ammo!" Lucy bellows. "You're just drawing more!"

Exhausted, I turn and follow her inside.

I'm fearful of what we might find here too. I have to be honest, I've already grown used to Lucy's company. Everything we know has gone, with the virus, with the explosion, everything has been taken away—the cars and planes and stores and televisions and radios—and now it's just Lucy and me, climbing up the back stairs of her house, sliding open the back doors, and entering the dark room. I don't want to lose Lucy now, like everything else.

Everything is everything. I still don't know what that means.

There are broken windows and shamblers in the house.

Lucy's hands begin to shake. I take the lead, shotgun out.

It's a horrible feeling to fear coming home; I remember my father, the beatings and the screaming. Of course, this is different.

It's dark in the house. There are clouds overhead, and the house is in shadows. I hear shuffling and moans coming from the blackness. I need light.

Lucy moves away and I hear a drawer slide open and then there's a beam of light in the darkness.

"Let's make sure the doors are shut and then look for Fred and Gus."

I nod. She brings out her pistol and moves through the house. I follow her. Again, I'm struck by how much she looks like a police officer, gun out, flashlight piercing the gloom.

We come to a large room, plasma television on the wall and big bay windows overlooking the backyard, letting in enough light to see the five or six shamblers milling about like they're at a cocktail party or a football game. There's dried, brown blood everywhere. They turn toward us as a group and lurch forward.

"Come on!" Lucy yells, her voice tight with worry. She dashes down the hall, and I jump after her. I can see the front door of her house standing wide open and shamblers in the yard turning to look.

A zombie steps out in front of her like a jack-in-the-box, and she barrels right into his arms. Lucy screams, and it's a sound I never thought I'd hear from her: too vulnerable, too scared, too panicked.

They tumble, and I can see the shambler's mouth opening to take a bite. I can't let that happen.

Something smashes behind me, and I know that the zombies from the living room are coming and I can see the shamblers outside making their way toward the open front door.

Lucy lies just inside, with a big motherfucker snapping at her face and neck. I reach them and kick Jack-in-the-Box with everything I've got and he flips over, but he's still holding onto Lucy so now she's partly on top. So I put my boot on his face and stomp as hard as I can. I can feel some dental work crack, but it's not enough because he doesn't let go. I stomp again. And again.

Finally something gives, his head flattens a little, and Lucy jumps up. She turns and looks back down the hallway.

"Knock-Out! They're everywhere." She kneels on the floor, recovers her dropped pistol, turns, and starts firing. I'm looking out the front door. The shamblers have made it to the stone steps and are working their way forward. I raise the shotgun and fire into the group, at the chest of a middle-aged woman wearing green gardening gloves and knee pads. She must've been in the yard when all hell broke loose. She takes the birdshot in the chest and falls backward onto her ass, taking two more of the things with her. It's like bowling, but with the undead. And if you lose, you die. Or not really die.

Lucy's gun is still popping, and my ears ring. I raise the shotgun to shoot again, I fire, and this time a zombie's head explodes. Even a broken clock is right twice a day.

More of the shamblers are coming from the street. Soon there'll be fifty or sixty. I've got to get the door closed.

But Jack-in-the-Box is lying dead in the doorway. I grab his feet and start to pull him away. The front-stoop shamblers are back on their feet, looking tattered and quite a bit worse for wear. I must've ruptured something in the gardener's body cavity, because black and green goo wells and drips from her mouth.

I give a great heave and pull Jack aside, hook the door with my foot, and slam the door shut with a crunch, but it sticks and rebounds a little. There's a green glove peeking from behind the lip of the door. I shove the shotgun in the gap, pull the trigger, shaking the house, and the green-gloved hand is gone and the door shuts. I throw the dead bolt as the door begins to shudder. The Welcome Wagon has arrived.

I turn back to Lucy and realize it's been ten or twenty seconds since she's fired. But now I know why.

She stands, heaving, gun out, eyes wide and frantic. There's a veritable dog-pile of shamblers on the floor. Seven or eight of them, all lying at her feet. I can't imagine what it must be like for her, murdering people in the front hall of her own house.

"Luce. Come on. Reload, and let's see if we can secure the house and find your family."

I put my hand on her shoulder.

"Luce. We're gonna be okay. Gus and Fred will be okay." I try to keep my voice low. And she looks at me. Some of the shamblers must've gotten pretty close when she popped them because a fine tracery of blood spatters her face and mars the beautiful hollow of her neck.

"Reload." I pull shells from the bandolier and feed them into the shotgun. I check my hammer; still hanging from the belt. She pops her clip, slowly feeds bullets into it. I know she's got another clip, full, but she's doing the right thing, keeping two loaded.

I go into the room Jack-in-the-Box came from and see boards have been nailed over the windows there.

"Lucy! Come here." She turns, gun in hand, and comes to me. "Looks like Fred had time to take precautions. He's boarded these windows. This is a good sign."

She's sluggish to respond. And that frightens me more than anything, really, that she might be losing it.

I put the shotgun on a table, grab her shoulders, and shake her. She looks annoyed and tries to pull away.

"Lucy! This means he wasn't caught flat-footed! He was prepared." Her eyes lock on mine. At first she's pissed, but then she understands what I'm saying and nods.

"So let's check out the rest of the house." I say, grabbing my shotgun again. I walk to the other rooms. It looks like Fred did a fairly decent job of boarding up the ground-floor windows. He ran out of lumber—who has that amount of lumber lying around anyway?—and started using doors. Bookcases. Tabletops. It must've been pretty hairy around here.

But where is he now?

Lucy stands beside me, looking at the ruin of her house.

"Lucy, if you were Gus, and scared, where would you go to hide? Your room?"

She shakes her head and turns to go back into the darker areas of the house. The front door is rattling and glass breaks somewhere in the house and the sound of garbled speech and moans can be heard, but I don't think they're inside.

We have to climb over the corpses in the hallway. It's a squishy, unpleasant thing, and I'm disturbed that I'm walking on the dead. Once I shared the common bond of humanity with them. Now? What are they? What are the shamblers? Do I still have some moral responsibility to them? Meemaw would say yes. Peepaw would say, shoot 'em dead if they're trying to get you. And yes, they are trying to get me. And people I care for. Emily in Iraq, maybe. Lucy, definitely. And Gus. I've never met the boy, but I'm fascinated that there's a child in the world that's half this woman. What will he be like? Will he have her eyes? Her hair? Her brains and confidence?

I want to meet him because meeting him will bring me closer to understanding her.

Once we're over the mound of the dead, I can see her face darken, worry for her child eroding her resolve. She's not thinking the same things I am, but at least her mind is working again.

There's a thump from below us, and Lucy gasps. It doesn't sound good. Thumps, in my experience, mean shamblers.

"Downstairs," she says, and she points at a door down a long hall. "Gus and Fred would've gone to the workroom. There are guns there. The safe." There's a wide opening on the left with a spill of light coming across the floorboards. The shadows aren't moving, which makes me think that room, at least, is devoid of shamblers.

I go first, keeping my shotgun to my shoulder, ready to fire.

I pop around the corner like I've seen SWAT teams do on television, and realize the reason they do it that way is it's better to get it over with. And it makes sense. My body wants to pop around the corner.

It's a nice dining room, made nicer by the absence of walking dead.

"The stairs are farther down the hall."

I retarget our front sector. I'm starting to think in television cop-show speak. Lucy's standing off to the side with her pistol out. She falls in behind me as I move toward the door.

"This is the one."

I open it quickly, like ripping off a Band-Aid or breaking up with a girlfriend.

The stairwell is dark. I hear another thump and some garbled moans. There's a shambler down there, no doubt about it.

Lucy flips on her Maglite, spearing the long stairwell with the beam, and whispers, "At the bottom of the stairs, it turns left. There's a long hallway running back underneath the house. There's a storage room, a little gym and laundry, and the last door is the workroom. It's got a safe. A gun cabinet. Fred had been reinforcing the doors and walls to make it a safe room. Just in case. It's a nice neighborhood, if that meant anything anymore."

"You're telling me."

I move down the stairs, holding the shotgun up with one hand and keeping my other hand on the rail. The carpet here is plush and springy, and I'm worried about my foothold.

When we reach the bottom, it's pitch black except for Lucy's wobbly flashlight beam. She's really upset, if the steadiness of her hands is any indication.

The carpet is still springy, and we're not making any noise.

I walk to the first door on the left, the one Lucy said is storage. I put my ear to it. Nothing.

I slowly turn the knob and then quickly push open the door. The flashlight beam jumps around the room, and I follow it as best I can. No shamblers.

We move to the next door. It's open, and Lucy shines the light inside, and for a moment, my mind assembles images and I have the impression of a shambler walking on a treadmill. But then the flashlight beam pans around and I realize it's just ironed shirts hanging from a pipe above an elliptical machine.

There's a loud thump, and it's obvious where it came from. The workroom.

We're as quiet as possible, going down the hall. It's become a habit, silence.

I go to the door and put my ear against it. There's a weird deep moan, a garbled sound, and then the door, right against my ear, bangs. The deepness of the moan lets me know it's a man. The shambler beats on the door, trying to get out.

I grab the door handle, look back at Lucy, who is pale faced and thin lipped, and turn the handle. It doesn't budge. Locked.

"I'm gonna have to shoot the doorknob."

"What?"

"How else are we gonna get in?"

She's quiet for a long while. Then she says, "Okay. But do it at an angle so you don't hit whoever's inside."

"Right. But it's a shambler."

"I don't care. If it's . . . Gus . . . I don't want—" She wipes her eyes. "Maybe I can save him."

I shake my head. "How?"

"A hospital. Maybe I can isolate the virus and—"

"Electricity. We don't have it. There's zombies everywhere. You think we'll just be able to walk into the hospital?"

She shakes her head, and I'm getting anxious. The beating on the inside of the door is louder now.

But it's her child and I understand what she's feeling and I realize I wasn't thinking about that so I say, "Okay. We'll capture him, keep him safe until we can figure out what to do."

She nods.

I stand back at an angle and pull the trigger. The doorknob disappears. Birdshot ricochets back and pings off my clear protective glasses. It's a good thing I've forgotten to take them off.

I inspect the door. The doorknob is gone, but the locking mechanism is still in the hole, so I reach in to fiddle with it and it falls into the workroom. I shove on the door, but it still won't budge.

"Lemme see the flashlight."

She puts it in my hand, and I kneel and shine it through the hole. My heart stops. I jump backward. There's a face right there in the space the doorknob occupied—milky eyes, mouth black and bloody and open in a snarl. The shambler isn't a happy camper.

I stick the shotgun in the hole, and I'm about to pull the trigger when Lucy knocks me aside. I sprawl over, dropping the flashlight.

"Goddamn it, Luce. It ain't alive. Whoever it is. And I don't think there's any others in there."

"I can't risk it. It might be Gus."

"Well, why don't you take a peek first? Will you be able to recognize him through the hole?"

She looks uncertain. For a moment, my heart rips itself from my chest and goes out to her; she looks so lost. I wish I could do something, anything, to make this situation better for her.

She dusts off her knees and kneels, pointing the flashlight in the hole.

Her shoulders start to shake, and I can see huge silent sobs wracking her body. She stands up and moves down the hall.

"Fred." She's crying now, truly crying. "It's Fred."

I don't know what to do with myself. Part of me wants to jam the bore of the shotgun in the hole, and part of me wants to try to figure a way to save the man, for Lucy's sake.

We both stay rooted in our own space in the dark hallway at the bottom of a big shambler-infested house in a shambler-infested city. Great plumes of radioactive smoke surround us. Now I'm positive those clouds were more mushroom clouds. And in this dark hallway, I feel very small and alone, especially since Lucy has succumbed to her fear, her shock. And her love. She's succumbed to love. It's her family at stake. My daughter is halfway around the world in Iraq, maybe fighting Al Qaeda, maybe fighting the undead. I feel a thin line of connection between Emily and me—the same feeling I would get when she'd stay with me, wear my shirt, and then when I put it on, her scent would linger and I'd feel her presence. I feel the thin connective tissue stretching away past the unseen horizon and right now . . . right now, I know she's alive and I'm glad of it. And I'm doubly sad for Lucy.

"I don't have to—" I say, dumbly, leaving the rest of the sentiment unspoken. *Shoot him.*

She's silent. I want to go hug her, and I'm ashamed, because when she said the shambler was Fred, my heart leaped and I was glad. Glad I still had her to myself. For a little bit longer. I shouldn't feel that way, but I do.

"Go ahead." She grips her arms like she's cold. It's impressive because she still has a pistol and the Maglite.

I approach her. I want to hug her, and I think about it. But as I get closer, she sticks out the flashlight and I take it.

"Are you gonna be okay with this?"

"No. How could I?"

I breathe through my mouth, like the big, dumb trucker I really am.

"Then I'm not gonna do it. I can't have you hating me for the rest of my life. You're the only doctor in town." It's my attempt at a joke. It doesn't go over very well.

I kick the door. It squeaks. The shambler—it's so much easier thinking of her husband as one of the nameless mass rather than someone Lucy loved—returns to banging on the inside of the workroom's door. Groaning. Making weird sounds.

"What are you doing?" Lucy has turned.

I kick again. I used to be in shape. I'm a big guy, and not all of it is fat. I'm a crappy shot, but I still have some muscle. The doorjamb splinters. I can hear the shambler inside the room become almost mad with bloodlust. We must smell scrumptious to him.

"Knock-Out. Don't. You don't have to—"

I lash out with my foot, one last time. The door crashes open. Lucy brings up the light.

Everything happens so fast, I don't know what I'm doing, but I'm doing it anyway.

The door folds inward and pops the shambler, knocking him back. I've got my hammer in hand and I'm moving into the room, toward the zombie—toward Fred. He'd been a medium-size man in life, rangy and athletic. But I outweigh him by fifty, maybe sixty pounds. I grab him by his neck and fall on top of him. He's twisting his head, trying to bite my arms. His hands grab my hair and draw my face forward, toward his black, snapping mouth.

It's like falling into a well.

I'm not really interested in becoming shambler-chow, so I raise my arm with the hammer and swipe his mouth with it. He's gonna require major orthodontia now. I give him another swipe across the jaw, which cracks and loosens. I turn the hammer to the side and shove the handle deep, deep into his mouth. I use my weight to hold it there, like a bit in a horse's mouth.

Then I hear Lucy screaming. She's saying a name, over and over again. And to my surprise, it's not Fred or Gus. The name she says is mine.

"Knock-Out!"

"Luce. Get some tape or something. If he keeps scratching like that, he's gonna get through my jacket. Leave some nasty welts."

"Fuck," she says, half laughing. The kind of laugher you hear at funerals, too forced and a little crazy. "You're a madman. Why the fuck didn't—" She stops and shakes her head.

She opens her mouth and then closes it.

"Hey, Lucy. It's kinda hard keeping him still. He ain't settlin' down. Can you find some tape or something?"

Wild-eyed, she turns and takes the Maglite off me and the shambler and goes to the worktable. I'm in the dark, holding the dead man now, and it's not my most favorite thing I've ever done. The man's flesh is dead—I guess—but he kicks and thrashes hard. I can feel his muscles bunch and contract beneath me, but slower than you'd think. Not like grappling with someone living, less frantic, but holy crow . . . so strong. His head twists and his body shifts, his face so near mine. The stench pours off him. *Eau de Deadman.* It's all over me, the stink.

It's hard to believe that this mouth has ever said Lucy's name with love. That this diseased thing has kissed her. His hands scratching at me have caressed her.

He's squirming. Squirming hard. At times I don't think I'll be able to keep control of him. His arms claw at the leather jacket.

He moans underneath me. We're like a horrible parody of lovemaking. To think, it's her husband I've held more tightly than her. Well, there was the shower. And the drainage ditch pipe, when we both caught fire. Ah. Good times.

I shove the hammer down harder. I hear something crack. It might be his spine. Maybe more dental work will be needed.

"These leather jackets were a good idea, Lucy," I say to her back, a little breathlessly, like I've been running. "If I didn't have it on, my arm would be shreds by now. Good thinking there."

"Shut up, Knock-Out! Shut up! This is no time to joke!"

"I'm not joking . . . God, he's strong, Luce."

"I'm looking."

"Hurry, please."

I turn my attention back to Fred, the shambler with the strength of a million men. I'm having a hard time keeping my arms on the hammer. My palms become slick with sweat. I hear Lucy knocking things over, rummaging through the worktable drawers.

"I'm losing my grip, Lucy! Please."

Suddenly, his face is bright again, and Lucy is standing over me, shining the light. His skin is blue green, and his mouth is open wider than any human mouth should open. It's ripped at the corners, rough, ragged tears running toward his ears.

But there's anger in his eyes. The dead man is furious at us. And I somehow feel like if we could figure out why he's angry we could heal him. The rage on his face is even more frightening than the fact that the motherfucker wants to eat me.

The light holds on Fred's face.

"Lucy! I don't think I can hold him—"

The room flashes white, and a hole appears in Fred's forehead. My ears ring from the noise of the gunshot. His hands loosen and fall away from my arms.

I don't know if Lucy is crying or not. I flop off the corpse, onto my back, and take in big lungfuls of air. I'm happy just to lie here in the dark, next to the corpse of Lucy's husband, and breathe. It's all I can do.

The room lightens; Lucy's lit a votive candle from the last house with a match. I can smell the sulfur of it. The scent comes through over the smell of her husband's remains.

It's gonna get real stinky in this house in the next couple of days.

Everything is quiet. The ringing in my ears dies, and I listen to Lucy sob and the house settle. Now I can see pipes and floor joists above me. It's a very nice workroom if you ignore the dead man. A glass-faced gun cabinet lined with rifles and shotguns sits next to the workbench. Fred must've been a hunter. A big five-foot-tall safe with combination dial and metal handle stands in the corner. It's got the word *Pinkerton* emblazoned on the front, under the handle, in old-timey script. It looks like a safe that movie bandits wearing bandanas blow up on trains: big, bulky, cast iron.

There are gold coins scattered around the floor. That's bizarre. Dollar bills. Particle board.

"Do you have a cat?"

"What?"

"Hear that?" I sit up. "That scratching. You have a dog or cat?"

Lucy looks around wildly. Her eyes fix on the gold.

"Shhh. Don't move," I say.

Scrrtch. Scrrtch.

"The safe."

Lucy jumps toward the cast-iron box, twists the dial backward and forward. She pushes down the handle and tugs the door open.

A boy falls forward onto the floor, followed by a shower of gold.

I've heard of Krugerrands before but never seen one. The safe was stuffed with them. And Gus.

The first thing he says is, "Who's he?"

The boy is sweaty and weak. And stinks of urine. Golden shower, indeed.

"Knock-Out, honey. He saved me. Saved us."

He looks at the remains of his father.

"Did he kill Dad?"

"No." Short and flat, her words. Lucy the doctor, Super Lucy, is back.

The boy nods. He's blond, a little pudgy, and has gray eyes. He looks happier now that he knows I haven't murdered his already dead father. I guess happy is relative.

Lucy cradles him in her arms, rocking.

"How long have you been in there, Gus?"

The boy touches her face, turns her head, and sees the burned hair. His eyes go wide, and he looks at me. I think he's beginning to realize that we've been through the shit-storm too.

"I don't know. Since last night," he says, voice not strong. But he doesn't look like he's gonna blubber either. He takes a breath, squares his shoulders, and says, "Dad and I were making lunch, when we hear this big boom, and the whole sky goes white. It's like lightning, you know? But it lasts too long. At least that's what Dad says. It's like a lightning bolt got stuck in the sky and the white light kept going." He swallows. "Can I have some water? There's jugs of it over there."

I look, and there are cardboard boxes full of gallon milk jugs. There's maybe fifty or sixty in there. Lucy looks at me and says, "Avian flu." She smiles sadly. "We were worried about a pandemic. We were just a little off. Every time we finished a jug of milk, we washed it, rinsed it, filled it with water, and brought it down here. Just in case."

I grab a gallon jug and look around for a cup. I can't find one, so I twist off the cap and bring the jug over to Gus. I tilt it up and let him drink. This seems to help.

"Hi, Gus. I'm Knock-Out. I sure am glad to meetcha."

He smiles. I offer my hand, and he takes it and we shake, man to man. His stare is solid, steady, and unlike any child's I've ever met before. He's like his mother.

"Y'all store any food? 'Cause I'm starving."

"There's MREs and canned stuff back there," Gus says. I want to ask him how he knows about MREs, but then again, he is Lucy's son. And Fred's. Fred might've turned into a ravenous murdering sonofabitch, but he seems like he was a formidable man before he took up shambling.

I dig in another box, pull out some brown glossy bags. There's a can of Sterno in the box and a pan. I take it all out and move to sit at the workbench.

"So what happened after that, honey?" Lucy brushes Gus's hair from his eyes. He blinks and moves his head away from her hand.

"We went outside, in the front yard, to look. Once the sky stopped its glow, we could see the big cloud. Daddy—"

The boy looks to his father on the floor. I stand and glance around. In the corner is a stack of wool blankets. Military grade, they feel rough and wiry, like Brillo pads. I take one and drape it over Fred Ingersol. May he rest in peace.

"The sirens, we could hear them coming . . . We went back inside and turned on the TV. The newsman was talking about a virus that caused seizures and . . . cannibalism."

"What else did the news say, baby? Did they say how far it had spread?"

"They said it was in New York and Chicago. Atlanta. Miami. Mexico."

"Mexico?"

"Shit," I say, and both Lucy and Gus look at me. "I thought you said it was just around White Hall."

She's giving us the thousand-yard stare, trying to figure things out.

"Maybe it takes longer to show symptoms than we thought. If that's the case, it could be around the world." She rubs her mouth with the back of her hand. "Or maybe it *is* airborne and we have a natural resistance to it. I just don't know."

"If it's all those places, then it's worldwide."

"It wasn't when the electricity worked," Gus says. He's like a little man, serious, well spoken. An equal.

"After the explosion, the news showed mushroom clouds all over. New York. Los Angeles. Canada. Europe."

"Oh no."

Goddamn. A fucking virus started World War III.

"But last night, right before the electricity went out, the newsmen said that the president and the . . . Chinese guy . . . that they were gonna talk. We heard honking and screaming. Mr. Milton came driving down the street, swerving. There was something wrong with him. He screamed at us and shook all over."

Lucy hugs Gus tight to her chest and looks at me. I open the MRE. Spaghetti with meat sauce. An army of smaller bags fall from the larger one. I don't need the Sterno; this has its own heating packet. Bread. Cheese spread. Salt. Pepper. Cocoa. And coffee. Sugar. Creamer. A wet wipe. Amazing how ingenious the American government was at one time. Now they've ingenioused the human race nearly out of existence.

I feel like Lucy wants some support with her son despite me just meeting him. So I become my grandfather.

"You want some cocoa?" I've never met a kid who doesn't want cocoa. Even in the height of summer. It could be the Sahara, an inferno, and kids will want more marshmallows in their cocoa. What is a marshmallow, anyway?

Fuck it, I'm gonna use the Sterno. Even the little extra light helps. I light the can and put the saucepan on the little fold-up rack that comes with it. I fill it with water and wait for the steam.

I don't have anything else to do with myself for the moment. But I'm starting to worry about the security of the house. The shamblers are beating at the front door and the back gate. I don't want to get caught down here, especially after the door has been kicked in once. I stand, go to the hall, and get my shotgun where I've dropped it. I feed it with shells until I can't put any more in it.

Lucy gives me a puzzled look. Gus too. They're looking at me like I'm crazy, but I'm feeling cooped up and claustrophobic. I take a deep breath, and, mirroring something I've seen both Lucy and Gus do, I square my shoulders and exhale.

I sit.

"Sorry about that. I got to roll. Just a touch of the nerves. I'm a trucker. But Luce . . . and Gus . . . we've got to secure the house soon."

Lucy and Gus exchange glances. He shrugs her off and stands up.

I hold out my hands. "I'm glad y'all are listening to me, but I didn't mean right now. Let's have some water. Let's eat some food. Gus, finish your story, and then we'll check out the house. Okay? It can wait that long. We'd hear something, I think. Lucy, did you close the door at the top of the stairs?"

She shakes her head.

"Oh shoot. Okay, stay here. I'll take care of that first."

Taking the Maglite, I walk into the hall, raise the shotgun, and tread softly on the carpet. On the stairwell, it's real easy to spot the shambler making his way downstairs. There's another behind him. There's a breach somewhere in the house.

I raise the shotgun, aim at the silhouette of the lead shambler's head, and pull the trigger. It tilts backward and then tumbles toward me, hitting the stairs face-first, then sliding further down the incline. It stops moving. I wish Lucy was here to see that shot.

I take a bead on the other shambler coming down the stairs and fire.

I'm not quite sure how, but I've missed completely. I didn't think that was possible with a shotgun, but you learn something new every day.

And this one shows me another thing new: it isn't beyond the undead to jump.

It launches itself in the air, and suddenly I can't breathe. I'm knocked backward into the wall, the Maglite spins crazily off down the hall, and only the shotgun is between me and the shambler. I can't see its face, but I can smell its breath, like dog food marinating in chicken grease in the summer sun. I don't need to see the foul thing to know he's there. And he wants to eat me.

I shove as hard as I can—I want to live more than he wants to eat me—and the shambler tumbles backward against the stairs. I stand as quickly as I can, put the bore of the shotgun in its face, and pull the trigger. It's only a boom. I've heard bigger ones in the last few days. The head before me disappears in a fine mist of blood. I can feel it on my hands.

What happens if its blood gets in my mouth? My eyes? Do I get the virus too? Was there blood on Lucy's face? Is there blood on mine? She said we all might have it already. I have to go with that. And there's no time to worry about it now, anyway.

I don't think I could do to her what she did to Fred. How could I? I've never, ever felt this way before. I can't kill this feeling. I'd rather die. And rise again.

I have the overwhelming urge to scream in the close

darkness at the base of the stairwell. But I force myself to stand and walk up the stairs into the light.

I catch another shambler in the hallway leading to the kitchen. There's a guest bedroom that Fred and Gus didn't board up. The zombies have beaten in the glass, and I can see twenty or thirty of them milling around just beyond the one caught on the sill, glass digging into his belly and holding him in place. One dead man claws at the back of his gut-caught brother and pulls himself up and over to flop on the floor like a fish able to move from pond to pond. I bash his skull with the shotgun's stock before he can rise.

There's no use trying to shoot into this crowd. But the guy stuck on the windowsill is doing a pretty good job of keeping them out for the moment. One fish at a time.

I shut the door. There's no lock. I hope I can get downstairs and back with hammer and nails before they can get in.

I run through the house, my breath wheezing in my chest. I feel a bit dizzy, but I keep going, shotgun in hand.

I nearly run over Gus coming up the stairs.

"We heard the shots!" he yells, but he's strangely calm. Maybe he thinks I'm a little deaf. With all the gunfire, inside and at close quarters, I could be getting a little deaf at that.

"They were on the stairs." I see he's picked up the Maglite I've dropped. "Listen, Gus, I need you to get your mother—"

Lucy comes out of the stairwell.

"Gus, do not just run off like that—"

She draws up short when she sees the expression on my face. "What's wrong?"

"We can't stay here. They're starting to swarm the house. So, listen. Gus. Lucy. Go get as much water and food as you can carry from the workroom. Bring them to the kitchen. But first get a hammer and nails. Gus. You go now. Run. As quick as you can."

He looks at Lucy, silently asking permission to leave, and she nods. I can see she doesn't want to let him out of her sight, but she knows she has to eventually. It might as well be now and make it quick.

He's down the stairs before the sound of my voice fades away.

"Why do we have to leave? We can bar ourselves in the workroom, we've got food, water—"

This is weird for Lucy. She's not thinking straight. It should be her saying this to me. Families are our great strength. Families are our great blind spot.

"Fred and Gus missed a room when they were boarding up. There's shitloads of shamblers flopping in, one by one. The guest room window."

Lucy starts off, down the hall.

"Wait. Lucy, wait."

She stops and turns back to me.

"I'm going to nail the door shut and that should hold them, but we've got to get out of here, Lucy. We can't just lock ourselves in the basement. That's a sure death. They can smell us, remember? What happens when we're the last folks alive in the city and there are thousands of them? Eventually they'll make their way here. We'd just be sitting in a pitch-dark hole waiting to die."

She nods. I watch the thoughts passing though her delicate features. God, she's beautiful, despite the blood, the grime, the burned hair.

"We've got to be able to run. Always."

"Right," I say. "We've got to get to the country. Arkansas hasn't got a lot of people—"

"But Little Rock—any city, really—is the last place you want to be. We've got to go somewhere with the lightest population density we can find."

I'm nodding now, because she's back.

Gus appears at the door to the stairwell. His face is ashen. He hands me my hammer. It has blood all over it. His father's blood. But he looks me in the eye, solidly, and puts a snarl of ten-penny-weight nails in my hand.

"Go get guns, get water, get food. Go to your rooms and get whatever—" I stop, not knowing how to say it. So I just *say* it. "Get your memories. Only what you can carry. Pictures of your father, Gus. Pictures of your husband, Lucy. You'll never be able to replace them. There ain't any coming back home once we leave. But do it quickly! Only what you can carry. We're gonna leave on the ATV. We'll be exposed, but we can go off-road, bypass cars, cut through yards. It'll be easier to travel than being trapped in a car."

"But—"

"Go!"

I turn and run to the guest room. One of the zombies is banging on the door already. The good thing is, it opens inward, so he can bang on the door all he wants, it's not going to bust open. Yet. Eventually, he might split it, if his friends join him. And one of the shamblers might remember how to turn a doorknob. Maybe. They remember anger. Sometimes it sounds like they almost remember a word or two.

I put nails every ten inches around the frame. In the hall is a bookcase. I knock it over, use my foot to break off a board, and nail it across the doorway. I hammer boards until I run out of nails.

I put the hammer back in my belt and go back to the kitchen.

Gus is there with his backpack stuffed full. He's got a pistol in a holster hanging from his belt. It looks heavy, blunt nosed.

"Your dad's?"

He knows exactly what I'm talking about. But he looks at me and says, "No. It's mine now."

I'm not going to get in some pissing match with a ten-year-old. I just boarded up a door to keep out zombies, for chrissake. The boy can keep his gun.

"Hey, do me a favor, will you?"

He stares at me and then nods once, slowly.

"Don't shoot me. All right?"

Lucy comes in the kitchen carrying a big box of water and MREs. She has consolidated. I remember I had some water boiling downstairs. Before the shamblers on the stairs. The ones in the hall and guest room.

"Did you . . . snuff the Sterno?"

She gives me a quick smile and then sets the box on the kitchen table. She moves over to Gus, puts her arm around him. Not in a lovey-dovey way . . . no. She touches him in the same way that the heartbroken are reunited with their true loves.

"We need glasses for the boy. Set him up with armor, bandana. Everything he might need."

"We should take a car," she says firmly.

"No. ATV."

"A car will protect us from—" She glances at Gus.

"Luce. The boy knows about the zombies. The world we know is over. And we always need to be able to run. You can't do that with a car. With the ATV we don't even need roads."

She cocks her head and looks at me as if she's seeing me for the first time all over again. I want to say that I can be stubborn, and sometimes I can be right. And in this case, I'm both.

I dig in my shirt pocket, pull out my last cigarette. It's bent but whole. I light it with a match. I miss my skull-and-crossbones Zippo.

The smoke tastes good. Gus watches me, curious. I'm big and hairy and ugly. I'm not a jogger or tennis player like his father. I'm a trucker. But his father is dead and I'm standing here in front of him.

I take another drag, ash on the floor, and then hold the cigarette out to Lucy. She glances at Gus. Then reaches out and takes it. She leans against the counter and inhales deep.

"I knew you smoked, Mom."

She looks surprised for a second.

"At night . . . before . . . sometimes I could smell it on you. You smelled like Granny. Smoky."

"It's a bad habit, honey. It can kill you if you do it too much. But you already know that, don't you?"

He nods.

I snap my fingers. I'm being a little hokey, but it's been a long time since Emily was a little girl and she always thought my hokiness was funny.

I say, "I just had an idea. I need a piece of wood. Yea big." I hold my arms out and make an imaginary square, four feet by four feet. "And some black paint and a paintbrush. You think you can find that for me?"

He's quiet. I can see his brain is working. The boy is a little scary. He hasn't cried; he hasn't shown fear. Just acceptance and understanding of everything that's come along. Zombies. Nuclear explosions. The change and brutal death of his father.

"And some more nails. And rope. Can you get all that?"

He nods again. He's chubby but has a nice, long neck and big hands. Smart features. He'll grow. Soon.

He turns and runs to the stairwell. Watching him move, I'm reminded he's only ten.

"So, what happened? Did you get the rest of his story?"

"Yeah. Bob Milton, our next-door neighbor, wrecked his car. Spasms. Lesch-Nyhan. Fred—"

She stops. I reach out and take my cigarette back from her.

"Fred went to the wreck to help him. Milton bit him. Gus pulled Fred . . . pulled his father back inside. They locked the door and watched the TV until the electricity went out. By midnight, the street was crowded with revenants. They started trying to get in. Fred boarded the windows, and Gus helped. But Fred started to have spasm problems. Cursing. Gus pulled him downstairs to the workroom. I guess it was there that Fred went into opisthotonus . . . a constriction of all the back and leg muscles. Horrible shit."

Lucy looks at the cigarette again. It's almost down to the filter. I take one last puff and hand it over.

"Gus is no dummy. He knew what was about to happen. And Fred did too. Gus convinced his father—who was already starting to spasm—to lock him in the safe. At least for a while, until they knew if Fred was going to—" She stopped there. Took a hard drag on the last of the smoke, looking out the window into the backyard. The rattling gate. Maybe it was the smoke that irritated her eyes. "So he dumped the Krugerrands on the floor and got inside the safe with a bottle of water."

"Shit. Smart kid."

She nods. "I can't imagine how hard it must've been for him. Or for Fred to turn the combination."

"Do you have everything you need?" She needs the change of subject and I'm happy to provide it. "I think you need to get all the medical supplies you can get. All the drugs, whatever you won't be able to find on the road."

"I lost my needle gun when we were running from the army. And it's useless without a lab anyway."

"Get what you can."

"I'll get Gus armored up too. I think there's some work gloves in the laundry room."

Gus comes into the kitchen carrying a two-foot-square board, a can of paint, and a brush.

"Here. Best I can do, Knock-Out." He leaves the board on the table.

"Your neck, arms. Protect them."

Gus follows Lucy out.

I hammer two nails at the top of the board, and once they're in good, I bend them over, creating loops. I feed the rope through the nails and tie it off, making a larger loop.

Opening the paint, I dip the brush in and, using my best handwriting, begin to write on the sign.

When Gus and Lucy come back, Gus has ski goggles strapped to his forehead and a black bandana tied around his neck. He's wearing a black motorcycle jacket, gloves tucked into his belt. A snub-nosed pistol in a holster. A hunting knife next to it, and a small Maglite. I have to remind myself he's just ten.

"What school did you get your medical degree from, Lucy?"

She looks surprised. "Dartmouth Medical School. I was a resident at Johns Hopkins."

I turn back and finish the sign. They watch me work.

It says, "Don't shoot! I'm a doctor. Dartmouth Medical School. Residency: Johns Hopkins. we can help!"

Lucy opens her mouth, shuts it. Gus smiles.

"Where will we go?"

"I don't know. Somewhere with very few people."

"This is the first time I'm glad I chose to practice in Arkansas."

Gus says, "We have to make for the Ozarks. There's nobody up there. And there's woods."

"We'll need to stay close enough to people that we can get food. Find other survivors. There's not going to be a harvest this year, I don't think."

The shamblers are in the guest room now, banging on the door. It's time to go back out into the world. We grab our bags, our boxes, and go back out to the back deck, down the steps to the fenced patio. The dead moan and rattle at the cypress gate. They can smell us. They can hear us. Everything we have is on our backs and in our hands. The rest is . . . abandoned.

I look at Gus, and his face is hard, mirroring Lucy's. She's got a look like an eagle's, fierce and uncaring. She's grinding her jaws, making the fine cords of her long neck stand out in relief.

I want to cry for them, this grim mother and somber child, since they can't do it for themselves. They need someone to burden their grief. To show them it is okay to weep, to feel for them the horror that's descended on us all.

Lucy looks at me and sees the tears streaming down my face. She comes over and stands by me. My burns are on fire. I want to scratch my ears, the back of my neck. She takes my hand and looks at me, her gray eyes luminous and questioning and large in the perfect clarity of her face. She kisses my cheek.

Then she looks back to the fence and the shamblers waiting there. It's as if she's thinking, *This is the reality of life. This is everything there is, and I can understand it, if I try. The end of the world. The undead. I can understand it. I can understand everything. I accept it.*

But that's Lucy. I'll never be able to understand her fully. I never want to. There are some things beyond comprehension, and saying that the evil upon us is just a virus, or a bad decision from an army general that ended our world, will never excuse or forgive it.

But I am beginning to understand what Meemaw meant. Sometimes life is too big for one person to understand. And you need to use something, a phrase, a song, a snippet of ribbon, to encircle and contain it.

Everything is everything.

3

WARFARIN

Tessa cared for the men. Their needs, all of them. They called themselves the G Unit. Twenty men under the command of Captain Hugh Mozark. Each man was young and scared and suddenly lost in the world.

The EMP wiped communications and the zeds ravaged the cities. The G Unit, like their forefathers before them, moved across the Great Plains, and if not for the automatic weapons and the armored Bradleys, they would have been as helpless as pioneers in the face of a wide, untamed wilderness.

At night, when Tessa had satisfied the captain in his tent, she brought around water, MREs, jerky scavenged from gas stations and convenience stores. She'd walk the perimeter to each of the men on watch, each man staring out into the dark fields, waiting for the dead. They looked at her with little boy eyes, and she'd crush them to her big bosom and let them cry. She hated Captain Mozark with all her heart, but she couldn't bring herself to hate these boys. These men.

Some men didn't want mothering. Some would grip her, hands tight on her back or on her ass, tearless, and want to take her into the Bradley, or away from the others, and put her on her back and spread her legs, even though she was old enough to be their mother. They were young, and the world was dead, but they still had needs.

Terrel, Keb Motiel, Blevens, and Jasper, they needed her that way. Terrel had a long salty dick and kissed sweet. Keb liked to smack her ass and rub it on her back door, and she avoided him as much as she could. Blevens was shy and came fast. Jasper liked dirty talk and to suck her breasts; he wanted her as a mother and a lover, and she tried to keep him satisfied, because he was bull-thick, heavily muscled, and could be dangerous if angered, or protective if sated. For one so young, he had a raw animal grace to him and knew how to move.

Lt. Quentin Wallis, second in command, didn't want to cry or to fuck, but he wanted to make sure they lived, all of them. And even though she was twice his age, Tessa loved him. He looked like Cass's daddy: tall, slim, and intelligent. Black as sin and noble as a king. Looking at him made her stomach flutter. She wished Cass was alive so she could have him. Cass was his match. But now she was dead.

And for that, Captain Hugh Mozark had to die.

They'd moved across the burning plains of Kansas, down into Oklahoma, toward the Ozarks. The cities still smoked a month after the end of everything, and their effluvium—vultures wheeling, smoke curling—drew crooked pillars up to heaven.

Tessa and Cass hid for nearly a month in the convenience store. They'd found it empty of both the living and the dead. Drawing down the aluminum-mesh doors, they hid in the back room, behind the register, eating cold food and drinking sodas and building a nest of wrappers. The dead rattled the mesh and moaned.

"Momma, why'd God leave us here like this?"

"God didn't leave us, baby. This ain't the work of God. It's the work of man, that's for sure."

"But he let it happen."

Tessa took up dipping tobacco in their convenient prison. Years before, she'd broken herself of smoking; six months of mood swings, shouting matches, and late-night ice cream. Cass, then a girl of ten, remembered that time with a mixture of fascination and wariness, like a biologist living in close quarters with a particularly vicious and intemperate big cat. But now she was back using. She preferred Skoal Apple Long Cut to the other brands, and her Skoal supplies were getting low. Taking a can from her pocket, she twisted off the top, dug thick brown and pink fingers into the dark tobacco, and stuck the pinch in her bottom lip. It tasted like apple orchards burning.

"Everything the Lord does, everything he lets happen, it's for a reason. It ain't our job to question him. It's our job to work through it, baby. To keep our faith."

Cass looked away from her mother, like she had when she was a girl, rolling her eyes. She put her disdain on display for Tessa.

"God don't give a shit about us. Or if he does, he hates us, sending the dead to eat the living. It's unnatural, Momma. And if God hates us so much to make something unnatural, I don't love him no more."

It was too easy for Tessa to slap, an old habit, a reflex. She never spared the rod and tolerated no insolence or back sass. Even now. Her hand came out, quick and open-palmed, and left behind nothing on Cass's cheek except a tear in the corner of her eye.

Cass, wiping her face with her sleeve, stood from their nest of wrappers and said, "I can't stay here no more, Momma. We gotta get out. Go to the mountains or something."

"Baby, the streets are full of 'em, the dead folks. The army will come. The police."

Cass laughed, a sound so lost and dejected Tessa couldn't believe it came from her own daughter.

"Five-o?" She turned away from Tessa and looked at the front of the store. The undead had moved away from the gate days ago and hadn't returned. But they'd seen them moving in the streets. "The police ain't never helped us. You know that. They shot Boo." The old bone of contention still had flesh. Cass's boyfriend, Boo, Boo whom Tessa forbade Cass from seeing after she'd caught them in bed together. Breaking and entering, the officer called it when Boo was shot dead climbing from a house with a silent alarm. But it only left Boo's body broken and ended Cass's trust of authority.

"Take a deep breath, Momma. You smell that? It's rotten meat. Rotten people. Piss and shit in the corner. Our piss. Our shit." She pointed to the walk-in freezer. They stayed in the back room because the flies were angrier near the walk-in and thickened the air like black smoke.

Tessa breathed, but all she smelled was the scent of burning apple orchards and tobacco. Her mouth, full of brown saliva, pursed. She spit.

"We will, baby, we'll leave. It's late now. Let's have a drink and sleep here tonight. We're still safe. There's a thousand places in this city but tonight, right here—" She pointed at the floor, firmly. "Right here is still safe. We know we ain't gonna go hungry. We know we'll have something to drink. To eat. That we won't be eaten."

"That ain't enough, Momma. Not for me."

They carried rifles and knapsacks full of clothing. They carried MREs and iodine pills. They wore full battle rattle and carried gas masks and vials full of Neumune pills to combat radiation sickness. They carried pictures of their loved ones and mementos of the homes that were forever gone.

In a pocket in her skirt, Tessa carried a tight, childproof bottle labeled Tylenol but full of gray-green cylinders of d-Con. She'd pilfered it from the convenience store. Warfarin, the d-Con box had read, was the primary ingredient. Deadly to rats. Call poison control if ingested.

In the day, as they moved across the plains, Tessa stayed in one of the two Bradleys, ordering and inventorying the rations, checking water, scanning the radio. The ammo, and whatever men could fit, rode in the other Bradley.

Mostly, Tessa simply sat still and swayed with the movement of the armored vehicle while the men flanked them on motorcycles and ATVs, ranging backward and forward, taking out any stray zeds. It was as if with the rising of the dead, they'd gone back a hundred years or more, crossing the plains on machines instead of horses, with Bradley Fighting Vehicles instead of wagons.

Tessa rocked with the movement of the Bradley, listening to the static—the ever-present static—on the radio and the distant pops of rifles. Ammunition wasn't a problem for the G Unit. Nor was food. It was the dead. It had been fifteen days since they'd heard from another living soul. She kept her hands in her skirt.

And she carried her hatred of Hugh Mozark.

He'd come into the Bradley the day after they picked her up. The tall, beautiful officer stood behind him in the backlit door, looking in. Wallis.

Mozark turned, waved a hand, and said, "Lieutenant. You may go." The beauty had stood straight and saluted.

Mozark filled the space. Hard faced and short spoken, he looked at her. She'd made herself smile, even though she'd come to kill him. She smoothed her dress. Tried to cover her breasts a little, even though she made sure she had showed enough to get the G Unit's attention. Cass was born when Tessa was young, sixteen, and now she was thirty-five and she'd never been pregnant again and had heavy breasts and deep hips. She knew what men wanted.

"What's your name, ma'am?"

"My name's Tessa, sir." She smiled again and pushed her arms together, making her tits swell. She had nothing except her body. And a bottle in her pocket. No daughter anymore, since the captain found her. So in the end she had nothing.

He looked her over slowly, with a lidded gaze. He wasn't tall or short or fat or thin. He was perfectly ordinary, she thought, looking him over. Cocoa butter brown with a complexion to match her own, freckles on his cheeks in a way that reminded her of Morgan Freeman but without the nobility, and a short-cropped afro going gray at the temples.

Standing in front of her, head bent just a little in the Bradley's compartment, he unzipped his fatigues and pulled out his cock. It was unremarkable, if thicker than some she'd seen. He flipped it with his hands, toward her face, like a dog wagging a tail.

She took it in her hands, warmed it in her palm and pulled back the foreskin, licked its head, and then did what he wanted. She put it in her mouth. He tasted gamy and wild. She thought of biting it off, and for a moment, while he pushed it into her as far as he could, holding the back of her head, she imagined him castrated, squirming and bloody, on the metal floor of the vehicle. But he might live through that and she definitely wouldn't. She'd do worse than unman him. He'd turn zombie before she was through. And he'd suffer first.

His cock pulsed in her mouth and the back of her throat, and when he came, she had trouble breathing. But she wouldn't swallow that part of him. Never.

"You're an old-school nigger."

She coughed up his semen and wiped her mouth.

"You," she said, voice hoarse. "You're as black as me."

"I don't even have to ask you, you suck me off. You're

like clay, ready to be shaped. Ordered. Ready to obey." He grabbed her breast, massaged it roughly until it came out of her top, and then he pinched the nipple until she yelped and tried to move away.

"All I require of you is to be what you are, obviously, already."

"Tessa. My name is—"

His fist caught the side of her face. In a world of abusive men, she'd never let any of them lay a finger on her. She knew how to hurt him with a gun or a knife. But she had nothing except her body now, and the bottle hidden in her skirt, and she didn't want to die yet, not before she could finish her task and lay her burden down. Rid this world of a living monster. Punish him. She touched her cheek and tried to look at him meekly, tried not to let him see the real intention in her eyes.

"Your name is bitch, or woman, or whatever I want to call you, understand?"

His dick was soft now, and he started to tuck it back into his pants, then stopped.

"Clean me up. Show me you understand your situation."

Face swelling, she used her hands, and he didn't stop her, didn't make her use her mouth again.

"You'll give any man in the unit a tumble. Or head. You'll feed us, take care of our clothes. You'll bring me my dinner separate and stay with me until I tell you to leave. Only then will you take care of the other men's needs. I won't go after any other man. Your pussy better be clean for me. I don't follow any man. Understand?"

Tessa nodded.

"You'll stay in the Bradley while we scavenge. You know how to write?"

"What?"

"Are you literate? Or are you a stupid nigger who only knows how to fuck and suck dick?"

"I can write."

"You'll listen to the radio. Scan the stations. Write down frequencies and messages, if any. Quentin and Reeves will show you how to operate it. If you can't get it, we'll throw your black ass out. We won't kill you. No. We'll just leave you."

"That's killing me. But if these boys can run the radio, I sure as hell—"

This time he used his left hand, planting his fist into her stomach. She'd have to remember that: he could hit just as hard with either hand.

There was nothing to say to Mozark, and she had no air to speak with anyway. She coughed and wished she could get the taste of his come out of her mouth. She'd take a dip when she was alone, if she could find some.

"We've made camp, woman. Get up, and get some food ready for the men. I'll expect you in my tent later."

Tessa woke up in a nest of wrappers and the smell of her own feces and urine in her nose. The convenience store was dark, but it was a clear night, and moonlight streamed through the lowered grate at the street. She and Cass had drunk most of the wine coolers from the walk-in and earlier, before bed, had progressed to the sweet Boone's Farm wines. Her mouth felt fuzzy, and her head pounded. She rose and went to the corner where they'd recently begun to relieve themselves; the toilet, ever since the water stopped running, was too full to use anymore.

When she returned to the nest of T-shirts and wrappers, paper towels and other soft items they had scavenged, she realized that Cass was gone.

"Cass? Where you at?" Her voice sounded scared, even to her. "Cassandra? Baby, where are you?"

Turning, she went to the front of the store and stared out into the moonlit street. The zombies were moving, down the wreckage of the old Vinita main street and toward the cornfields on the edge of town. Even now, at night, she saw the familiar faces of people she once knew beginning to rot and slough off: Cindy Cottar from the five-and-dime now missing her nose and half a cheek; Fred Anderson from Citizen's Bank who had declined her home-equity loan, limping away on a footless leg; Stephanie what's-her-name from Cass's hair salon missing hunks of flesh from her arms, legs, and most noticeably, her neck. And more, all of them shadowed and wreathed by a black cloud of flies, maggots pooling in their mouths and eyelids, dripping from ears and spilling from open wounds.

Above the shuffling noise of the undead, the constant buzz of flies, she could hear in the distance the faint hum of something she couldn't quite place.

A thrumming, insistent sound—she realized it was a machine. A big truck or off-road vehicle, maybe. An earthmover, maybe. It grew louder, and she could make out the higher-pitched whine of motorcycles or ATVs.

She ran to the back of the store, snatched up her purse, stuffed some cans of Skoal and one of the cleaner T-shirts from the floor into it, and went to the alley door behind the register in the storeroom. Cass must've gone this way to investigate the sound. The metal grate at the front of the store rattled far too much for her to have used it. They'd have been swarmed by zombies and Tessa would've awoken.

Weaponless when they'd first arrived, Tessa had found a broken old mop and stripped it of its gray cotton head. Now, in her flight after Cass, she grabbed it from the nook behind the alley door, snapped it over her knee, and stuck one half into the space between door and sill. If she and Cass needed to return, they'd still have a place. The other half of the handle, a jagged two-foot spear, she clutched in one white-knuckled fist.

The air was cooler here, and fresher than inside the store, even though the cloying stench of the dead hung in invisible streamers around her head. In some ways, the dead smelled better than her own shit.

She walked, quietly as she could, down the alley and toward the growing sound of engines buzzing in the corn.

"Zeds on the horizon! Zeds on the horizon! There's a cluster approaching camp, Lieutenant!" Jasper yelled. He lowered his binoculars and looked over his heavily muscled shoulder, back inside the perimeter, toward the command tent and Lieutenant Wallis and Tessa, boiling clothes in a galvanized tin basin, and the few off-duty men able to relax and sleep.

The camp lay miles from any town, so the cluster of

undead was strange. They found stragglers on the plains, and occasionally a small group, but a cluster meant something larger than twenty. Enough to batter their three-strand barbed-wire perimeter and pose a danger to the men. Especially at night. But the barbed wire was there just to slow them down enough for head shots—it snagged their flesh, what was left of their clothes, and set the tin cans hung from the wire to clattering. Sometimes they'd tumble and take other zeds down with them until the barbs ripped free of their flesh and they could rise again. They always rose again. It was obvious, at least to Tessa, that had they lived near Kansas City or Oklahoma City or Little Rock or Dallas or any metropolitan area, their defenses would never work, but they stayed in the farmlands and headed toward the mountains. They'd be all right as long as the barbed wire was there to alert them and the men remained vigilant.

It was a bright, blustery morning, with the wind freshening in the west and high, thin clouds skittering across the sky. The gray clouds that blanketed the heavens since the Big Turnover were gone, and the sun was warm. The clear day raised the men's spirits. There'd been no signs of radiation sickness.

"There's I'd say twenty-five of them, north of us a hundred yards. There's stragglers behind them too, maybe five or six. Don't know if the barbed wire will hold up if they all come battering."

Lt. Quentin Wallis stood, turned, and barked, "James, Blevens, and Roscoe—I want you guys on ATVs. Now. Outriding! Close enough to distract them, draw them off."

The three men jumped up and ran to the section of camp

designated as the motor pool. The buzz of engines sounded. The men turned their ATVs, the guards lowered the barbed-wire barrier that served as a gate to the camp, and the three buzzed out onto the plains, throwing dust toward the sky. They streaked away, over the rise, moving in oblique angles to the cluster of undead and then around their flank. Tessa shielded her eyes and watched, unmoved.

Lieutenant Wallis barked, "All men, north wall!" Some of the men snorted at his reference to the wall. "Hold fire until the outriders are out of the field of fire and the zeds are within range. No auto."

The men tromped to the barbed-wire barricade, rattling with gear, helmets. Full-battle rattle, the brass called it. Loaded for bear.

"Fuckin' trickass hos, these walkers waking me up from my nap," Keb grumbled. He slapped Tessa's ass as he walked by her as she worked. She slung the laundry paddle from the basin and hit his own backside with the steaming wood utensil. He jumped, unhurt but surprised, and wiped at the wet mark on his fatigues.

"They only nap you're getting, Keb, is them in your hair," Jasper said, low but not unfriendly. "Get your ass over here and take a target."

Moving fast and always out of reach, the outriders circled the cluster of zeds. The undead moaned, groaned half-decayed words. They moved after the loudest target, drawn to sound and smell. One of the outriders peeled away, pulling a pistol, and began executing the straggling zeds.

Lieutenant Wallis raised his radio and said, "OR1 and 2,

over. Lead the revenants within range and await further orders. OR3, continue on their back trail. Exterminate any and all stragglers. SOP."

"Copy that," came the crackling reply from the radio.

Tessa could see the ATVs' wheels, turning dust over at a median point between the cluster and the camp. The undead rotated slowly in a group and then shuffled forward. Their moans rose above the whistle of the wind on the plains.

Tessa put the laundry paddle down and walked over to stand behind the soldiers.

Keb said, "You come to give me some support, baby, while I kill these motherfuckers? Posted at the trap. The trap."

She ignored his words. She didn't like Keb even though she had to fuck him, and she didn't appreciate his glibness when dealing with the extermination of what once had been humans. There was something wrong with that, but she couldn't figure out what was so disgusting about it.

Wallis came and stood by her. "Steady, men. Wait until I give the signal."

Keb snorted. "This some Shaka Zulu shit, Q-tip. Ain't seen this many of them in a while." He turned his M-16, popped the clip, checked and replaced it.

"Agreed. We will exterminate, strike camp, and move on to avoid other clusters. Gas supplies are fine now but will be running low by tomorrow. Montfredi, go notify Captain Mozark of the situation."

A young man no more than seventeen, with big ears and a cowlick, flipped the safety on his rifle and bolted toward the command tent erected near the Bradleys.

Wallis watched the outriders with slate-gray eyes while Tessa watched him. He turned to her, smiled, and said, "Miss Tessa, please get this laundry and the food table packed and cleared away in the mess Bradley, ma'am. We need to be mobile quickly, just in case there are any more of these clusters about. It looks like they're nomadic. Just like us."

Tessa's stomach turned with the lieutenant's words; he did not scorn her for what she had to do here with the men.

God help her, Mozark would pay.

Montfredi scurried back among the men and said, "Lieutenant, the captain has asked for the whore—" He glanced at Tessa, then back to the frowning lieutenant. "He's asked that Miss Tessa . . . attend him."

"Private, what do you mean by 'attend'?"

Montfredi blanched, shook his head wildly as if denying anything relating to the request. "The captain is . . . he's, well . . ."

"Montfredi! Report!"

"He's vomiting, sir. Looks like shit, sir!"

"Miss Tessa, please see to the captain." He gave her a look, searching, and then added, "Montfredi will pack away the laundry and foodstuff." Montfredi swallowed, looked from Tessa to the lieutenant, and saluted.

Wallis raised his walkie and pressed the button. "OR 1 and 2, return to camp." He lowered the device. "Men! Once the outriders are clear, take aim and fire at will."

The ATVs buzzed across their view and circled around to the gate, having lured the zeds into the field of fire. A soldier moved the barbed wire out of the way once more and they rolled into the camp. Tessa paused, now watching the soldiers raise their weapons and begin to fire. Behind the men, with the wind at her back, the reports of the rifles sounded like popcorn in a microwave, small bursts and crackles, gaining intensity and dying like kernels in hot oil. The black figures of the undead stumbled and fell. Some kept moving, but with each revenant down, there were fewer targets and the remaining undead began to mist and slough off parts of themselves in the rain of bullets.

Tessa frowned, felt her gorge rise, and spat into the fire. That the dead could walk was bad enough; that they oozed and smelled like rotten pig and turned dark and noxious in the sun was worse. That they had once been human—had been children, had loved, owned houses and cars, bought tissues and bed linens, made desperate midnight runs to stores for milk and cheese—it was beyond imagining. God! It was awful. If they'd just turn into some other form less like humans, it might be all right. That they wanted to devour her made Tessa feel small and betrayed, and she couldn't sleep well anymore, not like when she spooned with Cass, even when they had been trapped in the convenience store.

The execution of the undead was so impersonal it nauseated her. These men could easily do the same to living people, she knew. Captain Mozark had been in Bosnia and Iraq. She'd heard the men talk.

Montfredi took the gloves from her and began to paw at the laundry pot. He'd retrieved trash bags. He popped one open and, with a grimace, began to paddle hot, steaming fatigues and underwear into the shiny black plastic containers.

The clothes would have to be washed again, Tessa saw. She sighed and turned to Mozark's tent.

Once out of sight of the lieutenant and away from the rest of the men, rifle fire still crackling behind her, she put her hand into her skirt, felt for the bottle. She withdrew it, popped the cap, and removed one of the d-Con pellets, kept it curled in her palm, now a little sweaty from her own excitement.

The stench of bile assaulted her as she entered Mozark's tent. Her eyes grew accustomed to the low light, and she saw he was on his knees beside his cot, retching.

Tessa approached and stood above him, looking at his crooked shoulders, his bent back, as he retched into the dull green mesh of the tent floor.

"You're . . . you're a terrible cook, woman. You've sickened me." He pushed himself from the floor and slumped heavily to the cot. "Bring me some water, whore."

For a moment, Tessa stared at Mozark, thinking she should kill him then and there. Her body filled with a tremor that went from her feet to her hands, and she felt herself filled with an almost obscene strength. She flexed her fingers and leaned over the captain.

A little grin creased his ashen face, showing white gums and bloody teeth.

"You hate me, do you?" He coughed, and his nose began to bleed. "Niggers hate their betters . . . always—" He turned his head, partially rolled to the side of the cot, and vomited again over the side, a weak stream of pale yellow bile.

This is what it must be like to be unafraid. But I'm not. I don't want to die now. And the men will kill me, for real, if I strangle him. But I could . . . I could wring his sorry-ass neck . . . tell them he choked to death . . . but on what? Montfredi saw him throwing up.

Tessa moved to the card table that served as his command post. There were road maps of Kansas and the Arkansas Ozarks, cigarettes, a bottle of wine, a battery-powered lantern, and a canvas-wrapped plastic canteen of water. Tessa crushed one of the pellets between forefinger and thumb, twisted off the cap of the canteen, and dropped the powder remains of the pellet into the canteen. She swirled it around and turned back to Mozark.

The captain dry heaved onto the crackly fabric of the tent's floor. His once mocha skin looked gray and sallow. Tessa smiled.

She came to him, placed a cool hand on the back of his neck. He groaned and feebly turned his head toward her.

"Here, Captain. Here, baby. Here's some water."

"Ah . . ." His mouth looked red and bloody.

She held the canteen to his mouth, and he lapped at the water like a car-struck dog. Tessa looked at him for a long while. Her chest felt tight, and her heart hammered against her ribs as if it were too big for her body. She found herself smiling.

"That's it, Captain. That's it. Okay." She took the canteen, stood, and went to the entrance flap of the tent. Mozark fell to his knees, then slumped on his side. His chest rose and fell slowly.

"It tastes . . . it tastes . . ."

Tessa pulled back the flap and yelled, "Lieutenant Wallis! The captain's sick! Really sick!" She turned back to the captain. "There ain't nothing as sorry to look at as an ashy black man down on his knees." She squatted, gripped his hair, and turned his face toward hers. This man would suffer for what he'd done. "You ain't no better than me. You a black-hearted nigger. But the difference between us is you'll be dead soon, like the zeds, and I'll watch when they put you down. Like you did my Cass."

But he was too far gone to hear. When she let go of his chin, he slumped to the floor.

Standing, she cursed. Then she moved outside the tent and turned the canteen over, pouring out the water into the Oklahoma dust.

It was dark and starlight washed the streets of Vinita in a blue glow. The growling, ratcheting sound of engines grew louder, and from the shadows of a doorway, Tessa watched as the corpses stumbled through the streets toward the fields only blocks away. She clutched her broken mop handle. One zombie moaned right next to her, and she gasped as the undead man lurched, belching putrid gas, and grabbed her.

He smelled like a sewer. Waves of septic stench and the rank odor of rotten meat made her gag and she felt her gorge rise in the back of her throat. Clutching the jagged handle, Tessa raised her fists instinctively, half to defend herself from the undead and half to cover her mouth from retching.

The pointed end of the mop handle caught on the zombie's

chin and sank five inches into the rotting skull—through lower mandible, black rotten tongue, sinus cavity—tilting its head back. Something gooey snapped, and the head lolled to the side, dripping black ichor. Tessa twisted out of its grasp, yanked the handle free, and ran.

She flew past a few zombies who had turned to follow her despite the growing noise from the unseen vehicles. Tessa, feet stinging as they slapped on pavement, banked down an alley, ducked into an open archway, through the door there, and began groping her way upward in the dark. Out in the open and away from the cloying stench of the convenience store, her nose had cleared and now, in the dark, she felt hyper-aware, every sense sharpened to a razor's edge. In the darkness of the unknown building she'd entered, she could only faintly smell the dead. It was musty and stale, and she found herself climbing black stairs upward, many stories.

Must be in Farmer and Merchants, she thought. The only building in Vinita with more than two stories.

She came into a large room, what must've been an office. The cubicles seemed mazelike in the light coming from the bay windows on the north wall of the room. She made her way through the dead, dull computers and overturned desk chairs. No zombies here. No living either. Just the husks of civilization.

At the window she could see north, out over the shorter buildings, into the fields. Banks of bulbs on big, mechanized tanks—or what looked like tanks—cast blue light in heavy arcs across the fallow land. ATVs and motorcycles circled the tanks like bees buzzing around a deadly flower.

And in the center of the flower, perched on the back of a war machine, stood a man pointing and yelling into a walkie-talkie.

Tessa's gaze followed to where he pointed.

At the edges of the light, a figure, desperate, burst through the corn, throwing long shadows behind her.

"No!" Tessa screamed. "Cass! No, baby!"

Even from this distance, Tessa could make out her daughter's form. Even if it had been miles, she would've know it was Cass, her run, the way she held her body, the arc of back and the long, muscular legs; she'd know her daughter anywhere.

It felt as if her heart stopped, dead still, in her chest. The zombies were ravenous and remorseless, most assuredly, but these methodical men drove a sinking feeling into the pit of Tessa's stomach.

Cass ran and Tessa could make out the zombies pursuing her, moving into the long light, moving as fast as their desiccated limbs could carry them. Cass limped and as she drew nearer the tank, Tessa could see she was nude from the waist up. And bleeding from her arms. They must've grabbed her, and she shucked her shirt to escape.

"No!" Tessa's voice cracked, and she banged on the thick office building window. She slammed her hand against glass. "No, baby!"

Helplessly, she watched as one of the ATVs drew near Cass and circled her. The masked driver dismounted, grabbed Cass's arm, and twisted, turning it over. He was looking at her wounds. He yanked her toward the ATV and pushed her roughly into the seat, and then he mounted behind her, one gloved hand roughly grasping her breasts and pulling her torso hard into his body. The zombies were gaining ground, and he popped the ATV into gear and approached the flower's center, moving away from the undead.

At the tanks, the ATV driver pushed Cass off, dismounted once more, and held her in front of the man standing on top of the tank. Tessa couldn't make out his face. She saw Cass stiffen and straighten her back, and she didn't have to see her child's face to know the expression on it—defiance.

The chief—the man standing on the tank—said something, and Cass replied, and the chief's body tensed a little with the words, and Tessa knew that Cass had smarted off.

"No, baby! Just hush." Tessa splayed her hands on the glass and breathed into it. "Hush, baby. Beg, honey. Beg for your life."

The chief said something else, and the ATV driver grabbed Cass's wrist again and twisted her arm, showing her wounds. She twisted and struggled in his grasp, but he didn't release her.

Everything Tessa knew ended then.

Four small explosions of crimson blossomed on Cass's body, across her back, and she slumped to the ground. When Tessa looked back to the chief, he was holding out a smoking pistol.

She slumped to the floor of the office, her back to the wall between her and the man who had murdered her baby. In the dark, musty air of the office, she cried and cursed; she cursed herself, her God, and Cass for her foolishness.

She didn't know how long she sat there, but the sun filtered through the streets of Vinita, casting long shadows into the corn, and when she stood, it was dry-eyed and with purpose. Looking out the window, she could see where Cass's body lay, and the path the men took.

I will kill that man, she thought as she moved back down the dark stairs. *If it's the last thing I do. He'll die at my hands.*

She moved into the street, making her way toward the clatter and light of tanks and the pop and crackle of gunfire. She adjusted her shirt, ripping the collar, showing more skin. She straightened her hair the best she could. Some undead had spotted her and she began to run, run to the tanks.

When she cleared the streets and entered the lights, keeping easily out of the reach of the zombies scrabbling after her, Tessa waved her arms and shouted for the attention of the chief.

An ATV intercepted her before she could reach him.

Barging into the tent, Lieutenant Wallis let Tessa and Montfredi know they'd be Captain Mozark's keepers and nurses until the G Unit could find someplace more secluded and stable.

"Ten minutes, people, and we're out of here. Understood? That means I want all the captain's things packed and ready to go, immediately."

Montfredi barked, "Sir! Yes, sir!"

Lieutenant Wallis turned and looked at his superior officer lying on the cot in the corner of the tent. He pursed his lips.

"We'll leave the tent behind. We've got three others just like it scavenged from a Walmart in Lawrence. Get the table, the maps, and his personal accouterments."

Montfredi hesitated. "Accuter . . ."

The lieutenant shook his head. Tessa could see that Montfredi's stupidity exhausted the young lieutenant's patience. Even if she'd never heard the word before, she could gather what he meant. But Wallis continued. "His things. Get his stuff. Pack it for him. The things he'll need."

"Yes, sir!"

Lieutenant Wallis peered at Montfredi, then squinted and shifted his gaze to Tessa. He looked her up and down. She raised her eyes, glanced at Montfredi's vapid face and then back to Wallis.

"You. Miss Tessa. You're in charge. Make sure Montfredi . . . make sure this . . ." He waved his hand. "Make sure this is all taken care of." He peered at her. "You are responsible, understand? I know you aren't army, but . . . the world has changed and you're with us now. I'd rather you be . . . this . . . than the men's . . ."

He bowed his head and looked at his feet, and for a moment, she wanted to go to him, to tell him it was okay. She was only doing this to get . . . to get . . . here. With Mozark in her power.

"I don't want you taking care of the men's . . . needs, the way you've been doing, miss. That part of your duties is over, understand?"

It was strange to say it like this, but she tried. "Yes, sir." She paused, cocked her head, and stared at the young officer. Dissembling came easy. "Least until Mozark gets better. He'll be wanting my company."

Lieutenant Wallis frowned, and in that instant, Tessa knew

that part of the young man wanted the captain to *not* get better, to go away, honorably, without killing.

He said, "You have free will, but the army practices a nonfraternization policy that your . . . extra duties . . . are in direct conflict with."

"You saying that the captain broke the rules? Shit, Lieutenant, I could've told you that." She winked at him and kicked out her hip.

I am not a whore, she thought fiercely. *He's blushing now, but he'd string me up or leave me for the dead to eat if he knew I was killing Mozark. Whatever else this beautiful lieutenant might be, he's an old-school soldier. He'll execute me for murdering the captain. I can't ever doubt that.*

"No." He shook his head, clenched his jaw, causing the fine line of his neck and chin to harden, and stepped closer to Tessa. She looked up into his face.

"It's wrong. What he made you do . . . it's one step away from . . . from . . . from *slavery*. From forcing another human to bend to your will, become property, to be used like a thing. An object." He looked at her with hard eyes. Even in the low light of the tent, she could see the taut lines of his cheek, the muscles in his cheek shifting. He raised his fist as if clutching at something that eluded his grasp. "I'll not allow the human race to slide back into barbarism on my watch."

He looked at his hands. It was a helpless gesture of confession, or a suitor proclaiming love. Tessa realized he was as uncomfortable with the conversation as she was. *But damn me if I'll show it.*

"So, until we're safe and sound, I expect you to

remain . . . chaste. If you want to mate with someone, I'll perform the wedding ceremony for you. I can do that. I am a minister too."

She stepped closer and patted his arm. "Thank you, Lieutenant. For a second, I thought you were about to propose to me."

The blush darkened only the skin of his throat and jawline. But she could still see it.

He brushed his slacks and stood up straight. "Are we clear, Miss Tessa?"

She knew not to push him too far.

"Yes, sir. We're clear." She turned, put her hands on her hips. "Montfredi, go get the laundry taken care of. Tie it tight and strap it to the top of the mess Bradley. I'll tend to the captain and his . . . accouterments. When you're done with that, haul your ass back here. You hear?"

Montfredi nodded, brought his arm up as if to salute, caught himself, and then dashed out of the tent. Lieutenant Wallis shook his head in disgust.

Tessa laughed and turned to attend to the blubbering captain.

The land became wooded, craggy, and uneven. The steady growl of the Bradleys grew as they labored up steep grades, and the men of the G Unit gave forced yawns to pop their ears. The Ozarks rose around them, and the zeds became fewer.

Tessa rode in the Bradley with Lieutenant Wallis, Montfredi, Keb, and Captain Mozark. Keb watched her with lidded eyes and occasionally flicked his tongue at her in amusement.

Tessa swayed with the motion of the vehicle, nestled among boxes of MREs and ammunition, plastic jugs of water and medical supplies. The radio crackled in its casing as the ATV outriders reported.

Captain Mozark grew more ashen. He lay still, and even his moans were listless. Blood trickled from his nostrils and welled, like tears, in the corners of his eyes. The interior of the Bradley smelled of human bile and unwashed men. Lieutenant Wallis studied road maps they took from service stations, rustling the paper in his dark hands. When she closed her eyes, Tessa imagined the dull thrum of the diesel engines as lawnmowers and the rustling of the maps as leaves on an autumn day. Cass stood before Tessa, pinioned by the afternoon sun, a brilliant fallen star, smiling. Their shadows grew long and black and Cass's face ceased to smile but began to grimace and then scream.

The radio squelched. Tessa jumped.

"Messy Bessie, this is OR2. OR2 on the ridge by Winslow. We got some live wires down here, moving across the interstate."

The lieutenant snatched up the radio. "Live ones, OR2? Transport?"

"ATVs. They've got two twenty-gallon tanks strapped to each vehicle. They're armed, but not heavily. Big man with a shotgun, a teen, and what looks like a young one, maybe eleven or twelve. They're all wearing freaky masks."

The radio squelched, then fell silent.

Wallis rubbed his jaw, then said, "OR1 and 2, move to intercept and acquire their gas reserves. Leave them their weapons and foodstuffs—"

Tessa exploded. "You can't do that, Lieutenant. They're alive! Just like us. You'd be leaving them to die! You can't—"

Wallis snapped his fingers loudly and pointed at her, signaling Keb to silence her. Keb lifted himself, leaned forward, and placed his hand on her shoulder, and whispered, "Baby, don't make me shut you up. I gots something for yo nasty mouth."

The radio squelched again. "Messy Bessie, they're carrying a sign. It reads 'Don't shoot! I'm a doctor. We can help!'"

Wallis expelled a lungful of air. He looked at the map, found what he was looking for, and spoke again into the microphone.

"OR1, OR2, and OR3 . . . escort the company north to the 540 junction. We'll rendezvous there and set up camp."

"Copy that, Messy, copy. Heading north on 540. Will radio with our position once we're in place."

Wallis set down the radio and squinted at Tessa. She realized he was furious.

"Miss Tessa, when I require your input regarding operations around here, I will ask you. Until then you are to remain silent like all the other men."

Tessa found herself, in some ways, more scared now of the lieutenant than she'd ever been of Mozark, because she loved the lieutenant and hated that she couldn't control her mouth. Now, in his eyes, she was a whore and a liability.

He continued. "But since you decided to speak out of

turn, I will address this once and once only, do you understand?"

She nodded.

"I am charged with the protection and survival of this unit, as you should know by now. This requires four major resources: gas, water, food, and ammunition. Of all of these, gas is the hardest to come by." He spread the map on his knee, flattened it with fine, articulate fingers. He sighed.

"It is not my intention to harm anyone, Miss Tessa, other than those that intend harm to us. Revenants. But I have, in my command, over twenty men. And you now. They are only three. We have to have the gasoline to survive. They could survive without it, possibly. These are the things I have to consider when making decisions."

He stopped for a moment, bowed his head, and passed his hand over his eyes, weary.

But when he raised his gaze, his eyes were fierce.

"This isn't a democracy. That world is gone, the one where everybody gets their say." He paused to let that sink in. "Above all, I value fairness and human life. But that does not mean I will be questioned in my decisions. Do you understand this?"

Tessa held her breath. She nodded again and then remembered the traditional soldier's response.

"Sir, yes, sir."

Wallis turned to the driver and said, "North, men. North."

The doctor looked nearly retarded, a big burly man with a half-charred head, eyes hidden behind goggles, and a gigantic hammer stuck in his belt. But his arms were thick with muscle, and he was tall. Two bandoliers full of shotgun shells crisscrossed his barrel chest. The two boys, the teen and the lad, stayed close. They all looked dirty, wary as feral dogs. None of them removed their goggles. Their hands never ventured far from their weapons. Even the young boy, a red bandana over his mouth like a Mexican bandito, kept his hand near the pistol at his waist. He watched the soldiers with a blank, reflective stare.

Lieutenant Wallis, hopping from the Bradley, approached the trio with his hand out, smiling. Tessa followed.

"Doctor, I can't tell you how glad I am our paths crossed—"

The big man laughed and looked at the teen. Tessa noticed the boy's fair skin and hard lines. He had a long, girlish neck. He nodded, looking at the larger man, and then turned goggled eyes back to the soldiers of the G Unit.

"I'm Wallis, and these men—" He smiled, waving a hand to encompass the waiting soldiers. "They refer to themselves as the G Unit. We came from Oklahoma, trying to find a less populated area. Our captain is sick. Very sick. Do you think you can look at him?"

The big man took Wallis's proffered hand and shook. He said, "I'm Jim Nickerson. Folks call me Knock-Out. And it doesn't look like we have much choice, does it?"

Lieutenant Wallis allowed a puzzled look to cross his fine, dark features. "I don't understand."

"Your men. They rounded us up, just like cattle, and brought us here. Not so much as a please or thank you."

"My apologies, Doctor. I asked them to escort you here because the captain requires medical attention."

Nickerson remained unmoved. He said, "What if we told you that we put up that sign just to keep folks from killing us at first sight, huh? What would you do then?"

Lieutenant Wallis blinked. "Are you telling me you're not a doctor?"

"No. I'm asking what you would do, that's what I'm asking."

The lieutenant stood at ease, placed his hands on his waist. "We would inventory your gear and take what we needed." The way Wallis said it, it was like he was saying, *We'd stop at the store and pick up some milk, flour, and eggs.* His face was blank, looking hard at the big man. Tessa felt her back go tight; the tension between the men spread.

"And if we fought back?"

"Each of my men is armed. We are short on fuel but not on food or ammunition. No, we have crates of ammunition."

Nickerson raised his goggles and squinted at Wallis. The way he did it, the deliberate slowness, the utter fearlessness of the action, frightened Tessa. The man had a callous, animal quality to him.

He was smiling, though it didn't reach his eyes. The two boys inched behind him.

"I just wanted to get this straight, so we all know where we stand." He spat. "Because now you understand how valuable we are."

Wallis remained still. The men around them began to rattle; they could feel the tension growing. Montfredi, his big ears standing out, looked between the lieutenant and the doctor like a rabbit caught between a fox and a hawk. Keb grinned, excited.

The doctor laughed and stretched, cracking his back. He dusted off his sleeves and pants and shook his leg to get the blood moving.

"Shit, it's been a long week."

He turned to the boys and said, almost as an aside, "We gotta trust somebody, sometime. And he was honest."

He turned back to the lieutenant. "We'll be glad to take a look at the captain." He stopped. "That is, of course, for a price. We require meals for all of us, protection from the revenants, and your promise that none of us will be..." Nickerson looked around at the hard faces of the soldiers who weren't busy setting up the perimeter. He rested his hand on his hammer. "None of us will be molested in any way. Nor stopped from leaving when we want, with all our belongings and vehicles. On your word of honor."

Tessa gaped at his use of the word *molested*. The way he used it didn't make her think of perverts. It made her more uncomfortable in ways she couldn't really come to grips with.

The burly doctor didn't fuck around, that's for sure.

No one flinched when a rifle fired. Shortly after, Montfredi squeaked, "Zed, Lieutenant! A onesy!"

Wallis turned to the men and barked, "Cudgels, boys. Axes and baseball bats, unless there's a cluster. That means five men on standby for execution detail." He sucked his teeth for a moment, then added, "If I catch one soldier on watch without a bludgeon to hand, there'll be dire consequences. Trust me on this, boys."

The men looked at one another.

"Now, Doctor, give me a moment and I'll have the men erect a tent for you. If you'll come this way."

Wallis took them to Messy Bessie, and Tessa followed. It was tight, close, and rank inside the mechanical beast with barely enough room for all of them. Tessa hung back by the door and peered into it. The captain lay on the metal floorboard, encrusted with vomit. His eyes were blank and he opened and closed his mouth like a carp suddenly pulled from a pool.

The teen pulled his goggles down around his neck, went to the captain, and felt for a pulse. He pulled back the captain's eyelids, looked into his eyes, and then turned to the doctor and said, "This man's been poisoned."

"You—" Tessa looked between the man named Knock-Out, the teen, and the little boy, who stared at her behind goggles, hand on his pistol. "You ain't a boy."

The woman straightened and pulled off her goggles and the cloth wrap from her head. Her long hair spilled around her shoulders in a mess, tangled and dirty from weeks on the road.

"I never said I was." She held out her hand to Tessa as if they stood in an office building or medical park. Tessa looked at the outstretched hand, trying to figure out what the woman wanted. Finally, she took it and shook. It was firm and paper dry.

"I'm Dr. Lucy Ingersol. How long has he been like this?"

"A month. Maybe a little longer."

"He seems to have ingested large amounts of an antico-agulant. I can't be completely sure, though. This isn't my specialty."

The big man rolled his eyes. "Luce, you're always saying that. There aren't any specialties anymore. There's just sur-vival. Anyhoo, you're the only medical game in town." He looked at the captain, shook his head, and said to Tessa, "Go get Wallis."

After Tessa retrieved the lieutenant, Wallis entered the Bradley, looked from the captain to Knock-Out to the woman, and paused only slightly when he realized the depth of his misunderstanding. Tessa noticed his jaw clench and re-lease, clench and release. But he recovered quickly.

Knock-Out grinned when Wallis offered his hand to Lucy and said, "I see things are not as I thought. And you must be Dr.—"

"Lucy Ingersol. We didn't mean to trick you."

"Nevertheless, you didn't correct my assumption."

"We've been on the road for two months and have traveled, in that time, about a hundred miles. Between the revenants and our fellow man scrabbling for food or gas—" She pursed her lips and gave her head a little shake. "You can't trust people, even now, when we should be helping one another."

Wallis nodded. "I understand. Thank you for helping us. We won't betray that trust."

Lucy nodded at his words, but her body, to Tessa's eyes, lost none of its wariness.

156

"Do you have any idea what's wrong with the captain?" Wallis asked.

Lucy nodded. The boy stepped forward and stood by the woman, his hand still on his pistol. He didn't remove his goggles.

"Your captain's been poisoned. By what, I'm not sure, but I think it's an anticoagulant. I can't tell if it's ingested or environmental." She bent and lifted his eyelids, showing eyes unfocused and red. His mouth still opened and closed. "Has anyone else shown similar symptoms?"

"No," Wallis said, glancing at Tessa for confirmation. "None have been reported."

Lucy rubbed her chin and stared hard at the captain.

"Look at his gums. They're bloody. He's had a nosebleed. He's starting to ooze blood from every pore. I didn't check, but I imagine he's bleeding rectally."

"Can you help him?"

"Maybe. If this *is* what I suspect, a large dose of vitamin K, regularly, will repair things. But I need to observe him for some time to see how the poison is getting into his system. And if we can find vitamin K in a pharmacy or hospital . . . I'm sorry, but honestly, I don't know if that particular vitamin loses potency—"

"You're talking to yourself again, Luce."

The boy finally said something. "That's okay, Mom. I'll remember what you say."

She smiled at her son. "Thank you."

Knock-Out shrugged.

"If it's not an anticoagulant, but something else, well . . . I have no diagnostic equipment. I have rudimentary medical supplies. A scalpel, needle and sutures, alcohol, some penicillin and insulin, and a couple of medical books that will let me rebuild some of what we've lost—"

"Rebuild?"

She shook her head and looked a little confused. "I don't know how to make insulin, for fuck's sake. Or penicillin. Do you? Not to mention medicine that'll treat typhus, or peritonitis, or any other nasty disease that comes with constantly living near the dead. How have you been treating your water?"

The look on Wallis's face wasn't one Tessa had seen before. He was . . . disturbed. The woman doctor had challenged him—not out loud, but enough. "Iodine pills and army-issue water filters. In Little Rock they have machines that can draw water vapor out of the air and make it potable."

"What?" She looked excited. "Really? We've got to get one."

"We just came from there," Knock-Out said. "Heading back through the dead into the city isn't my idea of a plan. There's no one alive. The whole population turned over."

The way he said that made Tessa think of dead fish bubbling to the surface of a stagnant pond. She'd seen her daddy's secret fishing hole turn over once. You could smell it for miles.

Wallis smiled. "With those machines, it takes a gallon of gasoline to make one gallon of water, so—"

She sighed and sat down near the captain. "That does us fuck-all good."

Lucy checked the captain's pulse, pulled a small penlight from a pocket, and shone it into his eyes.

"This man is seriously ill. If this world was . . . sane," she said, curling her lips around the last word, "he'd be in a hospital. I'll do what I can for him, but . . . I'm worried he won't make it. I'll observe him overnight."

Wallis stared at her, hard, and then nodded once. "You'll have the captain's tent. I've got to attend our fortifications."

"Barbed wire." Knock-Out chuckled.

"There's very little population around here, sir, and the clumsiness of the dead caught up in the wire gives us ample time to club them down. A little goes a long way."

Knock-Out laughed and held up his hands. "No, I'm not making fun. It's practical." He wiped his hands on his pants and took his turn sighing. "Only in Arkansas."

Night came, and Tessa remained by the cook fire. The camp was unusually quiet. They'd lost a man that afternoon.

Jasper and Buzbee had gone into the woods next to the interstate to forage firewood. They'd gotten separated, and the next thing Jasper knew (or so he said), Buzbee was stumbling toward him, blood all down his front, bite marks in his arms and neck, and two undead friends toddling after him. One was black and crusty like a charcoal grill, sex indeterminate, and the other was a young woman, thick around the middle and naked.

Jasper dropped the firewood and ran back to the interstate to call for help and wait.

They took care of the zeds.

But they'd lost one of their own. It had been over two weeks since they'd lost anyone. Jasper sat staring into the fire, and the men watching the perimeter smoked and stayed quiet.

Tessa watched Jasper and considered. She moved behind him, put her hands on his giant shoulders, and squeezed. He moaned and leaned back. Across the fire, Keb snorted and watched her with an angry expression.

"Rough day, baby, huh?"

He snorted. "Goddamn. Buzbee was a good guy. A real good guy. All I know is one minute, we're talking and laughing, the next, he's coming for me."

"That's gotta be hard on you."

"Real hard. He was a good guy."

She pushed her breasts against his back and ran her hands up and down his arms. "Well, you're off watch now. Try to relax. Get some rest." She put her lips by his ear. "I'll take care of you, sugar."

The back of his neck turned red, and he rose slowly. He picked up his pack and bedroll, his rifle and weapons belt, and slung it all over his shoulder.

She took his hand and led him toward the space between the Bradleys, where trysting, before Wallis's law, was common.

He was hard before the bag had been unrolled, and she barely had to move to make him come quickly. Afterward, they lay side by side on the bedroll, between the Bradleys, a small slice of star-strewn sky above them. She played with him then, stroking, trying to get it hard again.

"You'll protect me, right? Like that doctor. She has her big man to protect her. You'll be my big man, won't you, baby?"

Jasper snorted. "Of course. You're a good girl."

"Oh, yes, baby. I'll be your girl. Your good little girl. I'll do whatever you want me to do. How you want it?"

She lowered her head and took him in her mouth. He moaned, louder than before.

When she could breathe again, she said, "No. Not yet, baby. You big bull of a motherfucker." Her voice was husky, low—the tone she knew drove men crazy. They loved it when she praised their cocks. She spat into her palm. "You got to keep quiet. No moaning. They come looking for a zed, you don't keep it down."

When he was totally rigid, pointing up toward the stars like a tent pole, she got on her knees, lifted her leg and centered herself over him, swinging her breasts in his face. He latched onto one with his mouth.

"That's right, Jass. That's right." She lowered herself onto him.

He was vigorous, right till the end. He flipped her over on her back and, for what seemed like an eternity, pistoned her. The slapping of their flesh was almost too loud in the night. Her fingers found her clit and she managed to make herself come as he did, but it was hard, slow going, and she had to think of the captain, lying like a dead fish on the floor of the Bradley, and only then could she come. Shivers wracked her body, and her muscles tightened around Jasper, and he yelped with pleasure.

When it was all over, he slumped off and was snoring within minutes.

161

She rose, went to his weapons belt, and took his pistol and army-issue knife. She dressed, padded away on soft feet, knife in hand, looking for the captain's tent.

The doctor had to die. The captain could never recover.

Tessa crouched by the captain's tent, the muscles of her legs screaming, she'd been holding the position so long. Between the squat and the workout of fucking Jasper into senselessness, she could feel her muscles quivering and growing weak.

She hadn't heard any conversation for a long while, and the tent was dark. She counted to sixty, then rose, shaking her legs, and moved around to the tent's opening, knife in her right hand, a big handgun in the other. She didn't even know if the gun was loaded, but the knife would do fine.

In her mind, it played out like this: she'd come into the tent like a cat, locate the sleeping form of the doctor, and with one short, sharp stab, put the woman out of her misery. She'd flee, back to Jasper, and wait until the doctor rose and killed everyone around her, nobody noticing the puncture mark that did her in. Because everyone dies in this new, fallen world. Everyone dies. And then rises again.

She entered the tent silently and stood panting in the dark, trying to make out who slept where in the pitch-black interior. She made out a larger shape in the corner that had to be the captain on his cot. The shape over here, nearest the captain, should be the doctor.

She moved forward, knife ready, and paused over the black bundle of blankets.

What if it was the man? Or, worse, the boy?

Did it really matter? Once one was dead, he or she would rise and kill everybody else anyway.

Just stab them, you goddamn fool girl.

The sound of a pistol's hammer cocking behind her ear made Tessa freeze.

A small voice, a boy's voice, said, "What I can't understand is why you didn't just kill the captain."

Suddenly, flashlights lit the tent and a bleary Knock-Out and exhausted-looking Lucy roused themselves from their sleeping bags. Tessa realized, too late, that she had indeed been standing over the doctor, Lucy.

Lucy looked from her son, holding a pistol to Tessa's head, to Tessa, to the knife and pistol in her hands. Her eyes widened.

Knock-Out said, "What the fuck is going on here?"

"I thought something was funny." The boy's voice was high-pitched—girlish, even. "When Mom decided that it was poison, I was really surprised nobody asked the question, 'Who could've poisoned him?'"

"I said it could be poison, Gus. It could also have been environmental."

The boy nodded once, as if saying, *Okay, I agree with you, but that doesn't matter.*

"It looked like poison to me."

Knock-Out grunted. "You're ten. Your mother has a medical degree."

"I'm eleven. Last week."

Tessa hoped the boy would glance away from her, turn his

attention to the man. Maybe then she could escape, out and away, into the night. She still held the gun and the knife.

The child pressed the barrel of his pistol against her head.

"Don't even think about it. Go on and drop them."

After Tessa let the knife and pistol fall, Lucy snatched them up, threw them into a corner of the tent, and looked around blearily.

"I don't even know what's going on here." She buried her face in her hands and then looked at Gus in surprise. "Oh, baby, I'm sorry I forgot."

"It's not like you could've baked a cake." Gus waved the pistol at Tessa's face. "Ma'am, go ahead and sit down, over there by the captain."

"So, you were suspicious about this woman because . . ." Knock-Out looked uncomfortable. "I believe you, Gus, I do. I just want to understand how you came to this conclusion when no one else did."

Tessa sat by the captain. The boy's gaze never left her. He was frightening, the little one. The doctor was confused, the man appeared to be a brute, but this boy—just eleven!—had figured her out and waited for her.

"In school, they make us . . . they made us do stupid little activities in the workshops. They line up a row of similar items and one item that's different. You know, kid's stuff. 'One of these things is not like the others,'" he said in a sing-song voice, like a teacher.

The boy's gun hand never wavered. The bore of the pistol seemed enormous and black, and always pointing toward Tessa.

Tessa shivered. The fucked-up world had made this . . . this child . . . harder than the hardest gangbanger, and now, because of him, they'd turn her out to the zeds.

"Looking at the soldiers, seeing her here, she's so . . . I don't know, different from everyone else." His eyes darted toward her cleavage. "And it was the captain who had been poisoned. If it had been one of the regular soldiers, not the guy in charge, maybe it could've been something else, something other than poison."

"Gus. That's . . . that's impressive," Knock-Out said.

The captain moaned, a wretched, horrible sound.

The boy said, "So, I can't understand why you didn't just kill the captain. Why sneak in here to kill us but leave the captain to die of the poison?"

Tessa was poleaxed. Her voice, when she managed to make it sound, was raw and weak.

"My baby. He killed my girl, Cass. Shot her dead. And he raped me, turned me out to his men. You understand *that*, boy?"

He cocked his head, curious, like a bird.

"He needs to *suffer*." She spat on the ground. "You understand he made me into a whore for his men? It's a blessing that he killed Cass, or she'd be sitting here where I am now. But she never would've whored herself. She would've died first—"

The boy blinked at her. But the gun didn't waver.

"Someday you'll understand. Someday soon, looks like, when you get some growth on you. Maybe you'll see how men do women. Maybe this big motherfucker will slap your momma—"

"I don't think—" Lucy said.

Tessa went on, hoping to make them flinch or turn their attention away from her. But why was she talking like this, keeping their attention on her? She couldn't stop herself.

"Maybe he'll treat her mean. You know what men like to do to women at night, boy? They like to stick their dicks in them."

"Shut up, woman." Knock-Out stood. "Okay, I'm going to go get Wallis."

Lucy turned toward Knock-Out and said, "Wait. Let's talk this over."

"She tried to kill you, Luce. I don't care what you say. If we don't talk to Wallis about this, if we let her go, we'll never be safe. She could sneak in any night and try to kill us. And if Wallis discovers we knew and didn't tell, I'd hate to think what he'd do."

Tessa kept her eyes on the boy. "Maybe he'll argue with her and get a little out of control. Hit her. Hit you. Punch her to get her to shut up. He's annoyed now, but what if he gets mad? And your momma looks like she likes to argue. They ever fight?" Tessa licked her lips. She was desperate to distract them. "Or maybe you won't be able to stand what he does to her at night—"

Knock-Out raised his hand. "God help me, if you don't shut your fucking mouth—"

"See, boy? He's ready to pop me. He'd hit your momma, sure enough, she gets mouthy."

The boy said, "He wouldn't. Ever."

Tessa laughed. "You can't know that, boy. Men have needs."

"That might be true. But he's in love with her."

Tessa snorted.

The boy said, "Really. Look at him."

Knock-Out flushed all the way to his feet.

"Luce, I—"

"What're you saying, Gus? It's not like that between Knock-Out and me. We've never even—"

His face wavered, and then cracked. In that moment, Tessa saw he was just a boy. Just an eleven-year-old, scared and wanting to protect his mother.

"Mom, it's true. I've known it since the first day I met him." He smiled and looked at Knock-Out. It was almost a blessing.

Tessa heard another moan and smelled the exhalation of the dead. Lucy's eyes grew large, and the doctor shrieked.

Tessa's head jerked backward, hard scrabbly fingers on her neck and shoulder, and she felt herself being drawn up and back.

The captain has woken up. The thought skittered crazily in her head and then was gone.

He gibbered a little—or maybe that was her, trying to scream—and bit deeply into her neck. It was pain unlike she'd ever known before, blossoming outward. She could feel the tendons stretching and then ripping and the blood coming now, hot, down her chest, darkening her skin and spilling between her breasts.

The captain jerked her roughly back, into his lap, and worked his head back and forth like a lover nuzzling his beloved, but with hideous strength and gnashing teeth. Blackness pushed in around the edges and everything was going away when there was a tremendous boom and a flash of light and the captain's head rocked back, taking more of her flesh with it. His mouth fell open, and something dropped from the bloody maw. A piece of herself.

She couldn't scream; that part of her throat where speech came from was gone now. Tessa raised her eyes and looked into the smoking bore of the pistol that loomed at her like the mouth of a well. Beyond the pistol, the boy's face swam into focus, framed with smoke, frowning. His eyes were gray, Tessa saw, and his cheeks were smooth and fair.

She closed her eyes.

Cass. She could see her standing in the sun, radiant.

The captain was dead. Hugh Mozark was dead.

"Holy shit." That was the man.

"We've got to stop the blood—" The doctor's voice was strained and panicked. Tessa hoped the boy knew what to do. He was a smart boy. She prayed he'd know what to do.

Tessa opened her eyes one last time.

Then there was another flash, and a boom, and her pain disappeared and she felt herself pitch forward, into the well, and she fell into darkness.

They buried the captain in the median of 540 the next morning. A chaplain as well as an officer, Wallis said some words and commended young Gus on his vigilance. Then Wallis recited a short verse from memory. The men remained subdued, casting furtive glances at the doctor, her companion, and the strange boy.

On Jasper's insistence, they placed Tessa's body in the grave with Mozark.

"She was a good girl. A real good girl. She should sleep with the captain. For company," Jasper said. "They can keep each other company."

Keb groaned and began shoveling dirt onto the dead. Jasper joined him, tears streaming down his face.

"What you crying for, you stupid motherfucker?"

"I'm sad, Keb."

"Sad?" Keb jabbed his shovel into the mound of dirt and leaned against it. "That skeeze killed the captain. Why you blubbering for her?"

"I'm sorry she died. She was a good girl."

"Goddamn, you as dumb as they come. She was a ho."

"Don't talk like that about her." Jasper's face turned red. "She did what she needed to do to survive, man. That's all. Same as you. Same as me."

Keb sniffed, shook his head, and began to shovel dirt into the grave.

The doctor and her burly companion stood by the grave long after the men had returned to the Bradleys and begun to strike camp. The sun rose over the tree line, casting long shadows behind them on the dewy ground, and for the moment, the only dead within sight were those at their feet.

Slowly, Lucy's hand reached out and took Knock-Out's. They didn't look at each other, but their bodies grew closer until they were leaning against each other.

The boy stood a little ways apart from them, staring into the distance.

"What're you looking at, kiddo?"

Gus turned and smiled at his mother. His eyes flicked over her, over Knock-Out, taking in their clasped hands.

He turned back to where he'd been looking and pointed.

"See that bridge?"

In the distance was an overpass long devoid of traffic. Weeds grew high in the cracks of the asphalt, and at the interstate's edge, saplings rose and stirred in the slight morning breeze.

"Yes. Sure. I see it."

Knock-Out said, "What about it?"

"We need to talk to the lieutenant. I've got an idea."

Gus turned and walked back up the interstate toward the camp.

Lucy and Knock-Out put their heads together and then turned to follow the boy.

4

AS FIERCE AS THE GRAVE

The world loves the tomato because it is red. The apple is red too. But the tomato's flesh is the flesh of mankind.

Do the dead love the flesh of man because it is like a tomato? We'll never know. But I have my suspicions.

Not working the Garden today. Working the Wall. Five of us on the south side of the Bridge and five on the north, manning the murderholes. A cush detail, the South Gate, if you've got to man the Wall. Cush is relative, I guess. On the north side you've got what's left of Tulaville, Arkansas. Population zero. Living, that is. Beyond that, the interstate.

South, you've got migrant zombies from Little Rock and Hot Springs and even Pine Bluff. A little more traffic, but it comes in spurts. Not too much trouble manning the murderholes on either side.

And *man* is the right word. Most women don't chip in on the zombie disposal units, except for Sarah. Barb Dinews sometimes. They prefer scavenge units, which I'm not old enough for yet, even though I'm the tallest man here except for Jasper. But he's freak-show large.

Only fifteen or twenty women in all of Bridge City, so it

makes sense, I guess, having so few on the Wall. They work the Kitchens and the Garden usually, grow tomatoes and basil and squash and cabbages and cucumbers. Shoot crows and seagulls and whatever other flying creatures pass overhead, looking for food.

Always a line of men waiting to help the women, to tote and carry, fetch water, and just be near them. Reminds me of dreams. Dreams of school. Boys and girls. Recess.

"We've got a damily, ten o'clock." Blevens. Hurt his leg on the last scavenging trip, resigned himself to working the Wall, but not without a lot of bitching.

Damily: a little undead foursome (or moresome) that clings together. Scary, really, that they group like that—two adults, two children, all dead, coming for us. Almost as if there's something in them that they remember about being human.

This damily is a nuclear damily—one zombie charred beyond recognition.

Nuclear damilies are the worst. You get the stink of the dead *and* old charred meat smell.

A twofer. I think that's what they used to call it.

Today, the damily shambles up and joins the twenty or thirty others gurgling and moaning. The smell is bad, but the sound is worse: gargling, moaning, gibbering, glugging, clicking, slobbering. Nasty things, always hungry and totally without table manners.

We would set the table, years ago. Fork on the left, knife on the right. Napkin left. Glass left.

Now I have a bowie knife on the left hip.

"You think we can take out this bunch now? We're gonna

172

be at about capacity," says Ellroy. That's what all the men call him, but his name is Montfredi. They say he looks like a cartoon character, but I don't remember the character, or even the cartoon. I think. Years since I've seen a television with electricity running in it.

Working on something that might change that. I remember liking TV.

Blevens waddles up to the outer rampart, favoring his injured leg, looks out at the group of zombies trying to get in. Wrinkles his nose, sniffs, and then gives a nod.

"Let 'em in. There's another damily on the highway. We'll take care of these poor fuckers and leave them out here to gobble."

Me and Lindy move to the inset gates. No winches, the steel plates would be unmovable. As thick as my pinkie, they weigh almost five hundred pounds each, taken from the nearby foundry. I hate the weight, and the sharp steel edges can cut to the bone, but it's better than the plywood and tin stuff we had before. Too flimsy. Sounded like a drumhead when the zeds really started pounding.

Winch back the gates and the zombies shamble into the murderhole. They don't notice when we move the gates back into place behind them, lock them down with pins, and pick up cudgels.

I like a weighted ax handle for wet work. Lindy's partial to a Louisville Slugger, its business end full of screws and bent-over nails. Used to have the nails sticking out, but they kept getting caught in the craniums, and when the brain-crushed zombies fell down, they nearly pulled him off the ramparts.

The murderhole is a twenty-by-twenty space between the inner and outer gates, ringed by a walkway about six feet above the ground and connected to the rampart. The zombies' heads are right at our feet level.

This was all my idea. Some days I'm not too happy about it. Messy business, life. Unlife. Death.

Smashing skulls while the dead try to grab your feet is definitely an art. The dead dead slump to the ground, and the living dead stand on them. So smashing skulls gets easier but more dangerous as you go along.

This is why we're all sweating our asses off in motorcycle armor.

Takes somewhere between thirty minutes and an hour to smash all their skulls. Lindy and me are dripping at the end, and Ellroy brings us water while Frazier and Blevens—our elders—watch.

Spring has sprung, they say. Think of it like a revenant. Eventually it'll change, unless something is done. It'll change. Seasons are like that.

"Hotter than shit out here, boys."

"Least we don't have to worry 'bout global warming anymore."

It's hot. Feels like we do.

I was a kid, someone told me it was cow and pig shit and the methane from the shit that caused global warming. I laughed—it was so silly. But then the dead rose. So anything is possible. On a summer day, when there's forty, fifty of them banging on the gate, pushing to get in, to eat you . . . well . . . you can see the stink. You can see the gas rising from their bodies. Don't see why they shouldn't be like cow shit.

Question is, why don't they rot away? It's been three years now. Why haven't they rotted into nothing?

I should ask Mom, but I doubt she could answer. Hell, Knock-Out could give me just as good of an answer, really. Her answers are always missing something. His answers don't make sense, but they feel better. And the baby? Well, it's nice having some family. Wish she could watch TV like I used to.

I plan to give Ellie that. Television.

Blevens opens the inner gate and begins to double-smash all the skulls. I drop down, pull on my smock, the rubber gloves, and grab the ones he's double-smashed. You can't be too careful. Everyone has a headknocker in their belt and a pistol on their hip. Pistols are a last resort. The noise makes the zeds flock something fierce.

As fierce as the grave. They used to say that at weddings, I think.

No weddings anymore. Not enough women. Or maybe nobody's falling in love anymore.

Teeth first. It's horrible, looking into undead mouths, seeing the flesh hanging from black molars, but the metal, the gold and silver, are needed in Engineering, or so Joblownski says. Sometimes you have to smash a jaw with a hammer, just to loosen stuff up, and then pull out the goodies with pliers.

The naked zeds go right over the wall, into the river, to float or sink downstream. Not the best solution. But there are six billion of them and probably a hundred of us.

The clothed zombies, we take wallets, jewelry. We look at

tags in the clothing. Wallis wants info about zombie migration, and unless we plant tracking beacons on shamblers, looking at wallets is the best we can do.

"Got one from Jonesboro here. He's one of that damily that came calling." Lindy holds up an Arkansas driver's license. "Man, that sucks for you, Mark Watkins." He waves a wad of bills our way. "This sonofabitch has about three grand on him. He was fucking loaded. How bad does that suck, getting zombiefied holding three grand? Hope he got laid first."

Don't say anything. What do I know about getting laid? Of the few women here, none of them seems ready to let me devirginify myself all over her.

"Check his other pockets." Frazier finally speaks up. He's fat and pockmarked and doesn't give a shit about anyone but himself.

"I doubt he'll be holding any drugs," I say. Frazier's hair is long and braided into a white Viking.

He looks at me and scowls. "I don't give a shit what you think, you inconsequential little sparrow fart. Lindy, check the other pockets."

Feel like tossing the little troll over the side—and I'm big enough to do it now—but Blevens would try to stop me. My hands itch to do it, really. Mom and Knock-Out wouldn't be too pleased, though.

Huh. Guess it would be murder if I did that. Never really thought of it that way, but there it is.

I could snatch him up and toss him over, easy. I'm six feet now, and I spend every day knocking skulls and sliding around steel gates. Or hoeing and lifting bags of dirt. Just yesterday, I split the seams of my old work shirt helping Keb move a flat bottom on the docks. Keb laughed and asked me if Mom had dated Jasper before I was born.

I don't really know what I look like now—I remember wiping steam from the mirror in my bathroom, a lifetime ago, and peering into my reflection, waiting for facial hair, and now I have it, peachy, fuzzy, all over. I hope I'm ugly enough to scare the shitbag, Frazier.

And how do you get fat on the Bridge? We eat good, but there's never any seconds.

I stare back at him as long as I can. Think about tossing him and try to let that come through.

"Forget him, man. He's just an old, dried-up hippie." Lindy wads up the money and stuffs it into a sack slung around his shoulders. For some reason, even though it's worthless, he can't bear to throw it away.

I let reason win out. Reason. I feel like Mom.

Anyway, I've never actually been in a real fight before. At least not with someone living. Not before the Big Turnover and definitely not after. That's just wrong. But throwing Frazier off the Bridge might be fun. I'd like to see him splash.

"Hey, guys. You need to see this."

I drop a zed over the side of the Bridge and then hike myself onto the rampart.

"Holy shit."

"You ain't kidding."

The damily on the way wasn't a damily at all.

Riders. Horseback. And the dead, hundreds of them, following after.

* * *

I think she's a man at first. She's dressed like a man. She holds her body like a man, ready to fight.

When she gets to the gate, she holds up one hand, palm out, and hails us.

"Guards! My name is Wendy! This here's Jennifer. We need shelter." She shifts in the saddle and slaps her horse's neck, sending dust flying. "We've got info, from the south. News you need to hear."

Frazier scrambles to find the notepad that Wallis gave us with the words we're supposed to say, but I know it by heart and just say it without waiting for him.

I say, "Rider, we will allow you to enter if you swear, by all you hold holy and dear, that once entering our gates, you will do no harm to any living soul dwelling on this bridge, on pain of death. If you agree, make noises in the affirmative."

Wendy, hands going to her dual pistols, bellows, "Will we be allowed to keep our weapons?"

Shake my head. "Can't promise anything. We've never confiscated anything from anyone. But there's always a first time. And if you're holding something the quartermaster deems necessary to our community . . . well—"

"Well, what, boy?"

"We'll take it." I shouldn't say things like that, but I have trouble, sometimes, separating what I should say from what needs to be said. Maybe I'm like Mom. "You dense, woman? There are what looks like two hundred dead on your trail. You've brought them here. You are in no position to make demands. Now, you got maybe sixty seconds to decide if you want to agree and come in or stay out there and try to make your way beyond the horde of revs that've come calling."

She glares at me. It's like the glare I gave Frazier earlier. I hope mine has a little more threat.

Finally, she glances at the woman riding with her, looks back at me, nods.

"Go ahead and say it!"

"Fuck." She spits. "We accept."

"You may enter."

Me and Lindy pull the pins again, lift the steel gate, and slide them outward. The women and horses come into the murderhole, the animals tossing their heads and nickering. The zeds are right on their asses, ready to chomp, making a horrible ruckus.

It's gonna be a long day.

The husky woman who looks like a man—Wendy, she said her name was—looks me over when I come down from the ramparts. The zeds they brought are banging furiously on the steel gates, so I draw her inside the second gate, right at the Motor Pool. Ellroy stays with the other woman, helps her down from her horse. She's skinny, and might be pretty if she'd raise her head. Maybe.

Frazier gives me a sour look, and Lindy says, "What? You ain't gonna help us get rid of all these zeds? You better help with this."

"Yeah, yeah. Taking these guys to see Wallis and the Council. Be back soon."

* * *

"It doesn't matter what we do," Mom says to Wallis when we walk in. "People are going to start dying of cancer. The nuclear strikes pushed shitloads of radioactive material into the atmosphere. America, China, Europe, the cancer rates of the people who survived are going to skyrocket. And until civilization rights itself, which I don't see happening in the next century, there won't be any hospitals. So we've got to figure out a way to deal with the dying. We need to encourage suicide."

"That's absurd."

"Why? As far as we can tell, everybody turns revenant when they die. We're all infected. If someone dies inside the Bridge City . . . it's an untenable situation."

They look up at the woman and me as we enter. Mom cocks her eyebrow at me.

Knock-Out, who's cooing to the baby, smiles and winks. Keb, standing guard, puts his hand right on Wendy's breast and says, "Weapons on the table, mister."

She doesn't blink. I can see him figuring out that this is a woman. He takes his hand away from her chest.

She pulls two pistols, a sawed-off shotgun, a machete, some kabob skewers, a butterfly knife, and a long military-looking dagger from her person and dumps them on the table, one by one. Her back is straight, and if I didn't know better, I'd say she's mad. Or has a corncob stuck up her ass. Or both.

"Gots to frisk ya," Keb says, and gives her the once over, moving down her body. He stops at her shoes and lifts the cuffs of her jeans.

There's a shackle on her ankle.

Strange.

She walks up to the conference table and pipes right up.

"I'm Wendy. We come from Texas, me and my wife."

Wallis glances at me and I shrug, then nod.

"Who's in charge here?"

I can tell she's trying to make herself sound tough. Either that or she really is that tough. I haven't met a lot of people living on this bridge, but someone pretending to be tough scares me more than someone who is. You can't trust the way they'll act.

"We are. My name is Quentin Wallis. This is Dr. Ingersol and her husband, Jim Nickerson."

"Not husband. Consort, maybe. Knock-Out. Folks call me Knock-Out."

Wendy glances at him and then back to Wallis. He's stopped wearing his uniform since Mom insisted, but you can't hide the soldier in civilian clothes.

And he still keeps the hair high and tight.

"And absent is Joblownski, who's in charge of Engineering. He's a member of the Council."

Wendy clears her throat. "So, this here settlement is a democracy?"

"*No.*" Mom shifts and crosses her hands over her lap. "It's a shared dictatorship. We don't canvass the populace for their opinions, and they don't vote on major decisions."

"So, you just tell them what they're gonna do?"

"Yes. Right now, at this point in our . . . development . . . that's how it has to be."

"And these brutes I see standing about, they've got the look

181

of military about them. They make sure the people keep in line? They make sure folks do what you want them to do?"

Knock-Out brings Ellie over to me, lays her in my arms. She puts a chubby hand on my cheek and pinches me, hard, squealing. Her little fingernails are sharp.

Sometimes Knock-Out amazes me with how he picks up on things.

"Ma'am," Knock-Out says, "it'd save us all a bunch of time if you'd just tell us what you're getting at."

I clear my throat. Mom raises her eyebrow and gives me the look.

Wallis says, "Go ahead, Gus. Speak."

Careful here. I say, "Wendy? Can you tell us about what's on your ankle?"

She flushes. If she looked angry before, now she looks ready to pop. Her face is furious, if only for a moment, then is suffused with blood and she looks ashamed until the blood drains away, taking on the aspect of stone. Cold and remorseless.

She says, in a dead voice, "Slavers down in Texas. And they're heading north. This way. They know about you."

Wallis sits up straight. "What did you say?"

"There's slavers coming this way. We escaped, me and Jennifer. I killed . . . I don't know how many. Took as many of their horses as I could round up and rode hard, north. Toward you."

She sways a little. Mom stands, moves around the table, and puts a hand on her cheek, checking for fever.

I turn to Keb. "Go get the other woman. Jennifer. Bring her here, and tell Frazier and Ellroy to take the horses to the inner stable. Round up more men to man the North Gate. We need more hands at the Wall for the zeds on their trail. We'll figure out what to do with the horses later."

"There's fifty pounds of moldy oats in a bag on one of the mares. That should last them through a couple more days, but they need—"

Keb looks lost.

"Go on, Keb. We'll figure it out."

Wallis and Knock-Out are looking at me strange. Ellie gives a gurgle and goes to sleep. I watch her go, just like a little sunset in my arms.

Mom sits Wendy down at the conference table, brings over a bottle of Evian—a big gift. She cracks the seal on the cap and pours her a glass.

Wendy knocks it back.

"How long has it been since you've slept?"

She shrugs. "A week. Lost track. Since before we escaped. Caught some z's on horseback, but not for long. Lost three horses on the ride."

Knock-Out brings a tray with glasses to the table, a Johnnie Walker bottle blunt and amber in the light from the tent flap. Twists the cap and pours some for the woman. "I need you to tell us what you know. About the slavers."

She sniffs the alcohol. For a moment, she looks around at all of us, her eyes going from face to face. She was tough before, now she's lost and confused.

She says, "They took us outside of Rockwall. The undead from Dallas had mobbed and were roaming in migrant bands. Jennifer and I had holed up in a bank, living off vending machines, sleeping in the vault. We were hungry, but—"

"Safe," I say, remembering. Hard to forget spending a lifetime folded into a Pinkerton safe while your father claws at the door and gibbers for your blood.

She doesn't even nod. She looks at me, sucks her teeth. I take Ellie to the crib in the corner. Mom meets me there and lays her down. Ellie doesn't make a noise.

"Then they drove by, in armored trucks, a line of 'em. And police cruisers, talking on their PAs. Don't understand how they could've avoided the EMP, but maybe they were . . . I don't know . . . shielded or something. They told us they were gonna lead the undead away. Down Main, away from everything, and then shoot them. They said any survivors needed to head to the Chili's on I-30, where a transport would pick us up. Maybe five hundred dead folks were following, just trailing along. Once they passed, it was like it had just rained and washed the leaves from the street. No zombies anywhere.

"At the Chili's, there were men. They looked nervous, I remember. This was two and a half, three years ago. They had an eighteen-wheeler. They were all cops or army guys with big guns. They told us to get in. It felt wrong, but we got in anyway because the zombies were starting to come back—this was outside of Dallas and it was still burning, so there were millions of dead stumbling around, black and stinking from the nuclear strike—"

She stops, brings the whiskey to her mouth, and breathes into the liquor. I can see the moisture from her breath fog the glass. She swallows some and winces.

It's a long while before she continues. Mom looks at me, worried. Knock-Out places a hand on Mom's shoulder. Wallis steeples his long fingers and is still, watching, listening, thinking. I can't tell if he's as scared as I am.

"We drove north for hours. In and out of days, seems like, but might've been just a few hours. When we stopped, they circled the armored vehicles, keeping us in the cattle cars, waiting, while they rested. They didn't realize that someone was sick. When she turned, she killed most of the people in the other transport before they responded. They shot everyone, even the living folks. From then on, we had armed guards.

"Next day, we pulled into New Boston—north Texas—an army depot there. It's fortified, row after row of chain link. They separated the men from the women, put the women in a locked barrack, and put us in a holding pen. Jennifer—"

She breaks. I see it happen, I'm watching. Her face crumples, and I've never seen anyone as helpless as her, ever. I'm sorry now I was hard on her at the gate. I shouldn't have been.

"They wanted the women for their brothel. Sixty men, they became slavers just to get laid. They never let the girls see sun. They rounded up the men, walked them out to a field." She looks down at her hand, the glass in it, as if discovering something new. "The men. They shot them."

Her voice itself is like a gunshot.

"How did you—" Mom is wondering what everyone is wondering.

"They stopped me going into the pen. They stripped me. Two of them held me down—" She sobs once, loudly, and then shivers. "But they didn't put me in with the other women after. They laughed and beat me. Put me to work, being their dog. They had this collar, for the Dobermans that walked the perimeter. They put it on me and shocked me with a remote. Like a goddamned dog. That's what they called me. Dog. Bitch. I would've . . ."

Knock-Out pours her more whiskey. She rolls the glass in her hands as if warming it, but she's just looking into it, losing herself. She's not here with us anymore, she's somewhere else, somewhere back in Texas. She'll always be there, I think.

"I would've tried to . . . tried to . . . something. Kill them. Poison them. But they had Jennifer. I couldn't kill myself. I couldn't abandon her. So I waited and wore the collar and did what they told me to. I stayed their dog. I cooked their food. After the water went out, I carried their buckets of shit to the cesspool. I did their laundry. I tended their livestock." She drinks the whiskey, puts down the glass, raises her hands in an open gesture. "They didn't rape me again."

Before she looked like a man, but now, with the tears, she looks like a boy, maybe someone my age. It's hard to imagine what she's been through.

"They heard your broadcasts on the ham radio. They listened to your messages about the tactical superiority of bridges. They listened. There were more and more zombies coming every day, and it took more and more resources to wipe them out, so when your broadcasts came—telling how to distill water, to purify it, to fortify a bridge, to make a murderhole—they began preparing to move. The depot, all of us. North. I heard they were planning on wintering in Texarkana, some bridge there.

"The night before they were going to move, I was able to get us out . . . it seems so long ago. But it was just last week."

She's done crying now. Her voice is hard, but she's not trying to be tough. She's just telling it like it happened. I like this woman. I didn't like the woman at the gate.

She says, "At night, they would shackle me to a wall. I was entertainment to them. They took one of the doghouses for the Dobermans, sprayed it out with water, and threw some wool blankets in it. That was where I slept for a long time, until I started stinking. Then they didn't want me touching their food or washing their clothes. The big man there, Konstantin, he ordered them to give me a hutch near the brothel. They had these little portable buildings, like folks used to keep in their backyards for storing lawnmowers. This was my home. A glorified doghouse. But they let me wash and started making sure I had better food. At night they would chain me in, padlock me to a wall.

"But the night before we were supposed to move, the man on watch forgot to chain me. I don't know why, maybe the excitement of the day, maybe he was just distracted. I wasn't allowed anywhere but the laundry and kitchen, and at night I was supposed to wait on a bench beside my hutch for a man to come lock me in. There were always so many men about, I knew I had to wait. Like a good dog. And I always did. But this night—"

She makes a fist as if she's crushing something. "This night, he didn't come to shackle me. I only had a little time. I went back to the kitchen and took a knife, returned to the bench, and waited for him. His name was Jerry Mayfield. When he finally turned up, it was late and all the off-duty men had gone to the barracks. He was distracted and didn't bother to frisk me or even pay much attention to me at all. I stabbed him in the belly the minute he stepped into the hutch. He tried to yell, but I stuck the knife in his throat. He didn't take long to die . . . and there was blood . . . everywhere. When he started turning revenant, I led him into the main barracks. At one point, he was so close to me I didn't think I was going to make it away from him. But once he'd killed a couple of slavers, I ran to the guards at the brothel and screamed bloody murder. After they ran off, I set the women free and grabbed Jennifer. She was . . . she is . . . different now. The bastards . . . used her, used her hard. I slashed tires and had planned on killing the rest of the horses and cattle, but . . . I couldn't bring myself to do it and time was getting short. So I saddled two horses, took the rest. I didn't want to take an armored vehicle because they'd be able to hear it and follow. And the dead too.

"After a day's ride, it wasn't hard to loot houses for guns and ammo. Even some food. But we had to keep moving. It wasn't until a few days into our ride did we start getting a fol-lowing."

She shakes her head and looks at Wallis, points at his chest.

"Don't know how bad I hurt them, but . . . I know it wasn't bad enough. The gunfire stopped after a few minutes. So they must've put down all the revs I seeded there."

She lifts her glass and tilts it up, even though the whiskey is long gone. Knock-Out pours her just a bit more. "I don't know a lot, but I know this: They're takers. They want what you have. This bridge." She points at Mom. "These women. They'll be coming. Maybe not this month. Or the next. Or even this year. But they'll be coming, in force. They know where you are."

She closes her eyes.

Keb opens the tent flap with the other woman, Jennifer, standing beside him. Mom comes to her, shoos Keb away, and looks at me.

"I need Milly. Please go get her. And set up another tent, please, near the Garden, away from the others. These women need rest." She turns to Knock-Out and Wallis. "This tent is now an examination room. Leave the water and whiskey. I'll come update you once I've gotten them settled."

Mom smiles at me and then turns back to the woman, Jennifer. I run for Milly.

Wallis catches me on the way back to the Wall.

"I need you to outride for me."

That's the best thing I've heard all day. I don't get to leave Bridge City very often. And right away I know why and where he wants me to go.

"Mom isn't going to go for it."

"Let me take care of that. But I need your eyes. I can't trust Jasper or Keb alone for this, and I can't risk Knock-Out. So that leaves you."

"Don't get me wrong, I'm all for it. But Mom—"

"I'll deal with Lucy. It's time you start assuming some of the leadership responsibilities around here."

I don't know what to say to that. It's not like Mom is royalty. She, Knock-Out, and Wallis just turned out to be the best people to lead, that's all. And I'm just hanging around all the time. Probably because of Ellie. So I hear stuff. And I have a brain, unlike Keb or Jasper.

"All right. When?"

"In two days. I'm considering having you take the women's horses. This is covert, so you'll be going as quickly and quietly as you can. You don't want to pull up to the slavers with an army of undead at your back—"

He says it and then gets a funny look on his face. I laugh.

"Sounds like a plan."

"Indeed."

"I'm just glad I was here to witness the genius, Captain."

Wallis frowns at me. "Lieutenant. That's all I'll ever be. You don't assume rank without promotion."

"Oh? Sorry." I'm thinking about the Wall. The sun is going down, and I'm sure the boys are wading in zombies. I need to get back and help with the headknocking.

"So . . . no. You'll need to take a Bradley instead maybe. Or motorcycles. Loud ones. And ride slow. Draw as many of the dead as you can—swing through Fort Smith, Hot Springs, Arkadelphia. Draw all the revenant population you can to the south. But still get out and then don't draw any back here." He's deep in thought now, quiet and chewing at his lip.

"We should go see Joblownski. He needs to be in this conversation."

Wallis nods his agreement, shows his perfect white teeth, and claps me on the shoulder.

"Let's go."

The Wall must wait.

Joblownski tinkers with his still. He's got two: one for water, one for moonshine. And he can make the shine from anything. He can take a shoe, an ear of corn, three Twizzlers, and make a liquor that will get you high. Mom spends time with him, though not to get high. They're trying to get a filter that'll keep out the nastiest water-borne diseases from all the shamblers. A filter that's microns fine.

And that is fine with him. But today he tinkers with the rainwater distillery.

"When're we gonna be drinking from the river, Joblo?"

He glares at me, stands, dusts off his knees.

"Gimme a sec, boy, and I'll get you a cupful."

Wallis grins and sticks out his hand. It's something he does now, instead of saluting. He shakes everybody's hand. Everybody's. Knock-Out calls it "glad-handing."

They shake, and Joblo looks me over. "I've been thinking about your idea, Gus. We might be able to get the dam working. Trouble is, well have to go out and turn off all the electrical stuff in the town. You ever read *The Stand*?"

I shake my head. I was just ten when the world ended.

"Huh. That's too bad. Well, failing that, we can make little generators from outboard motors or anything that'll spin in the water. Give us a few volts, enough to charge batteries, maybe run a TV and the like, instead of using up gas. Might be able to rig some solar panels on the nearby houses, run wires over here to the bridge. But that'll take a shitload of human resources. Men always guarding our backs, my engineers—"

"Joblo, we can talk about this later. Right now I need to figure out the best way to draw zeds. We've got a problem. And this might be a solution. What's the loudest vehicle you've got?"

At this, Joblownski cocks his head, grins, and begins to talk in very excited tones.

It's near dark by the time I return to the Wall. Frazier spits on the ground in front of me and again I have the urge to chuck him over the Bridge, but Blevens and Ellroy are watching.

"So what's up with the lady riders, huh?"

"They had some info on gas reserves down south."

"Bullshit. There's more to them than that."

"No, that's it." I walk over to the rack and take out my preferred headknocker. I've got a belt for it back in my tent. "We're gonna head out Friday, see if we can find the reserves."

"We?" Ellroy looks at me. "Who's we?"

"Keb, Jasper, and me."

"Bullshit." This from Blevens. "The doc would never let you."

"Mom's cool with it. And it's time I start pulling my own weight around here, beyond the Wall."

"Shit, man, you need to start pulling your weight *inside* the Wall."

I laugh. "Screw you, Lindy. I haven't been fucking around in the Garden, making moon eyes at Cindy."

He splutters and turns red. Ellroy and Blevens laugh.

"Jesus Christ, you kids are fucking killing me. There's still fifty, sixty zeds at the gate. We've got to clear them out before morning. You know the rules. No dead by dawn."

Frazier is such a prick. I pull a lighter, a Zippo, and go around to the torches. Citronella. They smell lemony and drive away some of the flies. The shamblers follow us, and the flies follow the shamblers.

Lindy lights some torches on the other side of the murderhole. The night gets darker, and the zombies on the other side of the gate moan. Stars wink overhead.

Frazier and Blevens turn on electric flashlights, charged in the Bradleys. We check the inner gate. It's locked down.

Lindy and I open the outer gate and let in the dead.

In the early morning light coming through my tent flap, I pack my gear. I can't sleep late anymore. Those long Saturday mornings with cartoons and cereal are so long gone I'm having a hard time remembering them. The look of television. The taste of milk and sugary cereal.

I remember air-conditioning, and riding in cars. Riding in cars everywhere. I remember radio. And rock 'n' roll. And school, my classroom and teachers. There was noise all the time, the hum of a fan, the buzz of cars and whine of airplanes. Cars honked and their alarms chirped. People mowed their yards and blew leaves from their drives. Radios sang from above kitchen sinks. There was constant noise. The noise of industry and the fabric of life. Now, all we have is moaning. It's constant, except for those times after we've cleared the murderhole and the last of the zeds go over the side. Then suddenly it's quiet and the stars above draw our eyes up, up into the sky, and then I feel how small we are. Then the cicadas whir and something, someone—someone dead—moans out in the night. And then another moan. And then another. And soon they're all gathering at our gate again.

But I remember airplane trails across the sky, and the glow of halogen lights at night. I remember.

All that is gone.

It's hot in the tent, and sweat beads down my cheeks and drips off the tip of my nose.

The big .357, my headknocker, various knives and pointy things, I lay them all out on my cot. I oil the revolver and sharpen the knives. I spread out my armor, check and see if it still fits. I've grown a few inches since the last time I was outside the walls. The pants and vest don't fit anymore. The helmet is still okay. I guess the old noodle is still the same size.

The old noodle. That's what Dad used to say.

I can't remember his face anymore. I have some pictures, but they're like the river—I've looked on it so often, and even though it's always changing, it never really changes. I know every picture of him like I know this gun, or how to knock heads. I know it like I know the stink of the dead and the smell of wood smoke and citronella candles. I could scratch his face in the dirt, or on a stone with a piece of charcoal, I know every line of his face so well. But I can't remember the sound of his voice, the crooked smile, the smell of him. I can't remember the sight of him walking, how he'd move. But I can remember when he began to curse and spasm. I can remember him bent on the floor tight as a bowstring.

When I'm finished packing and maintaining my gear, I give the tent a look, checking out all the books stacked in the corner. There's Caesar's *Gallic Wars*. I've got *Roman Armaments and Siege Engines*. *A Guide to Building a Ballista*. And, most important, *Medieval Fortifications: The Feudal Way*.

If I don't come back, I'll miss them.

I wander down to the Mess, where breakfast is being served. As always, there's noodles and condensed milk. But today is a good day and there's fruit salad swimming in syrup. Canned Salad, the people call it. I get a bowl of pasta, some beans, catfish—which is what we mostly eat at Bridge City—and some of the Canned Salad.

Jasper, Keb, Cindy, Barb, and Dina are all sitting at a table and wave me over. Barb pats the seat next to her. It makes me feel a bit funny, Barb looking at me like that. She's plump, but not fat, and ten years older than me, I think. She was in college during the Big Turnover. They say she made it nearly five months living off the food she'd found in the apartment block she'd barricaded herself in.

Dina, like Mom and Knock-Out, has burns from a nuclear strike. Mom's always saying people are going to start dying from cancer soon. I don't like to think about Barb being dead. Or Dina.

Or Mom.

I sit next to Barb and she presses her leg against mine under the table. Her leg is warm and soft, and I'm having a hard time thinking.

"So," Barb asks, her voice low, "what's this secret mission you three are going on? Keb and Jazz won't tell us."

The men at other tables look at the women—three of twenty in Bridge City—and I know they'd like to toss me over the Bridge Wall and take my seat.

"Nothing, really." I take a bite of salad, follow it with coffee. "Some fuel reserves down there. Gas storage for Murphy Oil. See if we can bring back a tanker. Nearer the site, we'll rustle up a backhoe or something to be our spearhead and clear the roads for the tanker."

"Just you three?"

"Can't risk any more." Jasper is looking at me like a deer in the headlights—I think that's the saying—and Keb has crossed his arms. He's glaring at the women.

"That's right, ladies. Just like the Lil Prince says."

"Keb, don't call me that—"

"Shit, G, it's the goddamned truth. They's grooming you to be part of the Council, sure as shit."

I eat some more. Barb puts her hand on my thigh.

Dina, pretty even with the burns, says, "Well, we'll have a little party for you boys tonight, at the women's fire pit. You know, for the soldiers doomed to die and all that. Smells better there, less noise from the visitors at the Wall. We've got some whiskey we've been saving and some wine. I've invited Brandon and his friend too, and they said they'd bring their guitars. What do you say?"

I swallow. "We're leaving pretty early tomorrow—"

Jasper stares at me and says, "Gus, you don't get an invite to the women's fire pit every day. They invite who they want." Dina giggles. Really.

I've heard them partying at night down by the pit. But I

196

never really thought I'd be able to join the adults there until I moved out of the big family tent into my own, last year. Ellie came, and suddenly I wasn't the only kid anymore. Not like I felt like one anyway.

Women scare me. The women's fire pit is like the cool kids' table at school, back before the Big Turnover.

I'm so excited, I put down my spork and look at Jasper and Keb grinning like idiots.

"Um. Okay, I guess. That'd be great."

Jasper slams his hands down on the table. "Hell, yes! Keb, I told you Gus weren't no pussy!"

I don't really know what to say to that. But I'm glad I'm not a pussy.

Barb leans toward me, her mouth barely inches from my ear, and whispers, "It'll be fun. I promise."

Mom yells, "You're not going!" the moment I enter the Command Tent.

"Now, Luce, let's not get all excited about this." Knock-Out is holding the baby, bouncing her. Wallis looks uncomfortable and stands up.

She storms over to me, doing her best to shake the wooden flooring of the big tent, and gets right in my face.

"Negative! No. Absolutely not. You aren't going anywhere. I thought I lost you once. I'm not going to let that happen again."

"Lucy," Wallis says. "He's a man now. Old enough to make his own decisions."

"He's not an adult. He's just fourteen, for chrissakes. He should be in school, playing video games, having crushes on girls. Not leading an army of undead toward a pack of dogs who want to enslave us. In Texarkana, of all fucking places!"

"Mom, I—"

"Not a word, Gus!" She holds up her finger, old school. She hasn't done that since, since . . . I don't know. Since before.

She stands there panting, glaring at me.

"I'm fourteen now. It's time you let me start taking some responsibility." I can see her eyes, gray like mine, going back and forth. She's already thinking up a rebuttal. "Jasper, Keb, Frazier . . . they're starting to call me 'the little prince.' They think I'm too good to scavenge or fence-build, or gather wood beyond the Wall."

"He's right, Lucy," Wallis says, his voice serious. "I've heard the men talk. Everyone has to pull his weight at Bridge City."

"I don't care. As far as we know, I'm the only fucking doctor in the whole goddamned world. So that *does* make him a prince. He's staying here."

"Mom, I'm going. I don't live with you anymore. I've got my own tent. I do my time knocking heads at the Wall—I'm not too good for that! I'm ready to become a real member of our . . . our . . . whatever it is we have here. To contribute." I hold out my hand for her to take. A handshake. I know it's weird to do with your mom. But I don't know what to do. Hug her?

She looks at my hand like it's a zed.

"No, Gus." She won't cry. She won't. "Please. Stay here with me. Stay safe."

"Mom. I'm going with Jasper and Keb to make sure that *she* stays safe." I point at Ellie. Knock-Out still bounces her up and down.

Mom glares at me, her cheek muscles popping. She's grinding her teeth. She stays that way for a long time, and then she bobs her head. A nod. That's all she can give me.

She turns to Knock-Out. He's crying, tears running down his cheeks into his beard.

"Why are you crying?" Mom sounds surprised and offended.

"Because you can't."

The whiskey tastes like fire, like the heat from the fire, like the heat from her chest pressed against my arm. It tastes like her lips when she kisses me.

The men—I've forgotten their names—play guitar, eyes closed, and really get into it, stomping their feet and rocking their upper bodies in time with the chord changes. They hang on a chord—I don't know which one—and then go to another, hang on it for a while, and then back to the first. They're grunting and laughing and looking at each other, smiling.

There are words, but I can't make them out. They sound like iko iko or aikoaiko or something like that. It's hypnotic.

At the edges of the firelight, I can tell there are some men watching. I can feel their eyes on me. But then Jasper gets up, and Keb joins him, and they rush into the shadows, whooping and swinging fists, and whoever is watching starts yelping and cursing and then we're alone. I stay seated, kissing Barb. Keb and Jasper are laughing when they sit back by the fire.

Cindy sits nestled up to Jasper, and Dina has a hand on Keb's knee but is flirting with one of the guitarists, and they don't look friendly now, but I can't pay too much attention to that because Barb's breath is in my ear and then I've got goose bumps down my arms.

She pulls at me, and I realize she wants me to stand. I do, but not without some balancing issues. Her lips are on mine again, and her hand is behind my head, in my hair, pulling me down, but her hand is on the front of my pants too, and I don't know what to do with myself. All I can think of is that one piece of me that she's rubbing.

Then she pulls away, laughing, and starts dancing by the fire. She wants me to join her. She's singing under her breath and moving her hands like a belly dancer might. I don't know. I was ten when the world ended. I've read books. I remember some movies. That's all.

She crooks a finger at me and switches her hips and . . . damn . . . I wish with all my might that I could dance. The guitarists aren't even playing now and I want to dance. But Jasper and Keb are watching me, laughing, and I stay where I am.

Then one of the guitarists is up and dancing with her. The other one grins and begins to play. Instead of dancers matching the music, the music matches the dancers. Barb looks at me, shrugs, and puts her arms around the guitarist's shoulders and whispers in his ear.

I can feel the blood in my cheeks. I watch. My hands are balled into fists. I'm furious.

On my way back to the tent, Frazier stumbles out of the dark, coming toward me. River's on my left. My hand's on the concrete railing. The moon silvers the surface, and everything is quiet. The shamblers aren't moaning heavy tonight. We're pretty far away from either gate. The Garden is right behind us and the Command and Mess look like empty circus tents, ruffling in the breeze.

"Whaddya know. It's the little prince." He spits at my feet. Again. "Took your time getting back to the Wall. Left us there to knock heads for you. You stay back sucking your momma's tit? Huh? Hiding?"

I stop. This is really the wrong time for this. He gets up in my face. He's been drinking the old stuff, smells like. I look at him and can see the shambler waiting to come out. His breath smells rotten.

"Punk kids like you, having shit handed to them . . . I can't tolerate that." He jabs me in the chest with a finger.

Fuck. That hurts.

"You little brat. The world ends and we still got punk kids with rich parents buying their way outta—"

His last word isn't a word at all. It's a weird little sound. *Eerp!* Then I have him by the shirt and belt buckle, lifting him up and over the rail.

The splash, when he hits the river, is small and far away. Doesn't even have a chance to scream.

I watch the water for a long time. He doesn't come back up. I look around. There's nobody, but that doesn't mean nobody saw me. Not much I can do about it now.

Damn.

Should feel bad, but I don't. He didn't deserve it.

But he did.

Night Patrol will be by any minute. I should get back to the tent.

Morning now. Gear up after a bad sleep. Bad dreams. I'm stuck in the TV, trying to get out. But I can't. There's a face on the other side of the screen, but I can't make it out, so I smash the glass and come through, slip bloody and gashed over the lip and begin to fall, fall through the air, until I hit black water.

Sweating when I wake. It might be a hangover from the whiskey. Or the dream. Maybe it's just the sun's up and my tent is hot.

At midpoint of Bridge City, Joblownski winches down the motorcycles to a barge below. It smells like fish and hickory. We're right near the industrial smoker where the catfish pulled from the river meet their final end.

Joblownski, when he sees me, hands the winch control to Wilkins and waves me over.

"Here's your new armor, Gus. Check it out. I've had Wilkie work this leather bandolier into the fabric for extra rounds. And here—" He points to the chest piece. "I've fitted

202

it with easy-grab bludgeons. In this case, a couple of camping hatchets. Fastened with Velcro for quick release."

"The chest piece looks good." He fits it on me. Jasper and Keb walk up looking bloodshot and tired. Big night for them last night, I guess.

Me too.

I check the hatchets, rip them out, one in each fist, and grin at Keb.

"Double fisted," Jasper says. "Nice. Hey, why didn't we get fancy new armor?"

"Yours fits you. His didn't."

I Velcro back the hatchets without any difficulty. On the leg armor, instead of holsters, he's got Velcro rip-away .9mms. And extra clips. Already loaded.

"Won't that make it hard to draw?"

"If you need a quick draw against the revs, there's nothing I can give you that will keep you alive. But if you take a spill with this gear? You won't lose all your weapons." He picks up three small pieces of metal-studded leather.

"These are called gorgets. They go over your throat. You know how the revs like biting necks. They have buckles around back and should fit easily under your helmets. Come over here and check this out, boys."

We all follow. A couple of new engineers join us. Now that I'm checking it out close, the motorcycle looks different from usual. There's a rack soldered to the handlebars. And a big cast-iron bar welded a couple of feet in front. The rack holds an M16 and an A-Bolt .30-06 with scope.

"Damn, Joblo, you sure got us mounted for bear." Keb

snaps his fingers and then slaps Jasper's chest. "Posted at the trap, dog. The motherfucking *trap*!"

"I have no idea what you're talking about, Keb, but yes, you've got some armaments. Each of you has a grenade launcher attached to the M16, your old military-issue stuff. Use those to take out vehicles or clusters of revs if you have to. Shotgun too, for close work. There's extra rounds in the bags. The big bar out front is to knock over zeds in front of you. And since you'll be riding at night, I've mounted a rear headlight on each of your bikes, so you can check out how close your . . . herd, I guess . . . is."

Jasper looks at Joblo and says, "Does the seat eject, Q?"

Keb and Joblo laugh.

I watch them. "What?"

They stop laughing and look at me.

"You know, Gus. James Bond?"

I point to one of the new engineers.

"That him?"

"No. James Bond. Double oh seven? British spy?"

I shake my head.

Keb says, "You telling me you don't know who James Bond is, Lil P?"

I don't say anything. I don't like when this happens.

Two men, new looking—I can't help but think of the big one as James Bond—come over to us, nodding, smoking grape vine, and harness the bike. We roll it over to the concrete side of the Bridge where they've knocked a hole and they winch the bike up and drop it the hundred feet to the party barge waiting below.

I don't know why they call it a party barge; maybe because it can hold a large party of people. But it can fit our three bikes and us and take us downstream to the dam.

Wallis shows up, pulls me aside, and briefs me on the plan. Again. It's pretty simple. Take as many zombies as possible to the slavers. Get back alive. He'll have the Bradley waiting for us on I-40, outside of Arkadelphia.

He slaps a case in my hand.

"Flare gun. You might need it to signal us. Wish I had a radio that worked, but the ham radios are just too big to carry." He puts his hand on my shoulder and gives me a look. He's trying to be friendly and doesn't know how. "You weren't with the unit, but I still feel like you're one of my men. I want you to come back safe. And make sure Keb and Jasper get back safe too. They're big and deadly. And loyal. But they barely have a brain between them. You are in charge." He slaps my shoulder hard then, and says, "Your mother won't be seeing you off. Ellie's got a fever, and she needs to monitor her. But Knock-Out asked for you to wait just a bit."

After Wallis leaves, I watch as they winch down Jasper's and Keb's bikes. Keb tries to joke, but I'm not biting. I'm glad he's smart enough not to rib me about last night.

"Looks like you're on your own now." Knock-Out's voice, behind me.

I turn and he's there, hands on his hips, looking at me, shaking his head. I don't know why he's doing that, the head shaking.

I've known this man since I was ten. He was there when my father died true death.

True death. I've never thought of it that way before. He had something to do with Dad's end, but it was Mom who pulled the trigger.

It had to be done.

"Listen, Gus," Knock-Out says. "I know I'm just some guy, and I've never tried to replace your . . . your dad. You know? You're your own man. Even when you were young. Ten when I met you. So I just want you to let me talk to you, man to man. Can we do that?"

Don't see any problem with it, but can't say I really want to have a heart-to-heart either. We move over to the side of the Bridge, away from the motorcycle winch, toward the smoker stinking of hickory and fish, and stop there.

Knock-Out leans on the railing and stares out past the dock and rock-pilings below us, out at the river. There's a pair of seagulls diving into the Arkansas's brown waters. The sun shines off the surface, turning brown water blue.

"Your mom is broken up about your leaving. Ain't no doubt about it, she's terrified you'll not come back."

Don't know what to say, except, "I know."

"But it's more than that really, Gus. These slavers. You growing up with a .357 on your hip and knocking heads every day. Now with your leaving, Luce is reminded that the world, her world—the world she could control and define— all that is gone. And you, her son, are the first generation of the new, undefinable, uncontrollable world."

He pauses, spits, and watches as the spit falls to the river below.

"Does that make any sense?"

"Maybe. I think so. James Bond."

"What about him?"

"I didn't know who he was." Jerk a thumb at Joblo, Keb, and Jasper. "They thought that was weird."

"No." Knock-Out looks very serious. "It's not weird. It's just this new world we're living in."

I get it. I'm not stupid.

Knock-Out sighs and says, "Above all things, your mother needs understanding. She needs to be able to comprehend what's going on. That's why Bridge City, I guess, is important. It's a community, and she sits at the top. Her never being able to figure out why the dead rise has eaten away at her these last few years. It's worn away her sense of order."

"It doesn't seem to have bothered you."

Knock-Out puts his hands on his hips and looks at me. "Or you either. You want to know why?"

I wish he'd just get to the point.

"When I was a boy, I watched my father beat my mother to death. He was dead drunk. And when he came for me, you know what I did?"

I don't understand. He's talking about himself, but it's so much like . . . like when Dad died. I can't speak. I never knew that about him.

"I locked myself in a closet and cried until the police came."

"Yeah. Okay. I see what you're saying. We're alike, you and me."

"No, the point is, for you and me, the worst thing that could ever happen has already happened to us. But for Luce, it hasn't. For her, the worst thing would be to lose you. Or Ellie."

He coughs and then touches his side as if it's sore.

"You okay?"

"Yeah. I'm fine." He stands straight and puts his hand on my shoulder. "I need you to promise me you'll bring yourself back. For us, for your mother. For the community. You might not think so, but you're needed here. You might not know it, but people look to you for guidance."

"I'm just a—"

"No, whatever you're gonna say isn't true. You're not a kid. I don't think you ever were one. Yesterday, when you told Keb what to do, did he argue?"

"No, but—"

"Has Wallis entrusted you with this mission? You, a fourteen-year-old boy?"

"Yes."

"You're a leader. Get used to it. Acting like you're not is just lying to yourself and can hurt us all."

His hand rests on my shoulder. He squeezes and I can feel the warmth and pressure, even through the armor.

"You're important to us. To everybody here. You came up with the idea for the bridge. You came up with the idea of the murderholes. The chain-link fences. You're a leader. We need you." He pauses, turns away from the river, and leans back against the rail. "I came to find you last night, to talk. And I saw."

He saw. He knows what I am. A murderer.

"I don't know what he said to deserve it. Or if he did. I don't know anything. I don't even know what I saw." He turns and looks at me, and I've never really looked at him this closely. He's got green flecks in his eyes. He's big, but I'm bigger now, I think. I remember when he let me out of the safe, all the times he's made me laugh. All the times when he's thought of me when Mom didn't, brought me gifts, protected me.

"This is a different world, Gus. And the fact that you did what you did . . . well, I'm going to keep it between us. It's a hard life you have to lead, and I think that all this head-knocking and the undead, it can make you . . . strange. But you shouldn't have done it." He wipes his eyes, and I can't tell if it's the smoke from the curing fish or real tears. Probably real tears. But you never know with Knock-Out. He's harder than all of us, I think. But he's softer too.

"And you can never do it again. If I ever discover that you have—" He stands up straight and rests his hands on his hammer. "I'm gonna tell you one last thing you already know. Or you better know. Human life is precious and it should be protected at all costs. The biggest crime is taking another human life. I'll say it again: life is precious. It should never be wasted. Never be thrown away."

That's what I did when I murdered Frazier. I threw his life away.

"I need you to promise me you'll never take another life. Ever."

The silence draws out and I can hear the moans coming from the Wall. The seagulls bank and wheel and caw in the sky. I look at Knock-Out. He's standing there, hand on his headknocker, bristling with hair.

"I can't do that."

He looks stunned. His mouth opens as if to say something and then he closes it.

"I'm riding south to try to stop the slavers. You think I might not have to kill some? No. If I'm supposed to be a leader, I can't promise you not to kill. But I can promise you this: I'll never kill again in anger." I shrug. It's the best I can offer him. There's too much at stake.

He swallows, looks hurt. I can't blame him. He's got a murderer for a step-son, and he's got to keep that secret if he wants to stay with Mom. Everything is different from the television world we used to have.

"Okay. If that's all you can promise, I'll take it." He slumps a little then. "That's all." He coughs again, but it's more of a nervous cough. "Know that your mother and I love you."

He slaps my shoulder, pulls me into a hug that lasts for a long time, and then walks away. I go to the rail, feeling like I'm gonna puke, and look out over the water, away into the trees on the far shore. Then, after I've controlled myself, I turn and get harnessed to rappel down to the dock.

For an hour or so, Joblo pilots us downstream toward the Ozark Game & Fish boat ramp. I haven't ridden on a boat in years, even though I helped oversee getting the boat dock fixed to the main downstream pylon. My idea, actually.

It's a little frightening, looking into the brown water, not knowing what could be under the surface.

The bikes wobble and shake when Joblo runs the party

barge right up on the concrete. The forest has worked itself up to the edges of the pavement and the trees hang over the road.

"Gonna have to send a team down here to clear this brush. It's the only boat ramp within twenty miles." He spits and shakes his head, moving to the front of the barge. He unlatches the aluminum gate at the front of the boat and begins pulling planks of wood.

I go over to him.

"Had an idea on the way down here. Go into town, find some delivery trucks, you could probably rig up an elevator to the boat dock with their rear platform lift motors. If you had some heavy-duty batteries being constantly charged from a water genny. Like we talked about, with a prop. Run the genny into the batteries and from there into a breaker or something. To lights, to the winches on the elevator."

"Hmm. Might work, but it depends on the amperage we get out of the prop gennies . . . a regulator on the charger . . . hmm . . . It's worth a try." He shakes my hand. "Be careful out there."

"I will."

"See you in a day or two. You best be getting on."

"Right." I turn, stop, look back. "Before the elevator, you might want to think about just a good old zip-line, for a quick exit."

"Why would we need a quick exit?"

I shrug. If he can't see it, he's a moron.

* * *

211

Once we start the motorcycles, there's no way to hear anything except your own thoughts. The noise means we have to get moving. It's important we get to the major highways quickly, so we'll have some room to move. Everything will be over real quick if we hit a cluster of zeds on these back roads.

When you start making noise, it's real easy to find yourself surrounded.

We head east, to Ozark, Arkansas, cross the bridge there and hit I-40. Through the river valley, wreathed in forests, the medians now full scrub-brush on the smaller highways. Trees and forest growth push in tight to the asphalt on the back roads. Taking it easy until Clarksville, where we start picking up some stragglers. They are rising from piles on the ground, shrugging off whatever sleepiness makes them quiet and inactive. Not a lot, maybe twenty or thirty, doing their damnedest to keep up. We roll slow between the derelict cars. Jasper's got a cooler bungied to the rear of his bike, and it's filled with food and energy drinks and coffee. Keb's toting two big forty-gallon containers of extra gas. I've got some extra ammo, the flare gun, and, well . . . me.

I can see them snorting something when we take breaks. I'm not an idiot. I know what they're doing. Looks like the murderhole finally turned up the goods. Frazier would have been happy.

Gonna have to deal with it.

By the time we hit Fort Smith, there's at least a hundred zombies on our tail. We're still rolling slow.

It's hard, just riding at barely more than a trot. Every instinct in you screams for you to gun it, to get out of there.

Because being the head of an undead parade can end only one way, really, unless you're lucky.

Your ears get used to the constant, massive drone of the bikes and the ruckus of the dead, and you just steer. But it's tiring. Going slow. Your legs are always out, balancing.

Keb's got this uncanny ability to barely roll and doesn't have to put out his feet, but Jasper and I do.

When the sun goes down, we pull ahead before the light totally dies and eat some and talk for just a few minutes before the zeds catch up.

"We've got to ride straight through until morning, guys." I shake open the map Wallis gave me. "It's gonna take us days for the whole ride. Wallis wants us to take the state highways to Hot Springs and from there east to I-30 and then south all the way to bypass Little Rock. He thinks we'll run into too many zeds there." I wave my hand at the trees lining the highways and the brush growing in cracks on the asphalt. "But I say we dump these revs, haul ass east on I-40 to Conway and Little Rock, pick up a few thousand, and then head south. That might take two days, no sleep. How much of the cocaine do you have?"

Jasper's eyes go wide and Keb grins. "Oh, the little prince wants to get his snoot full? Is that right?"

"How much?"

Keb raises his shoulders and opens his hands. "No clue, Lil P. Mebbe coupla eight balls. Maybe a little more."

"Give it to me."

"Not just no, but hell no. Ain't giving you shit."

"I promise you'll get it back."

He lids his eyes.

"I'm not fucking around, Keb. I'm in charge. Give it to me."

Slowly, he pulls out a cellophane bag rimed in white and hands it over to me. It doesn't seem to be very much at all.

"Shit, Prince, be careful with the blow, man! Wrap it up! Don't hold it like that."

He thinks I'm gonna dump it. I laugh, and he gives me a strange look.

"Don't worry, Keb, we need this. If we ration it out, it'll keep us awake, able to do this right. This stuff will save everybody."

Jasper laughs. *Just say yes to drugs.*

"Yes," Keb says. "Lemme have a little hit before we get started again."

I check my watch. It's seven and the sun is totally gone now. The zeds are getting closer.

"No. But at ten, I'll let you have some."

"Fuck, Lil P, just a taste?"

"At ten."

I see him tense for a moment. Maybe he's thinking about chucking *me* over a bridge. But he won't. Jasper and Keb might need me to survive, but without me there'd be no going home to Bridge City. He curses and stomps off to his bike.

We dump the zeds and roll. Fast.

At ten, we all do lines off the upturned mirror of Keb's motorcycle. My heart tries to beat its way out of my rib cage, and

I feel like one gigantic erection, pulsing and needing somewhere to go. I drink water and snort the cocaine deeper into my sinuses.

Keb's laughing when the cluster lurches out of the dark into the headlights. I rip the hatchets off my chest and jump into the middle of the damily to start headknocking before I realize I don't have on my helmet. It's hooked on the handlebars of my bike.

Not much I can do now. I put down one, smashing his face deep into his cranium, sending goo flying. I hear Jasper yelling. Keb is still wrapping up the cocaine bag.

"Keb, goddamn it! There's revs!" Jasper bellows.

I laugh and whip around, knock away the arms of a couple more shamblers, and put the two hatchets deep into their skulls. I've been headknocking at the Wall every day for the last three years. If I know anything, it's how to crush skulls.

Getting the hatchets out is a tougher proposition, so I just let them fall buried in the shamblers' craniums and pull a kabob skewer out of my sleeve. I plant it deep in a woman's eye socket, kick out with my big treaded boots, and knock down her buddy, a stringy moaner missing an arm. His one good arm leaves a slime trail down my Kevlar leggings, and I stomp, hard, on his skull, sending its contents spurting through ruptured bone and decayed skin.

I pull the dual .9mms, turn, and step forward to meet a dead girl, semifresh, no more than two months shambling. I stick the barrel right in her mouth, midmoan. Her hair jumps a little when I pull the trigger, and smoke pours out of her mouth as she falls.

I really like Joblo's armor improvements.

My ears are ringing from the gunshot. When the ringing goes away, I hear cicadas whirring in the trees at the interstate's edge. Then, in the distance, a moan.

"Damn, Lil P, I ain't seen nothing like that shit in . . . well . . . a long-ass time, yo." He laughs, throwing his head back far enough for me to see silver glinting in his mouth, even in the glare of the bike headlights. "You're like a little Bruce Lee or sumpin'."

Japser pats me on the shoulder.

"Nice work, Gus. You're getting really good at that. They had you surrounded."

Blushing, I think. It might be the cocaine, though. I grab my hatchets, wipe them off on the semifreshie's clothes. I leave the skewer. I've got lots more.

The moaning from the side of the road is getting louder, the zed drawn by the gunshot. Maybe the light from the bikes too.

We do one more line each, and I take back the cocaine. It's not like I could kick his ass or anything, but Keb doesn't say anything or argue about not holding the drugs.

The motorcycles roar and we're back rolling, in the dark, toward half a million undead.

By dawn, we've hit Little Rock. The shamblers, at least the ones caught in our headlights, are coming out of the brush, rolling down inclines and shuffling up exit ramps. We're going five miles an hour. A fast jog, really. When they get in front of us, we either run the bikes right at them, knocking them silly with the ironwork crossbars, or we try to avoid them. It's not too hard, but it's getting harder with every mile we get into the city.

One manages to grab part of Jasper's chassis and we drag it a couple of hundred feet, leaving a black skid mark on the pavement.

It's the clusters of cars blocking the interstate that cause real problems. We have to move the bikes into the median or on the shoulder to get around them.

Another surprises Jasper from behind an SUV. Grabs his arm. Yanks it to his mouth and starts gnawing, but Jasper's gear means the shambler is losing teeth rather than enjoying dinner.

If there weren't, oh, maybe a thousand zombies tottering behind us, I'd find it funny, and the cocaine is wearing off. Jasper pulls the zombie close and smashes his fist into its face. It doesn't let go. He pulls out his headknocker, a big stake hammer, and pops it a good one between the eyes. It falls away. Probably dead, but we don't get off the bikes to check. There's a damily working its way up the shoulder toward us, too close. A woman and two little boys. Another woman trailing behind.

We roll.

The moans are really loud now. I can hear them over the thunder of the bikes.

I have no memory of the layout of Little Rock from when I was a boy. Maybe I've been trying to forget. But the sun rises, and I can see we're among buildings. Shamblers are everywhere, coming for us.

I hold up my hand to Jasper and Keb, and we stop for a moment but keep the bikes running. I turn to look behind us.

A wall. An ocean. A wave. Coming. Moaning.

Thousands. Maybe more.

We roll up a rise to an overpass and a zombie falls from above, a leaper, and lands in front of us, a sack of goo exploding into a hundred streamers across the pavement. I have a fleeting memory of stomping on ketchup packets when I was a kid.

The leaper zed tries to rise even after impact. Jasper runs over him with his bike and stops, keeping him pinned.

I stop, turn around, and check on Keb. He's shaking his head, looking at the road behind us. From here we can see the extent of the mob. The horde.

This must be what rock stars felt like.

Keb, Jasper, and I look at each other and Keb flips up his visor. I follow suit.

"Holy fuck, Lil P." He shakes his head. "It's unbelievable."

"Believe it."

We sit there. Watch them slowly coming up the slope into the shadow of the overpass, the morning light washing over the wreckage of their faces to show every bit of decayed flesh in detail. Everything has this dreamlike, rosy glow, and I can hear the cicadas whirring in the trees beyond them, rising and falling like waves cresting and crashing on some far-off beach. I wonder what Mom would be thinking if she could see the real me. The me that chucks people off bridges and huffs cocaine like a vacuum.

I feel tired. I don't know if it's the cocaine wearing off or the realization that I'm such a shitty human being. Or both.

"Guys!" Jasper's yell interrupts my thoughts. "This pus-bag is clawing at my boots. We gotta go."

And we do. Ride the wave.

South.

On the far side of Little Rock, we pull ahead, maybe four hundred yards, and do as much blow as we can in the time it takes the horde to catch up. By now, I feel like an old pro, snorting huge lines with a hundred-dollar bill.

I have no idea where the bill came from. Keb, I guess. "Tradition, baby. Tradition," he says, and he winks at me, snatches the rolled-up bill, and huffs down a line. *It's weird holding money*, is all I can think.

We remount, fire up the bikes, and lead the horde south.

Horde is a poor word for what they are. *Horde* points to in-telligence of some sort—or at least intent—I think, and these things have none now, I'm sure of it. Maybe the freshies, the ones with a brain still intact and not a piece of rotten meat sloshing around in a skull full of putrefying juices. I'll grant they might still have something going on upstairs. But I doubt it counts as thought. No. They just have instincts, raw and ravenous.

They call a group of geese a gaggle. A school of fish. A flock of seagulls. A murder of crows. A team of horses. A pack of dogs. A pride of lions.

We went through all of this in school. Everything has a name.

But what do you call a group of undead? Never mind one

this large. A damily won't cut it, as Knock-Out says. Maybe an extended fam-damily?

Next stop, I'll see what Jasper and Keb think.

Still tweaking as we roll up on the roadblock. No way to get the bikes across or around.

Someone guessed we'd be coming. *And* they devoted the resources to drag cars and trucks and SUVs across the highway all the way to the tree line. I can see where big treads hauled them over. A backhoe, maybe. Or even a Bradley. The woman said they took her to an army base; it could be a Bradley.

I dismount and take off my gear, preparing for the long hoof.

We'll never make it. Never. Might be able to lose the horde, but we'll never make it to the slavers' territory without transport.

There's fifteen thousand dead at our backs, moaning like, well, whatever it is you call a group this large.

"What the fuck you doin', Lil P?"

I unsling my shotgun, check my headknockers.

"Getting ready to run."

He pops the straps on his M-16, lifts it, chucks a grenade into the launcher.

"Why?"

It takes the horde a long time to work itself through the breach. We blew three vehicles into parts, dragged the bigger stuff aside, and rolled through, smelling burning rubber and gasoline.

"Bottleneck is gonna stretch out the group!" I yell to Keb and Jasper. "Gonna have to slow down even more, if we can."

No one looks happy.

"Uh . . . well, let's get far enough ahead for another bump," Jasper suggests.

Sounds good to me.

Keb spots the rider first and is off like a flash, revving the bike, making his front wheel pop off the pavement. The man had been sitting on an ATV, idling, surveying the road. A sentry. The moment he sees us, he drops his binoculars and wheels around and bolts south. Keb points at the retreating figure, looks to me, and I nod. The best rider among us, he disappears down the interstate, moving around burned cars and SUVs.

Jasper revs his bike, but I hold up my fist in the stop signal. He guns it down. Even through his visor I can tell he's disappointed.

In an hour, Keb returns. He's bleeding from a graze on his arm, but he's got a man trussed and over the backseat of his bike. We pull ahead of the horde and stop but leave the bikes running.

Keb pops his helmet, shakes out his lengthening dreads, and says, "Check it, Lil P." He walks over to the man and points at his pants, his jacket. "Army. A slaver, no doubt."

The man mumbles through the gag that Keb has on him.

I point at it. "Let him speak, if he has anything to say."

"Awright, yo highness. Awright."

When he can speak, the man looks at me wide-eyed. "Slavers? We ain't no slavers."

Keb, Jasper, and I glance at each other. News to us. The woman could have been lying, but I seriously doubt Wendy would've faked the shackle. And Mom said that the other one, Jennifer . . . she'd been raped many times. The evidence was all over her body.

"That right? Not slavers? You mean you don't have a bunker full of girls? Your own little whorehouse?" This from Jasper. I'd never heard him so bitter. Or intense.

And that makes me pause. I've always thought of Keb and Jasper as outlaws, wild men constrained by no law. Seeing how disgusted Jasper is with this man, it makes me reconsider him. And Keb. And Bridge City. People want order, order and stability and, if not righteousness, then at least individual respect where the strong can't abuse the weak.

I think back to the night before last on the bridge. Frazier's last sound as he fell.

The soldier is grimy, greasy-haired, and nearing starvation.

"Almost got away. Little four-wheeler. He tried to go off road, took a spill, and I snatched the little bitch up, easy as shit, Lil P."

I look back toward the . . . horde. We need a word for them. Getting closer and closer. We're gonna have to move in the next few moments.

A lone revenant—a girl, it looks like, at least through all the bloat and char—shambles up, out of the brush on the shoulder. Keb runs over to her, kicks her down, and stomps on her head until she stops moving. He's snarling as it happens, and I see the man watching him.

"So, you say you and your little group aren't slavers, huh?" I try to keep my voice light.

"No! I don't know what you're talking about."

"Where are you located, then?"

He shuts his mouth and looks around. I nod at Keb and Jasper.

Jasper unslings the man and dumps him onto the concrete. We remount our bikes.

"Ain't you gonna untie me? Hey! I told you I ain't involved with that! Untie me!"

The moaning is so loud now, it's hard to hear anything other than the slaver's blubbering.

"You don't seem to get it. You'll tell me everything I want to know, or you're zombie food. There's no deals to be made. There's no angle for you. It's total honesty. Or death."

He doesn't take long to decide.

"You won't leave me here?"

"No, we won't."

"Lil Prince, don't go making promises you can't keep."

"Shut up, Keb." I turn back to the slaver. "Spill it."

He starts to talk, but Jasper interrupts, grabbing the man and slinging him over the back of his bike, facedown.

"Too late, fellas. We need to skedaddle. Our tagalongs are getting a mite close."

We fire up the bikes, roll maybe a few hundred yards more down the interstate, as slow as thunder. On the bright side, the horde is getting back into a tight cluster after straggling through the breach.

We have to do some spring cleaning before we can stop. There's a little group of zeds coming toward us from our front sector, as the old members of the G Unit might say. We stop, fifteen feet shy, drop our visors, cinch our gorgets, and get our headknockers up. Once everyone is ready, we wade in. There's a sketchy moment when two of them grab my swinging arm, but Jasper's there, crunching skulls with his tent hammer. Keb's a blur with the crowbar, jabbing with the forked end, clubbing with the curved.

When the last zed is down, we clean our bludgeons, store them, and once again dump the slaver onto the concrete, this time in the middle of the putrid remains of the cluster we've just wiped out.

Strange. When I was a kid I would dream about doing stuff like this—

The slaver blubbers again, but we ignore him. Keb turns up the mirror on his bike, and I can't see any problem with doing some more blow. I've been up thirty-six hours now, and I can feel it. A line or two will hit the spot.

We do the lines, and I walk back to where the slaver lies on the asphalt. I'm thrumming all over, energized, and he looks at me with wide eyes as I rub the residue of cocaine over my gums like I've seen Keb and Jasper do. It numbs my teeth, which is bizarre, not as a feeling, but the fact that it feels good. I could use some water. My mouth is tacky.

"So, where were we?"

He's crying now, for real, terrified. No more bravado, like

Wendy, no more posturing. He knows he's a hairbreadth from shambling.

I squat. He's facedown on the pavement, eye-level with the black pulp of the strangest fruit known to man: zombie noggin.

"Hey. Hey, man." He quiets a little. He needs to hear what I have to say. "Listen. Tell us everything. The slaves. Your plans about us. Where you're located. You spill it all, right now, I promise I will let you go unharmed."

"Lil P, you can't do that shit, man."

"Goddamn it, Keb. I can do whatever the fuck I want." I stand, walk over to where he's watching me. "Don't contradict me again. Why do you think they put me in charge of this mission?"

I'm angry, but Keb gives this half-amused, half-distracted shrug, as if he's saying, *Hey, what's it to me?*

What he *does* say is, "It's cool, Prince, it's cool. I'm here to bring you back home in one piece, doctor's orders. It's your ass when you get there, though."

I turn back to the slaver. My skin's itching a little, and I scratch at my arm as I get in the slaver's face.

He doesn't need any more prodding.

He spills it all or, at least, everything he knows. A mean son of a bitch named Konstantin is in charge. It's hard to get a clear picture of the man from the slaver. The slavers don't have any heavy armaments except a couple of .50 cals mounted in the rear of Jeeps. Of the near fifty Bradleys they have—New Boston was a motor depot, after all—none of them will start, and there's no one there with the wherewithal or tech savvy to make them run again.

They couldn't figure out why the Bradley's wouldn't start. Thought it had something to do with the radiation that caused the zombies.

Idiots. And they don't even know about the EMP.

Jesus.

They heard our ham radio broadcasts and have set up camp on the Fulton Bridge over the Red River a few miles out of Texarkana. They've got chain-link murderholes set up at the south end, and they just spear the zeds through the fencing and then go in and clear them out.

They plan on moving north, through Hot Springs, toward us, in winter, when there'll be less growth and more visibility.

They don't think we'll give them any trouble. They don't know about the G Unit or the Bradleys—a couple of things we didn't mention, of course.

When he's done, I pull a knife. Put it at his throat.

"The slaves." I prick him hard enough to make him start to bleed. Actually, I stick him harder than I mean to, and the tip of the knife slips a half inch into the soft underside of his jaw. It's too easy to slip. Too easy to go further than I want.

The shamblers are closer now, moaning and making wet, phlegmy sounds.

He gives me a look that's half pure hatred and half self-disgust. The blood is coming now from his jaw. I might've slipped the knife all the way into his mouth. No way to tell, really. "Yeah. There's around sixty women. And they've started luring men into camp with promises of food, booze—" He glances from me to Keb to the shamblers getting closer and louder every second. "I ain't got nothing to do with that! I don't. I'm just a scout."

"You're taking men now? What do they do?"

"Latrines. Bait for the murderholes. Labor."

About what I figured.

"And you're coming for us to get more? Is that right? You need more slaves?"

"They need more workers to build walls. Without 'em, they'll be stuck with just layers of chain-link."

Yeah, buddy. Say *they* all you want, but you're still a goddamned slaver.

"One last question."

Jasper waves. "Hey, gents! It's time to move. You got maybe a minute."

"Last one. You fuck any of the women?"

He looks into my face and his eyes go all shifty. "Yeah. Couple of times. It's how they keep us in line. Reward us. If we work hard, we get to visit the whoreho—the women's tent."

I hold up the knife. "It's a good thing you told the truth. Otherwise I would've staked you, you filthy little shit."

I spit in his face.

Then cut him free.

Keb looks at me like I'm crazy, and Jasper shakes his head like I'm a retard. Maybe I am.

The slaver wastes no time racing off. He's favoring one leg, but he clears the interstate and the trees before I can get back to my bike.

"That was a motherfucking mistake, Lil Prince."

"Probably." I don't know what I'm becoming. It's too hard

to think with the cocaine making my head pound and my heart hammer. "I gave my word."

To Knock-Out, not some worthless slaver.

"Who the fuck are you, man? Why's your word so important? Huh?" He waves his hand behind us. The zombies are maybe fifty yards away. "Look at this shit. You ain't got the luxury of having pride, man. Your word ain't shit."

"I don't expect you to understand this, Keb. But if we don't act human, we won't be human." I twist in my seat, look back at the horde of zombies shambling toward us. "Without that, without something like honor, or commitment . . . fuck . . . without knowing something sure other than we're going to die, what the hell are we? We're just like them. Just hungers running crazy."

"The zeds are real. The slavers are real. Pride don't matter when you're shambling. All that other stuff is make-believe bullshit, Lil P."

"Maybe, Keb. But if we don't act like it's real, then it never will be." I slam down my visor, kick start the bike, and roll, south.

Eyes bright, tails bushy, thanks to the blow. Starting to consider divvying up the remainder between the three of us so we can each snort to our own heart's content, but I don't know what we'd put it in. Or if Keb has any more of those hundred-dollar bills. We make another pit stop, snort some lines with an efficiency that comes from habit, and roll on down I-40, southwest. Taking it slow. But it's hard. With my heart racing, cocooned in the roar of the motorcycle, I want to gun the damned thing. Put this mass of undead far behind and breathe fresh air.

But we can't. We watch the road, we watch the zeds shamble after us. And we have to roll slow.

Flash of light to my left.

The explosion takes out Jasper and his bike in a blossom of yellow fire and smoke and for an instant I'm lost and then I'm ripped from my bike and tumbling head over heels through the air. Something tears at my back and my helmet hits the ground, hard.

I have, burned into the undersides of my eyelids, a vision of Jasper in three pieces, spraying blood, each piece of him twisting away from the others.

No clue about Keb.

I lie in the grass, on my back, looking at the sky, watching the smoke rise above me. All I can think of is getting up, moving away from the zeds coming for us, but I can't seem to get my arms and legs to move the way I want them to. They move, but there's a lot of pain, and I'm so clumsy, I feel like I should just lie here until I can get my limbs to move together. But the zombies are getting closer.

I push my body up and a big bloody chunk of Jasper is right next to me. Or it might be Keb. I don't know.

I look back at where we came from. The wind blows smoke from the burning wreckage across the interstate and into the tree line, obscuring the undead. Maybe it will keep them off me, distract them.

No, here they come, through the smoke. Close. Thirty feet, maybe.

I stand. It's really hard to move and my ears ring, like when the big guns on the Bradleys fire. Deafening. I thought the Harleys were loud.

What the fuck caused it? An RPG? A mine?

I walk. Away from the zeds and the burning wreckage. Something's wrong with my ankle and the pain is starting to come through now, bright and shooting and in the end it's gonna kill me.

Might be shambling just a little faster than the shamblers.

There's a buzzing and I don't know if it's my ears still ringing or it's something else.

I walk. I hear the shamblers behind me. Soon I'll be able to smell them.

A crackle.

My helmet muffles everything, so I pop the visor. Gunfire. The buzzing of motorcycles.

I trip on some debris, hit asphalt, and roll. The hatchets dig into the meat of my pecs and abs but stay attached. Joblo will be happy to learn his Velcro did the trick. Doesn't look like I'll get the chance to tell him, though.

I tumble down the shoulder into the high grass and force myself onto my hands and knees.

The shamblers stand above me, on the pavement. Some look my way and slump down the hill. Others peer ahead, in that blind, fumbling way the zeds have, toward the highway. I put a hatchet into my left hand and, with my right, rip a .9mm from the Velcroed holsters. The sound isn't much of a concern right now.

I take aim, fire. Aim. Fire. Aim. Fire.

I miss one before the end of the clip. Most of the shamblers peeling off the road to gobble me are prone now, but there's a thousand more where they came from. And the pistol reports have alerted them that I'm being scrumptious over on the interstate shoulder.

Maybe two hundred more turn and begin to shamble toward me.

I run. My ankle is screaming, and I'm having trouble keeping my balance, but I can handle the pain. It's better than the alternative. I feel something tearing down there and know I won't be able to run for very long. Maybe a few more seconds. In that time I can get far enough away to at least eat a bullet.

I won't shamble. I won't turn like Dad.

I'm away from the shamblers, and they don't look too happy about the situation. If they could run, they'd be hauling ass to eat me. But all they can do is gimp along, gnashing black teeth.

I rip the other .9mm from its holster and place the barrel in my mouth. The gunmetal tastes oily and I remove it on instinct, it tastes so bad. I don't want to die. But I won't shamble. It's hard to put it back in my mouth.

I'm looking at the mass of zeds when the zombies start to dissolve and the air around them fills with a black mist. It's like tea bags being dunked in steaming water. Then I hear big chain guns, .30 caliber or larger.

A pair of motorcycles pulls in front of me. The riders hop off and have pistols out and in my face faster than I know how to deal with. They're yelling something but I'm still looking at the zeds behind them. Tea bags in water.

Maybe I should let them shoot me. At least I wouldn't have to taste the gun oil again.

Knock-Out wouldn't approve.

I drop the gun and they knock me down, truss me like a hog, and sling me over the back of an ATV.

Looks like I've found the slavers.

It's an hour or two ride, and we're going fast, leaving the zeds behind, the thousands of dead, to mill around and look for someone else to chomp on.

I hope no survivors wander through that area. That stretch of interstate is gonna be kinda rough for years. If you think about all the individual lives those zeds represent, each one with a life and a history and a bank account and family up until the Big Turnover, it's like a whole town on the hoof, and I feel a great loss as the sound of their lowing diminishes and passes away. There go ten thousand aces in the hole.

When we pull into the slavers' camp, I twist uncomfortably to check out their fortifications. Chain-link, mostly. Piled-up cars too. If we had gotten here with the zeds, the fences would have crumpled under the weight of the horde. The zeds would have wiped out the slavers.

A thought strikes me. What about the women? They would've been zombie-chow too. At least that didn't happen. Silver linings and all that.

They drive through many layers of chain-link fencing until we get to the bridge. They've set up tenting, much like we have at Bridge City.

Everything looks a little disordered here. All the men are in fatigues and armed, heavily. They look at me with cold, uncaring eyes.

Yeah, well, fuck you too, gentlemen.

The ATV rolls to a stop outside a big tent like the one Mom, Wallis, and Knock-Out operate from. Two slavers snatch me up under the armpits, hoist me into the air, and bring me into the tent.

There's one of those folding chairs set up and they dump me into it, hands still tied.

A man, small, with short-cropped hair brushed forward like Caesar, pulls up a stool and sits down in front of me, puts his hands on his knees, reversed, so that his elbows stick out at sharp angles. He's hard with muscles, and he's angry.

He's scary angry, really, like he's never been happy ever, not once.

"This him?" he says over his shoulder.

In the shadows of the tent behind him, a wavery voice says, "Yes. That's the one. The Prince."

Oh. Our old friend. The blubbery slaver who spilled it all.

And I let him go.

Caesar puts his face right in mine, like he wants to bite off my nose. His breath smells like peppermints and aftershave.

"Okay, young man. My name is Konstantin. Captain Konstantin." His eyes search my face. "I'm merely a captain. Not a prince. So forgive me for speaking harshly."

"I'm not a prince. That's just a stupid—"

He holds up a finger and shushes me.

233

"Tell me about your defenses. Tell me everything about your community—"

"I don't think tha—"

The blow, when it comes, totally surprises me. Catches me on the ridge of my eye. Zygomatic . . . Mom tried to teach me the human bones.

My zygomatic is fucked now. I felt something crack when he hit me and I can't see anymore from that side.

The pain is just outrageous. The human body shouldn't be allowed to feel this much pain. I'd cry if I could, it hurts so bad, but I think I've pissed myself instead.

With my good eye, I can see when Konstantin raises his fist and shows me the brass knuckles.

"Let me ask again." He brushes an imaginary fleck of dust from his fatigues. He's not looking at me at all now. "Tell me everything about your community. Everything. And let's start with the king."

"The king? We don't have—"

He spares my head this time. So I've got that going for me. This time he slams his brass fist into my chest. Something goes crunchy in there too.

I didn't think I could feel more pain than my fucked-up face but . . . well . . . as Mom always says, the human animal is an amazing creature.

Konstantin motions to his goons, and they move me to a wooden table.

"Okay, little prince. This looks like it might take a little while. So why don't we all get comfy? Yes?"

One of the men takes my arms, puts them on the table,

and feeds zip ties through the holes I'm just now noticing in the tabletop. They splay my hands flat.

"Are you right- or left-handed?"

"I'm . . ." It's hard to talk. I make my mouth move. I don't want him to hit me again. "I'm left dominant."

"Hmm. Nice." He cocks his head and nods at me, like he's appraising something a tiny bit more interesting now. "I am a leftie too. We'll focus on the right, then, for starters."

When he takes out pruning shears, holds them in front of my face, just so I get the idea, clamps them down on the tip of my pinkie—*snick!*—and that little bit of *me* detaches itself and rolls across the table, leaving a trail of blood, I scream. I scream.

I scream.

I'm sorry, Mom, Knock-Out. I'm sorry, Ellie.

I'm so sorry.

"So, tell me about your king, little prince. Tell me about your home."

I tell. Everything. Everything I know.

And some things I don't.

I pass out a few times.

This man, Konstantin, it's hard to believe that he really is here, that he exists. How can another human be this . . . this . . . inhuman?

Above the pain, beyond it, I think of Frazier. I shouldn't have thrown you away, Frazier, like you were useless or something. I shouldn't have killed you. I thought you were a shithead and that seemed to matter and be enough.

God, I'm an idiot.

Why did I let the slaver go? Principle? There's no such thing as principle as little bits of *you*, of yourself, are being cut away.

When I come to, there's not much left of my hand. Just index and thumb, giving it the look of a bloody claw.

Konstantin had pruning shears and questions. And he questioned and pruned. Down to my palms.

You think of yourself as tough. You think of yourself as different. All it took was three fingers for me to tell him everything. Everything I knew. By the second finger, I was brainstorming with him, trying to figure out the best ways to enslave my family. My home.

Like: focusing fire on the gates, RPGs, big-caliber weapons.

Dislike: finding barges upstream, setting them adrift, knocking all of Bridge City sideways.

Dislike: catapult with zombies.

Like: targeting the Motor Pool gas reserves.

Like: sending another "escaped slave" to infiltrate and sabotage.

Like: Joblownski and Mom. To be taken at all costs.

Like: outposting at the Dam, where our boats are stored.

Really like: using flat bottoms to take the dock.

Really like: killing the ones who resist, putting the ones who submit in chains.

* * *

They've thrown some water on me to wake me up, and it's washed away some of the blood and piss, but I smell horrible. And it's river water; I can smell the muddiness of it. No telling what infections I will get now.

My face is okay, other than my eye. Konstantin left my face alone after the first wake-up call.

I told him everything he wanted. And more.

I'm sorry, Ellie. So sorry.

It seems I'm a prince. My mother is a queen. And Knock-Out.

He's the king.

Konstantin orders them to strip me. A goon comes with the bloody shears that trimmed my hand and starts cutting away my clothes, the remnants of my armor.

They strip me bare. Naked as the day I was born.

More naked, really. They've stripped me of three fingers.

Konstantin says, "Crucify him. Their little fucking prince. Put him at the north gate as a warning to any others who might be about. As long as he'll last. When he's done and revivified, cut off his head. We'll dunk it in wax for a keep-sake."

Mom is an atheist. Dad was too.

Now I know why.

When they stake me to the telephone pole, it's a major effort.

"Why don't we just kill him now?"

"Fuck that, man. You want *him* on your ass? The man expects a show."

"A show? For fucking who? These unholies?"

"Naw, man. For us. The troops. Them."

I manage to crack an eyelid. There's a chain-link pen with Visqueen roof and flapping sides. A troop of hollow-eyed men watch as these idiots try to figure out the best way to crucify me.

Obviously, they've never done it before.

"Hey." I can only manage a whisper. "Hey, retards."

"The bait is talking, Jeb. You hear that shit?"

I don't have the strength to keep my eyes open so I just assume the idiots are grimacing at me or something. Then I feel the fist. He's hitting me. But it's a faint feeling.

"Hey. Water."

"The meat wants water."

"Let's give it to him." Laughing now. Then I feel it. Taste it. Piss. They're pissing on me. On my face.

It stings, the urine. I didn't think I was still capable of anger, but there it is, red hot, in my chest, like a burning ember. God, to see these men dead, I'd give the rest of my hand. My soul. To see them all dead. Everyone.

"Douche. You need to make an X with . . ." It's hard to breathe. I'm having trouble getting used to the idea that these morons consider me a latrine.

"With what, bitch?"

A boot hits my ass, bowling me over. Then my chest, where Konstantin pummeled me with the knuckles. The crunchy rib goes crunchier, and I howl. I didn't think I had the strength to make that much noise.

"Yo, what's that? You hear that, man?"

"No, shithead. All I hear is this little bitch's crying."

They're back to trying to figure out the best way to lift me up to the I-30 traffic sign. Finally they decide to tie some rope around my waist, throw the rope over the crossbar of the sign, and hoist me up.

That's what they do.

It's pretty painful, but by now I'm kinda, I don't know, half dead.

When they've hoisted me high, the rope cutting into my waist and balls, the idiots stop. They're on collapsible ladders and have me up there, oh, I don't know, maybe fifteen feet high. Pretty high. Everybody for miles around can see me, it feels like.

Some shamblers are at the fence, looking at me, pawing. Moaning.

I guess the only good thing about being crucified this high is I'm not gonna get eaten.

"What're we gonna do with his hands? Aren't we supposed to stake them or some shit like that?"

Geniuses. I don't know how Jesus had it so easy. At least the Romans were efficient.

"No, just cut some line and we'll tie out his arms. Right. You get me?"

"Yeah. That's a cinch."

I try to laugh, but the ropes they're throwing all over me are cutting off my breath. I want to breathe, so I stop.

A cinch.

Fucking idiots.

When they're done, they've got me pretty much in the crucified position, more or less. I can feel myself slumping to one side because the rope is slipping off my mangled hand.

Einstein notices and fixes it. He takes his knife, stabs it through my palm, making a ragged hole, and then feeds the rope through the hole. I can feel it go between my bones. It's a miracle he doesn't cut an artery.

But he doesn't. It's all about the show.

I thought I knew pain. I thought I knew it.

I spend a day on the sign, I think. My last day. At one point, Einstein or one of his breed comes with a fishing pole with a sponge tied to the tip and dabs water on my face.

When I have the energy, I open my eyes. There's guards working the fencing. Stabbing zeds in the eyes when they come to call.

One slaver, they call him Bonzo, he's a crack aim with a slingshot, knocking down zeds one by one.

I can't believe I didn't think of slingshots. Something must've been wrong with my head. Bonzo's smart. I'd save him.

The downside is that the bodies pile up outside the fence. You don't want a pile of stinking dead undead rotting your air. At least I don't.

And you don't want to have to go outside your fortifications to try to get rid of the dead.

Murderholes are still a better practice. This makes me feel good for a moment, and then the pain returns. Fuck Bonzo.

What I can't figure is why Konstantin was so fixated on the king. Now, looking back at my short, sorry life, that's one question I have. Why did he keep cutting off bits of my fingers and asking about a king?

Maybe he's jealous. Maybe he wants to be king.

Sorry, Knock-Out. I don't know why I chose you over Wallis. But that's what the man wanted to hear.

He wanted to hear about a throne. He wanted to hear about a crown.

So that's what I told him. What he wanted to hear.

The pain comes in waves. It grows and swells, then ebbs and recedes, like a tide.

It's not just a feeling, really. It's become part of me, of who I am. I am pain, and my awareness travels out, away from my body.

The worst thing is, I'm gonna turn. Not today, maybe not tomorrow. But I'm gonna turn.

That's hard to stomach.

Sometimes I muster the strength to reel my awareness back in, open my eyes and watch as Bonzo and the other jackasses who've killed me shoot the zombies at the fence with slingshots. When he misses, I can hear the chain link ping and reverberate. And, of course, above it all, the moans of the dead.

I beg for water. That's not good. The begging. But it's like I've never tasted water before and I need it, bad.

They laugh, piss on a sponge and dab my face with it.

God help me. I drink. I drink whatever they give me.

The sun has gone down and come back up. New morons at the fence.

I won't make it another day. I don't want to, anyway. I just want the pain to go away.

"You hear that, man?"

"Naw. It's just the meat moaning."

"No, not that. That."

There's a buzzing and a low rumble. From where they've crucified me, I can see something on the interstate leading away from the bridge, up I-30.

Holy shit.

Thousands of them, thousands coming toward us. And in front, Keb. Riding a Harley and waving. Not like he can see me. But he's letting the guards know that he's bringing them a little present. Right down their throats.

One of the morons screeches and scuttles off. Behind me I hear a siren wind up and scream. Men holding M-16s rush to the fence. The slaves in the Visqueened pen start to scream, and I hear one douche bag yell, "Don't let them out! Leave them there if there's a breach! We're loading the women into the trucks."

God, I hope that sonofabitch dies.

They start shooting at Keb, but it's too late. The zombies hear the sirens and smell the scrumptious human flesh scurrying around behind those thin little fences.

Keb stops, kicks the kickstand, and parks the bike right in the middle of the interstate, motor still running, pretty as you please, then yanks his rifle from the rack. He runs off, down the shoulder, toward the trees lining the road. Some zombies follow him, but the majority come for us. And the majority is thousands. Almost as many as when they took me captive.

Keb makes a move that's pretty easy to read even at this distance. He's chucking a grenade into the launcher and aiming it right at me.

I hear the report, and then the outer fence gate disappears in a boom and explosion of fire and smoke. Something whangs off the sign they've tied me to.

And then Keb is gone, running into the tree line, away from the zeds, the gunfire, his bike. He's gone, God love him.

It doesn't take long for the horde to reach the outer fence.

There's frantic bellowing and yelling, and behind me I can hear them firing up what sounds like diesel engines and clanky machines.

I hear his voice. His voice. Konstantin.

It's faint and hard to pick out over the noise of the evacuation.

"Secure the women and armaments, goddamn it.

Goddamn you, soldier, secure the slaves! If we lose even one, I'll have you as bait!"

Four extremely stupid slavers are firing into the mass of dead moaning at the fence, and someone hastily parks a cargo truck in the breach Keb blew open.

The fence looks like it's gonna hold for a little while. But the zeds get a rhythm going, rocking back and forth, pushing. It's hard to tell what's causing the rocking motion, but most likely it's zombies shoving. Groping from the rear. They're packed so tight the ones in front can't fall, and they surge forward, making the fence cave inward.

When it does cave, the front zeds drop flat with the fencing. The others tromp right over them, moaning, doing the whole undead thing.

The slavers who stuck around, firing into the mass, the shamblers catch them as they try to climb over the truck they parked in Keb's breach. One guy screams so high it sounds like an animal keening. Four of the zombies start to chow on his arms and legs, and the rest of them use him like a bowl of onion dip at the old-time parties, scooping big gobbets out of his middle.

The rest I can't see, it's blocked by the truck. But the zeds are getting *down*.

I never thought a sight like this would make me happy, but there it is, happiness. It's the last time I'll feel it. It's sweet.

The zeds shamble forward to the inner fence. The slavers have a little common sense. They have two rings of fencing.

It's kind of elementary watching the way the zombies go through the chain-link. It's like, after the first section, they've learned. Singly they've got the intelligence of a mayfly, but together, they've got the intelligence of a chicken or dog. An animal that can remember how to do things. We used to have a dog, Cookie, that knew how to open doors with her nose. She could even pull open drawers. Just a dog.

And here's thousands of former humans with some cranial juice going on. Enough to walk, grab, bite. So maybe together, in a big ole group, they can take care of fences, easy.

I wish I'd been able to go to more school before the world ended.

None of the slavers even *thinks* about me. I've been so focused on my pain and watching the zombies take apart the fencing, I haven't paid attention to what my fellow human beings are doing. And they obviously haven't worried themselves with me. The sound of machines retreats. Behind me.

I'm left, crucified, looking down at a sea of undead.

Damnation.

That's what they are. *A pride of lions. A flight of angels. A damnation of undead.*

And then the zombies break the second fence and pour through the breach.

The tide comes in. It washes around me.

Hours of moaning beneath me. Hours.

At times, when I come into consciousness, I think I've already died. Other times, I realize I'm moaning louder than the shamblers.

You see pictures of Jesus crucified, and he's looking down, at what's below him. Mary. Her girlfriends. Other people, I guess. My parents are atheists. Were atheists. I guess I am too. I don't know all the details of the religious stuff. But I've seen pictures.

Damn, I've got sympathy for a guy who had to go through this. At least his tormentors knew what they were doing.

Mine were idiots. They tied me, tight, around the chest, so I can't really lean forward and look at the ground or anything that's below me.

I know there are zombies down there, pawing at the sign.

Thank God they hung me high.

Or maybe not. It might be better to die now. I can't thank God. Thank stupidity.

Pain, white, overwhelming.

I've passed out, I think. And come to. Behind me I hear a very faint rumble of vehicles, the chatter and pop of automatic weapons.

There's moaning below me, but not nearly as much. Within my field of view are a couple of shamblers that can't shamble anymore. They're draggers. No legs.

The party is over except for the zombies below me.

They're like a little choir. Two baritones and a tenor. Two males and one female. The rest have gone to follow the slavers.

Every once in a while I feel something hit one of my feet. A hand, maybe. No biting, though.

I want to die now. I want to die.

* * *

The sound of gunfire wakes me. I'm trying to see below, but anymore I don't have the energy to open my eyes.

I want to die.

The shambler choir stops and suddenly the horrible pressure around my groin, my chest, my hand is gone and I hit the pavement.

God, that hurts. It just keeps getting worse, the pain.

Keb says, "Holy shit, Lil Prince. Your chance of winning any beauty contests is totally fucked now, man."

I'm too tired to even scream when he picks me up, slings me over his shoulder, and walks me through the breaches in the fencing to his bike.

There's the rumbling of an engine. His Harley. I feel water, clean fresh water on my lips. The sensation is so bright, so electrifying, I could cry. He adjusts my body and then there's wind, brisk wind, and I pass out.

The world loves the tomato because it is red. Like man's innards. His guts. Its pulp reminds us of our pulp, so easily exposed.

And *so* delicious. I'd eat one of them like a fucking apple right now and drown myself in water and whiskey.

I'd fuck Barb silly.

They're looking at me, in a ring. I remember this from the days when TV worked, the ring of worried faces. But there's more, there's something else.

"Is that . . ." I try to talk, but I sound like Gollum or something, my voice all low, scratchy and evil.

Mom looks behind her.

Wallis says, "Lights. Joblo rigged your water gennies. So now we've got some lights. Some battery chargers too."

Mom cries, paws at me. I try to sit up, but Knock-Out looks down on me, shakes his head, and winks.

I force myself up, and they back away. I've only got one eye working right now. It feels like they've bandaged my whole head.

"What?" It's hard to figure everything out. "What happened? Where's Keb?"

"He's taking it easy. He rode you straight home, thirty-six hours after . . . after . . . well, we don't really don't know what happened. But he got you home. He's been sleeping it off."

I nod. "Keb. He saved us all. Not just me. They killed Jasper . . . they questioned me . . . but Keb, he brought them all in. The zombies. Thousands of them. Keb brought them in."

I'm quiet for a minute, remembering.

"What a sight to see."

Mom cries even harder now, and there's nothing I can do to stop her. But then she stops, the tears wiped away, like she's decided, just then, that that was enough.

Wallis sits down on a chair in the tent—*our* command tent—and looks at me. I know I've got to spill.

"Where's Ellie? Where's the baby?"

Milly comes into the tent as if she were waiting for the question. Ellie is there in her arms, gurgling, cooing, swaddled in blankets.

I stretch out my hands to take Ellie and . . . stop. There's only one hand there.

My right hand is gone halfway to the elbow.

There are still tears running down Mom's cheeks, but her face is blank. "It was putrid, honey. I had to amputate, otherwise you would've . . . you would've died."

I shouldn't be alive anyway.

So I say what needs to be said. "Thank you, Mom. I know that must've been hard for you. But I've got another." I hold up my left.

Everyone laughs and I wish Keb was here with us.

I tell them everything, and their smiles fade. Everything. Knock-Out barks a funny little laugh when we get to the subject of royalty.

"Me? King? What the hell were you thinking, boy?"

I hold up my hand. "I wasn't. He was cutting off my fingers and he seemed to want . . . he wanted us to have a king. He wanted me to be a prince. I don't know why. Maybe because if he takes us, he'll be king. I think that's what he wants."

"Shhh." Mom. She must feel horrible, but I wish she'd just let me be.

Wallis presses his fingertips together. He's figuring things out.

Knock-Out looks at me and I meet his gaze. Not much to say, really, but I understand now. Death is too easy and always waiting. I've been down its throat.

Ellie coos and Milly lays her in my lap. I look away from Knock-Out, his face streaming with tears, down at her little face, pink and perfect. For a little while, everything is better.

"They won't stop. They'll be coming for us."

Wallis says, "Then we'll be ready."

The world loves the tomato because it's red, and its flesh is the flesh of man.

Today is my day to work in the Garden. I'm not very much help now. My janked ankle hurts more than my missing hand, but Mom's got me on some pills that deaden everything and make the sunshine bright and soothing on my skin.

Barb, kneeling near me, says, "No. Dig in the soil like this, Gus. Break up the dirt and let the fertilizer get in the soil."

"I can't." I can still feel my missing hand. It tingles. Sometimes I imagine it around Konstantin's throat. Like it's off living a life of its own now. That's a nice thought.

"Oh." She says it, but she's not embarrassed. She's just forgotten that my hand is gone. Like I do two hundred times a day. "Well, let's get the basket and find the ripe ones, then." She looks up, beyond Bridge City's trusses, toward the blue sky and thin, watery sun. "It's a beautiful day."

We pick tomatoes. We laugh and Barb touches me, on the shoulder, on my knee. Once, she falls silent and puts her hand on my crushed cheek.

5

THE BEAURACRACY OF THE DEAD

MINUTES OF THE TULAVILLE RECLAMATION COMMITTEE

DATE: May 23, 2018
TIME: 9:00 AM
PLACE: Command Tent B
Present: Chairman Joblownski, Engineer Richards, Engineer Broadsword, Citizens Fulcher, Werk, Hammond, Bilyeu.
Absent/Excused: Co-chair Ingersol (Gus)

Secretary: Myself, Barbara Dinews

ITEM: Jim Bilyeu, formerly of Ozark, Arkansas, explained to the committee the location of a galvanized tin warehouse, thirty miles distant, allegedly full of bricks, lumber, and, of course, galvanized tin. Bilyeu also informed the committee of the location of Winger's Chain-Link and Siding Emporium, forty miles distant.

His proposal is to take the eighteen-wheeler reclaimed from Tulaville Shell Truck Stop and outride to Ozark, with escorts, including a Bradley, and retrieve the building materials for use in the Tulaville Wall project.

Heavy debate ensued.

PROS: Dearth of building materials for fencing project, needed brick reinforcements for North and South Gate murderholes, plywood for further development on Bridge City.

CONS: Ozark, Arkansas, population before Big Turnover around 5,000. Estimated. Zombie populace medium to heavy. Fuel expenditures, both gasoline and diesel, would be heavy. Human resources, heavy.

MOTION: Engineer Richards moved to send a motorcycle team to scout the warehouse and chain-link depot and determine zombie population density. Citizen Hammond seconded.

ROLL CALL VOTE
AYE: Joblownski, Richards, Broadsword, Fulcher, Werk, Hammond
NAY: Bilyeu
ABSTAIN: Ingersol (Gus)
VOTE: 6–1–1

MINUTES OF THE RESOURCE ALLOCATION COMMITTEE

DATE: May 15, 2018
TIME: 9:00 AM
PLACE: Command Tent B
Present: Chairman Joblownski, Lucy Ingersol, Jim Nickerson, Engineer Broadsword, Engineer Richards, Co-chair Gus Ingersol, Keb Motiel

Secretary: Barbara Dinews

ITEM: A contentious meeting. I don't know if I understand all the implications of it.

First item of business, Gus presented Joblo with a list of required fuel, vehicles, and munitions for what he kept describing as a "day jaunt," which had me, and I could tell the other engineers, puzzled. Joblo denied the request.

Lucy said, "Joblo, just get us the damned gas and guns."

He looked startled. "We need that for Tinman, Lucy. I thought I made that clear."

"I don't give a shit. You'll give us what we want or I'll never so much as look at the smallest scratch on your hand, I won't diagnose you the next time you have the sniffles, I won't set any broken bones. You'll be out."

His jaw dropped. "But why?"

Lucy stood. "It's simple. Because we need it, and we're gonna have it. I don't want to bulldoze you, but I will to get what I want."

"Lucy . . ." Knock-Out raised a hand, tugging at her sleeve. "You don't have to be so . . ." His voice was weak, and his clothes hung on him.

"You shut up. This is important."

Gus said, "She's right, Knock-Out. This has to happen, if not for you, for everyone else. This will happen more and more often, every year."

Knock-Out let his hand fall back in his lap.

"So what's it gonna be, Joblo?"

The requisition was granted.

There's something going on here I don't understand.

MINUTES OF THE POWER & LIGHT COMMITTEE

DATE: May 25, 2018
TIME: 5:00 PM
PLACE: Command Tent B
Present: Chairman Joblownski, Engineer Richards, Engineer Broadsword, Co-chair Gus Ingersol, Keb Motiel, Dina

Secretary: Barbara Dinews

ITEM: Amperage from prop gennies is enough to keep boat ramp elevator batteries charged but not much else. Needed: more props (or larger ones affixed to permanent housing), gears, the machinery of electrification (see addendum provided by Engineer Richards). Especially needed are more car/truck batteries.

PROPOSAL: Scavenge expedition to Helman & Son should provide Bridge City with enough large truck/heavy equipment batteries for more wattage and usage. Electrical lighting. Engineer Broadsword mentioned needing refrigeration units for the winter when game becomes scarce and foraging becomes more problematic and strung farther afield. I heartily concurred, having spent my time in the kitchens. Movies for general populace were requested. (Morale issues were brought up and then tabled by Co-chair Ingersol, to be discussed in Morale Committee Mtg.)

PROPOSAL: Gus wants to make an attempt to restart the dam works, bringing large-scale electricity back to this whole region. Most committee members were a bit dismayed by the idea, which would involve fortifying a permanent outpost there, cutting numerous outgoing electrical lines. And a turn-off expedition, which would involve going into homes where closeted zombies might be hiding. It was agreed that there would be casualties.

Gus, playing devil's advocate to his own idea, pointed out that, tactically, it would weaken our position, having two locations to guard. However, after 9/11, the dam was fortified by the Feds to prevent terrorist attack, so that should lessen some of the workload. However, the zeds aren't quite terrorists. But everyone knows that the slavers are coming. Sometime.

Heavy debate followed.

PROS: What is there to say? Electricity. Civilization. Higher standard of living.

CONS: Weaker tactical position. Joblownski pointed out a reliance on technology that will eventually die unless we can, in the next few years, procreate madly and ship all the rug rats off to MIT at the age of four. Otherwise, we're looking at wearing loincloths in twenty years. He gave an extensive speech about how knowledge has been lost and how it will take a millennium to regain it unless we take chances. We need to find more people. Phrases and words to define for later meetings: Biomass. Reciprocity. War of attrition. Scalable education. Renewable technology. Feudal states.

MOTION: Not really a motion. Joblo and Gus ignored us all, chatted for a while about the difficulties of reclaiming the dam, and then planned an expedition for tomorrow with Keb,

Broadsword. When reminded that they needed a majority in committee to assign community resources, they laughed. Gus asked, "Should my mom start charging for her services? Should Joblo? For that matter, should I?"

I responded that Doc Ingersol and Joblo were a doctor and an engineer, respectively.

Joblo informed me that Bridge City, the gennies, the murderholes, the dock, the garden—well, most of what makes Bridge City what it is—were all Gus's ideas initially. All news to me. Explains why Keb sticks to him like a bodyguard. I just thought he was a cutie. Didn't know he was a brainiac. Assumed it was his mother calling the shots.

Was a cutie, should repeat. His face is sorta lopsided now, and, well . . . the missing hand is disconcerting . . .

ROLL CALL VOTE (not like it matters)
AYE: Joblownski, Richards, Broadsword, Ingersol, Motiel, Dinews (yes, I'm making them give me a vote, even though I vote along)
NAY: None
ABSTAIN: Nickerson
VOTE: 6–0–1

MINUTES OF THE HOUSING, GARDENING & ZONING COMMITTEE

DATE: June 11, 2018
TIME: 8:00 AM
PLACE: Garden

Present: Chairwoman Dr. Ingersol, Co-chair Dina Matthews, Engineer Richards, Citizens Hattie (last name unknown), Gus Ingersol, Keb Motiel, and Knock-Out

Secretary: Myself, Barbara Dinews

PERSONAL ITEM: Nobody has ever asked for any of the minutes to these meetings we keep having. It's becoming obvious that this is just a journal I'm keeping that could, at any time, be looked at by whoever wants to. I never thought that the end of the world would finally make a blogger of me, but there it is. This Underwood is pretty neat. Once Joblo showed me how to thread ribbon and set me up with a table in the command tent, I've been clacking away. Other than cooking, scrubbing pots, and planting seedlings, it's something for me to do. It's obvious by now that Wallis (who doesn't seem to want to attend any meeting), Doc Ingersol, Knock-Out, and Gus are the real players at Bridge City. Joblo is like a mad professor. The rest of us are just here to observe what the Big Four decide for us.

I've got to be honest. That kind of frightens me, four people running our lives. But between them, they've got it worked out, I must say. I've never seen anyone argue more viciously than Knock-Out and Wallis, or Gus and Knock-Out, or Doc Ingersol and Wallis or . . . well, you get the point. I can tell they're not in some weird power play. You'll hear them talking and then, all of a sudden, Doc will stop, turn her body a little at an angle to the speaker, and say, "Is that right? Well, here's points 1, 2, and 3 that go against what you're saying." Then it'll be on. Big argument. I say argument, which it is, but it's obvious they're all enjoying the debate. And it's never personal. They attack each other's ideas. They don't attack each other.

Doc Ingersol usually wins. I guess that means she's the boss lady.

And that makes it okay, I think, that, like it or not, they're our leaders.

PROPOSAL: Not much discussed, though someone suggested composting zombies for the gardens. Doc Ingersol mentioned how much disease can come from a single dead body. Knock-Out pointed out that, in essence, we'd be eating our own dead, which sickened most of us, except for Gus, who laughed. "They eat us! It's only fair." Keb shook his head and made crazy motions around his ear.

It's weird that Gus doesn't have a right hand anymore. He gestures with it like it's there. And, honestly, I can see his hand there; I know what gesture he's trying to make.

Keb told the women at the fire circle that the slavers crucified Gus on a traffic sign. That they chopped off his fingers and then drilled a hole in his hand and put rope through it to string him up.

It's kinda hard to believe that someone could do that to another person. And Gus is different now. He can't look me in the eyes.

I wish I hadn't kissed that guitar player.

MINUTES OF THE ZED DISPOSAL & TRACKING COMMITTEE

DATE: July 18, 2018
TIME: 11:00 AM
PLACE: Command Tent
Present: Chairwoman Ingersol, Co-chair Gus Ingersol, Co-chair Quentin Wallis, Co-chair Jim Nickerson (Knock-Out), Engineer Joblownski, Citizens Hattie, Keb Motiel, and the general populace

Secretary: Barbara Dinews

ITEM: Zombie accoutrements, IDs from wallets namely, have been found from as far away as Nashville and Denver. This means they're migrating. A discussion followed about the possibility that clusters in excess of 100 or more might batter our city gates. Joblownski assures us that the murderholes can accommodate much larger numbers, but closing the currently manual double doors will be problematic. However, now that there is minimal electrical power, he could jury-rig winches that could open and close the steel doors even if zeds were in the way.

Gus and Wallis pushed preparing for the worst, which would be thousands of undead at the gates. This could conceivably happen, since we've been seeing more extended damilies and what the outriders are calling mega-damilies on the move.

However, right now, Joblownski assures us we are safe. He reminded us all that with the recollection of the large stores of chain-link fencing from Ozark, we're beginning to establish concentric rings of chain-link fencing, and he's designed multiple levels of murderholes, funneling all the migrant revenants toward the master murderhole. He displayed his designs on graph paper. They seem logical, though I have doubts they will hold—just chain-link fencing—if a mega-damily of a thousand or more comes battering.

Joblownski (and Gus and Wallis) argued we should focus our attention on the slavers who will be coming. He insists on another reconnoiter as to their position. Wallis tabled the discussion, wanting to keep that private for the moment.

This makes me nervous.

ITEM: To date, we have harvested two hundred pounds of silvered, gilded teeth. We have fifty or sixty pounds of change and over a hundred and fifty thousand dollars in reclaimed paper money—which is worthless except for use as kindling or toilet paper. But people like to look at the money. Some of them cry.

MINUTES OF THE LIVESTOCK & STABLING COMMITTEE

DATE: August 2, 2018
TIME: 8:00 AM
PLACE: South Gate
Present: Chairman Gus Ingersol, Co-chair Quentin Wallis, Co-chair Lucy Ingersol, Engineer Joblownski, Keb Motiel, and the general populace

Secretary: Myself, Co-chair Barbara Dinews

ITEM: Knock-Out couldn't attend the rancher's arrival, but the rest of the Big Four were there.

The rancher is a sour little man, raw-boned and rangy, prone to laughing too hard to hide his sadness. Somehow, he's survived in the Ouachita Mountains for the last four years, keeping cattle and horses. He came through the outer ring of chain-link, leading the cattle, with only a few undead trailing him.

When we brought him inside the protective ring, away from the murderholes, he pointed to a large bull—his only bull.

"That bastard right there will trample any goddamned rev in sniffing distance. He's meaner than the devil. Probably will trample the living too, only I'm too smart to get next to him. But keep any people away."

We haven't had any real need for provisioning livestock until now—except finding food for Cookie, the stray dog that ended up at our gates. We lost a man trying to get her into the city, and so she is quite loved and becoming too fat as well. As to the livestock, Joblownski, with two assistant engineers, immediately came up with a solution.

"We'll pasture them on the south shore, in a ring of chain. Since the revs don't seem attracted to cattle or horses, maybe the bull will act as an extra line of defense. I know—" He waved his hands. "I know. It's laughable. But we should test. It'd be nice if we had three tons of roving, zombie-stomping bull to our south."

So we tested in one of the concentric rings guarding the southern shore, where there is ample grass and water. After the animals checked the perimeter and settled down near a large cottonwood, Joblownski and Keb went to the outer gate, unlocked and unlatched the chain door, and let in the few zombies waiting there. The bull—who Dap, the rancher, calls Satan—snorted, roused himself, and began to saunter over to the men and the undead.

Joblo ran away, and Keb danced backward, leading the revenants inside the chain. There were only three: two men and a child. Keb brained the fastest rev with his headknocker, dropping it in its tracks, and then turned tail and ran to the inner ring, through the gate, to rejoin us. Satan chased him. Dap, his mouth full of tobacco, laughed merrily, watching as the bull stood breathing heavily behind the chain-link fence. Then a rev moaned, and the big animal wheeled and tromped off.

It's amazing what short work three tons of bull can make of two zombies. More were gathering on the outer ring, pawing at the chain. We considered letting them in as well, but relented. Eventually they'd find their way down the sluice-way to the murderholes, so we could keep count, harvest metals, and perform tracking.

Dap tells the committee he knows the locations of two more ranchers keeping their cattle and people in the highlands. Maybe twenty or thirty head more cattle and fifteen or twenty more people, not including a few dogs, which the zombies *will* attack, strangely. Man's best friend becomes man's best snack.

We, immediately and on the spot, requested Dap to outride, find the ranchers, and invite them here. We showed him the ins and outs of life on the bridge, the progress of the Tulaville reclamation, and the "great" wall that is now beginning to take shape around the neighborhood closest to the bridge.

He agreed.

Our little community is growing.

THIS DARK EARTH

MINUTES OF THE TULAVILLE RECLAMATION COMMITTEE

DATE: August 8, 2018
TIME: 8:00 AM
PLACE: Command Tent A
Present: Chairman Gus Ingersol, Co-chairwoman Ingersol, Co-chair Jim Nickerson (Knock-Out), Engineer Joblownski, Engineer Broadsword, Keb Motiel, and the general populace

Secretary: Myself, Co-chair Barbara Dinews

ITEM: It was with happiness mingled with sadness that Engineer Broadsword debriefed us on the events of the Ozark Galvanized Tin, or Tinman, mission.

They recovered four tons of chain-link fencing, ten tons of bricks, unknown amounts of lumber and galvanized tin. In this, the mission should be considered a success.

However, on the exit from Ozark they encountered an extended damily—numbering in the hundreds—which swarmed the outriders and escort vehicles. Five men were lost: Montfredi, Stevens, Wilkins, Bilyeu, and Hammond. Morale teeters, a strange mixture of delight at the new building materials and grief at the loss of the men. Montfredi is especially mourned.

To make it worse, it seems the damily that got Montfredi is heading this way, trailing the fleeing raiders. It could be here in a couple of weeks. God, I hate to think of towheaded Montfredi shambling along with his ears flapping. (And I find this odd, the prediction of a damily battering the gates—it smacks of meteorology, which we all know is, or was, consistently inaccurate. I can't help but think of the book Daddy always read to me when I was a girl, *Cloudy with a Chance of Meatballs*, with food falling from the sky. God, I miss him. I imagine he didn't make it out of the Dallas firestorm. But this new book we're writing would be titled *Sunny with a Chance of Zombies*.)

Joblownski brought out stores of his moonshine for the wake. The women of Bridge City conducted an emergency meeting and allowed the remembrance to be held at the women's fire. Many of the men became ecstatic, it being their first time. The poor boys.

MINUTES OF THE BRIDGE CITY SECURITY COUNCIL

DATE: August 14, 2018
TIME: 10:00 PM
PLACE: Command Tent A
Present: Chairman Gus Ingersol, Co-chairwoman Dr. Ingersol, Co-chair Jim Nickerson (Knock-Out), Co-chair Quentin Wallis, Engineer Joblownski, Engineer Broadsword, Keb Motiel, and the general populace

Secretary: Myself, Co-chair Barbara Dinews

ITEM: Strange to be woken by Gus. He came to my tent and scratched on the fabric. I could hear the usual moaning of revs, and it was hotter than the dickens even at night, and the cicadas were making a horrible racket, but Gus was very quiet and soft spoken. Almost hard to hear.

* * *

"We want you to attend this meeting, Barb." He smiled at me, remembered himself, stopped smiling, looked away toward the river, looked back, and smiled again.

"What meeting?" I asked. I really had no clue.

"Slavers," was all he would say. So I made myself as presentable as possible and followed. Gus is tall and takes long strides and I had to jog, almost, to catch up. He wasn't looking at me. He was doing whatever he could to *not* look at me, walking fast, staring at the river, looking at the stars, and finally, half wanting to slow him down and half wanting him to pay attention to me, I reached out and touched his arm. Unfortunately, my hand fell on his stump. It felt angry and hot.

He stopped and looked at me.

"Gus, I'm—" I didn't know how to say it. "I'm sorry for what happened."

He laughed. A little nervously, I think, holding up his stump. "It was just a hand . . . I've got another. The redundancy of the human body—"

"No, I don't mean—" I tried again. "Not your hand, though that was . . . horrible." I took his other hand, held it in mine. I felt his nervousness in the tension of his fingers. I dug my thumbs into the hard calluses of his palm, massaging, trying to loosen the tension there, like Dad had shown me so long ago.

"I mean the night . . . when I danced with that other—"

He pulled his hand away and looked at me. Hard. As intensely as only he, or his mother, can with those gray, almost

265

animal-like eyes. Wolf's eyes, maybe. He squinted a little and tightened his shoulders as if awaiting a blow. Even missing a hand, he's worked shifts on the Wall, and he remains as massive and muscular as ever. Possibly the largest man in Bridge City now that Jasper is gone.

Then he sighed, and smiled. His shoulders relaxed, and I was powerfully reminded that he is just a boy, really. Not uncertain, like any other boy I ever knew. No, not that. But inexperienced.

He has the raw intelligence of a man. But wary. I wish I hadn't kissed that guitar player.

"It's nothing," he said. He waved his missing hand in the air, and I could see the gesture he was trying to make. "Really. It's nothing," he said again, leaving me wondering if he was talking about our history or his hand.

Gus might be a boy or a man. I can't tell which. But whatever the case, he's complicated.

Wallis and the Doc looked up as we entered the tent, and the Doc's eyes went back and forth between us two, maybe three, times. Knock-Out, bald now and looking for all the world like David Carradine on *Kung Fu*, dandled the baby on his knee. I sat by him, put my pencil and paper on the table, and made googly eyes at Ellie. Knock-Out grinned and gave her to me, and for a while, everything was all right. The dead, the living, the undead, they're all minor problems. Holding this smiling, chubby baby is like holding your own soul, unborn, all the possibilities unexplored, all the wrong roads and mistakes untaken. She's pink, and fat, and has cankles. She smells like love, and the world we've almost forgotten. She put a chubby hand on my cheek and then moved it down to my neck and tugged on my collar and explored my necklace.

I could have stayed like that forever, holding Ellie. Maybe it's my body telling me something. Maybe it's the world, the scarcity of life now on this new frontier.

Knock-Out, wasted and no longer looking like a black, burly bear, winked at me, took the baby, and walked her over to Doc Ingersol, who pulled out a breast and stuck it into Ellie's mouth.

Wallis stood, pointed at a map, and spoke. "Stevens, on his last run, marked the slavers' retreat back to New Boston, where they knew they could find shelter in their old camp." He stabbed at the map with a long finger. "They lost many of their soldiers and slaves in the retreat, but they've been more actively recruiting . . . if you can call it that . . . making forays into Oklahoma."

Wallis paused, wiped his face. It was close, still, and hot in the tent. The moans of the dead came through the tenting canvas, and the cicadas sounded even louder.

"They've found a cache of fuel, it looks like, and an engineer or mechanic skilled enough to resurrect some armed transports from the Army Depot. But that's not all."

Doc Ingersol, Ellie held close to her breast, said, "Don't mess around, Wallis. Get to the bad news so we can make some decisions."

Wallis ground his teeth at the interruption—I know it must be hard for him, a former military man, to have a council of equals. He took a sip of water and continued.

"All of our scouts—Stevens, Ransom, Sunseri—report more and farther-flung patrols around the Boston base. Ransom was nearly caught by one. And Sunseri, on his way south, spotted a small cluster of zeds and thought he heard a motorcycle. We have to assume they're scouting us too."

Gus cleared his throat. "Um . . . Mom?"

She smiled at him and patted the seat next to her. He walked over and sat down.

"Do you remember our trip to Costa Rica?"

"Yes . . . but what on earth does that have to do with why we're here?"

Joblownski, leaning past the silent Engineer Broadsword, waved his hand at her. "Doc, let him talk."

Wallis sat back down and poured himself some water from a ceramic pitcher. Joblo's new still has reputedly been producing water as clean as bottled. I poured myself a glass. It was quite nice, but there was a hint of charcoal.

"You remember the zip-lines we went on? Had to stand in lines for hours?"

She nodded.

"I'm thinking deer stands."

Wallis laughed. The council members have become used to Gus's oblique way of getting to the point.

Joblo stood, excited. "I hear you. We put them on the ridge. With the walkie-talkies I've managed to get to work. Sniper rifles."

"Hold on, everyone." Wallis stood and walked around the table to put a hand on Gus's shoulder.

"Slow down and tell us what you're talking about."

Gus tapped his finger on the map. "Here. This ridge. We place deer stands in the tree lines, men with scoped hunting rifles, flares, radios. Spread them out over miles." He ran his finger along the map. I was beginning to see it.

I began scribbling in shorthand, stopped, and asked, "But why did you mention the zip-lines?"

He smiled at me as if he had been waiting for someone to ask that question.

"Revs will cluster around trees or buildings where they can smell or hear the living. The zip-lines will give anyone in deer stands the ability to get away, quickly, unless they're totally mobbed, which is unlikely." He turned back to the map. "We dig ditches that will be hard for Bradleys to cross."

"They must've recruited some mechanic or engineer who understood the effects of the EMP enough to combat it. To repair the damaged electronics or replace them," said Joblo.

"These will be moats, actually. Here. Chop down miles of trees across every approaching road and train track. This will help in keeping out the zeds as well, so we can consider it a quality of life issue."

"Moats? It's like we're going medieval," I said.

Gus raised an eyebrow and looked at me. "We have no electricity. We live in a fortified enclosure, under siege, with guards on the walls. I'd say medieval is exactly what we are. In fact, it's what I had in mind when I designed the bridge defenses."

"Oh." I looked around the command tent and saw expressions of dawning understanding. Knock-Out just smiled. When he saw me looking at him, he winked.

God, he looked horrible. I did my best to smile back.

Wallis grunted, drained his water, and then said, "Okay, all that is fine and dandy, but it has nothing to do with what we're talking about. The slavers are mobilizing. They'll be coming for us. What are we gonna do?"

Everyone remained silent for a while. Then Knock-Out stood, brushed his loose-fitting jeans, and spoke.

"This bridge, this community we're building here, right now it's the most important thing in the world. Did you know that?" He looked around at me, at Broadsword and Joblo and Wallis. Then, coming to Doc Ingersol, he put his hand on her shoulder and squeezed.

"After the bombs went off, and the dead rose, the televisions and radios stopped working, we were lost—Lucy, Gus, and me. But we made our way north, through the masses of living dead, and found Wallis. And together, all of us, we've made this community. This city. And as far as we know, it's the only place like it in the world now, where people live free with some semblance of safety. Who knows what it's like in California or New York or China, for that matter? We were lucky to be so remote. This is our *life* now."

He stopped and bowed his head, giving us all a good look at his newly bald skull.

"We can't give this up, what we've made." He spoke very quietly into the stillness of the tent. "So that means we have to defend it. Or take the war to them. But we can't run. We'll never run."

There was no dissent. Wallis smacked a hand down on the table.

"Agreed. We've worked too hard here and in reclaiming Tulaville to let some filthy . . . goddamned . . . slaver come take it all away from us." The profanity, coming from Wallis, made me nervous. He's a religious man, conducted services on Sunday. And when he said "goddamned," the look on his face was terrifying.

"So, I think we should do both. Take the war to them, right down their throats, like Gus and Keb did, but this time with greater purpose. More aggressively. And that means we have to muster a militia. Maybe even institute a draft."

"A draft will never work, so let's take that off the table right now." Doc Ingersol's eyes shone bright, alarmed.

"Why not?"

"Okay. You've got a draft and my number comes up. I refuse. What are you gonna do about it?"

"Kick you out of our community. Put you beyond the wall."

"Are you going to lure the revs away?"

"No. Waste of manpower."

"So you're saying you're going to kill the people who refuse."

"No. I'm not. We're just going to put them beyond the wall. Maybe downriver."

"You'll waste the gas?"

Wallis fell silent.

"I thought so. You can't kill people who refuse, otherwise we'd be the slavers." She pulled Ellie's mouth from her breast, covered herself, and then said, "Quentin, I think you'll be surprised at how easy it will be to form a willing army. Everyone here is thankful for Bridge City. We're not going to let it be taken away from us."

Gus coughed. "We have to take the fight to them. It's too dangerous otherwise."

Wallis peered at him, and Joblo said, "What do you mean?"

Gus held up his missing hand, and I could imagine him holding up his index finger to make a point.

"We're all infected," he said. "Every one of us. And when you die, you rise." He let that sink in. "So, if I was attacking us, I'd have snipers picking off people inside the gates, so that the general populace could be turned against itself, giving the advancing army room to maneuver. Shoot enough people, you've created a small force of saboteurs right in their midst."

"The attacking army has the same weakness," said Wallis.

"True. But their army isn't confined inside walls, fences."

"Hell, son, it's a risky business all around. If everyone rises, it's a three-way running battle. There's always another army nipping at your heels or eating away at your insides."

Gus nodded in agreement. "Yes. But I sure would rather be on the other side of the fence from the revs."

There was a pause then, and people helped themselves to more water, and Wallis shared the last of the Johnnie Walker. It went quick, but not before I managed to get a glassful.

"So here's the way I see it," Wallis said. "We need to know how we're gonna take the fight to them. Motorcycles worked once, but we lost Jasper and nearly lost Gus. I don't want thirty-three percent of my force lost. When you're a commander, that's a not unreasonable expectation. We don't have enough people to lose. So whatever ideas you have, make sure they take into account the welfare of the attacking force." He looked around. "Understood?"

There were general murmurs of acceptance.

"How long until the slavers will be mobile? Any idea?" Gus asked.

"Stevens says most of their manpower is currently occupied flushing out and capturing pockets of survivors in Oklahoma, Louisiana, and the panhandle. It looks slow, but they're gaining momentum. And the fact that they have gas reserves makes them especially dangerous."

"How long?"

"Five to ten months maybe. No way to know, really."

Grumbling and coughs. Engineer Broadsword rubbed his face as if stemming tears. Joblownski cleared his throat and said, "We'll figure something out."

Doc Ingersol, holding the baby, stood and waved everyone away like she was shooing a flock of chickens—her manner of dismissing a meeting. "Yes, we will. We'll have to."

Everyone filed out of the command tent, hushed and somber, except for Wallis and Knock-Out. Doc Ingersol gave Knock-Out a kiss and whispered something in his ear. He smiled wearily in return. I can't imagine how hard it is for them. It doesn't look like Knock-Out is going to make it. He and Wallis put their heads together and begin to talk. I wish I could have stayed and listened.

I have no doubt what they discuss will affect us all.

Gus walked me back to my tent, and when we got there, I didn't wait. I kissed him.

He was surprised. He should have been. I wouldn't want to be with him if he wasn't surprised.

"Wha-what?" he stammered. "What was that for?"

"For including me."

"I don't know what—"

"Yes, you do. I saw your mother's expression when I came in. I wasn't expected. And you didn't include me because of the idiotic minutes I've been taking. No one has even asked to look at the minutes."

His face went from surprised to embarrassed to serious all in a moment, and I don't know if it's because I saw through his ploy or because of the minutes or because of the kiss.

"They are important. We just don't know how important they are. Yet." He looked down. Beyond me at the garden. Out at the river.

I kissed him again and this time there was more than a little heat in return.

When we separated, he said, "You're important too. You ask the right questions. You listen with all of your head, don't get all emotional, and don't jump to conclusions. We need you to help us, as a group, as a community. To help lead."

When he said that, it sent shivers down my spine. My arms rippled with goose bumps. They claim power is the ultimate aphrodisiac. It's not like he was giving me a crown or anything. But to be more of a part of the councils, to have a voice in the future of our community and, consequently, the future of humankind . . . well, that's something. That's something.

More than I ever expected in college, that's for certain. More than any doctor could have given me. More than any rich man.

I tried to get him to stay with me for the night. He blushed uncontrollably, tried to rub his face with his missing hand. He stammered. I love him for it.

I laughed and remembered he's still so young.

So now I'm finishing these "minutes" in my tent, by light of an LED flashlight, clacking away. God help the person who ever reads them. They'll brand me a power-mad hussy.

They'll be wrong.

6

THE ENGINEER

Dap rides point, I follow, and Klein and Fulcher bring up the rear. The constant sway in the saddle chafes my ass, thighs, and calves horribly, even through motorcycle armor, but it beats working on the Wall.

Two days in the saddle, moving fast to keep ahead of the dead. A long time, longer than I'd like to admit, since I've been this close to them, outside the Wall, without people and multiple barricades between them and me. You can't relax outside. Every noise is threatening, every broken twig a possible shambler. I hear them moaning through the trees, in the brush.

"We're not gonna make it tonight, Broadsword," Dap says, looking back at me and the others. Klein has his shotgun and hammer, and Fulcher has one of the old army M-16s and a crowbar tucked into his belt. I've got my pistol and a lever action .30-06, which makes me feel somewhat like a cowboy. And a trench shovel for a headknocker. But then the horse shifts, I almost topple off—again—and the illusion of cowboy is gone.

"So what do you suggest?"

"Revs don't fuck with cattle or horses, so I suggest we put on a little speed, get up over this ridge, pasture the horses somewhere before sundown, and find some nice trees to bunk down in."

"Trees?"

"Hell, Eric, how do you think I kept my cattle alive for the last few years alone? Get used to bunking in trees." He pats his saddlebags. "Don't worry, pard, I got some stuff for you. And with luck, down by this crick, we can find magnolias."

"Why magnolias?"

"Easy to climb."

"Fulcher. Hop down there and brain that shambler, will you, before his friends get here for the party?"

"Why me?"

"Because you're the lowest man on the goddamned totem pole." Dap grunts and shifts in his nylon hammock. "I can't climb down over you, now, can I?"

Fulcher remains quiet. He's scared. I would be too.

"Gimme a sec and I'll get down there with you." Might as well help him out. If he's ever gonna become an engineer, he'll need to see us doing more than just distilling water and running gennies and collecting bricks. Hiding behind the Wall.

No thanks, just an exhalation of air. "Tell me when you're ready," I say at last.

Getting in and out of the small nylon hammocks Dap gave us is easier said than done. I swing my legs over to one side so I'm sitting, ass waffled by the weave. Hand on a branch, I tilt forward and try to find another branch with my foot.

No dice.

I lean more and almost fall out of the hammock. In the end, I'm hanging from my hands and scraping at the trunk with my feet.

"Goddamn, boys. Ain't you ever camped before?" The tree rustles and the shambler below moans louder. From farther off, another moan answers. Then another.

"Shitload of 'em out there." Klein clutches his shotgun to his chest.

"Better get down real quick and get those headknockers ready. If you don't take these out quick-like, we're gonna have to run for it. A mob forms around the tree, we'll be stuck. For good." He spits, not caring that we are below him. "Broadsword, there's a branch to the left of you. Put your foot there."

I snag the branch with my boot, steady myself, and find my way lower in the tree until I'm even with Fulcher. We look at each other, nod, and then drop to the ground. The shambler stands closest to me. It immediately issues a garbled, phlegmy sound and, wheeling, lurches at me. My collapsible trench shovel is strapped to my thigh with Velcro, so I walk backward, rip it out, flip open the blade, and screw it tight. Gotta keep distance between me and these things.

Numerous moans sound from the darkness of the woods.

Dap curses. "Christ on a crutch. That's an extended damily. Time to run, boys."

The shambler totters in front of me, the smell overpowering. It's like a walking sewer full of dead pig. I nearly choke, but the silhouette grows and lurches, so I raise the shovel and swipe it across its head. Hard. With everything I've got.

The shovel, nearly ripped from my hand from the force of the blow, shudders and rebounds, but the zombie goes down.

I hear Dap scramble down the tree. I get the impression he's rushing, but the flash of steel in the dark tells me he's cutting the hammocks and stuffing the white nylon into his rucksack.

Dap and Klein drop to the ground, next to Fulcher and me.

"I said run. It's time to run."

"Which way?"

He points. "Stay together."

We move, hunched over in a skulking trot, our boots ripping at the earth, cracking twigs, making entirely too much noise.

There's a damily between us and the horses, which nicker and rear.

It's not hard to tell the horses aren't happy. Horses do not like dead people. In fact, they're pretty adamant about stomping them.

"Ain't nothing for it, gents. We've got to deal with these bastards. To arms."

Everyone hoists their respective headknockers. A shovel, a couple of hammers, a tire iron. Hammers are the preferred headknocker, I've noticed, but I like the army trench shovel because it's bladed as well. If you can get one down, a couple of well-placed jabs and you can separate the head from the shoulders.

We wade in.

Dap has always seemed to me to be a sour, squirrelly little

dude, but he moves like lightning. He's dropped one rev with his hammer and moved on to the next before the rest of us know what's happening. I push forward.

One of the revs is fresher than the others. She spasms forward, grabbing me. Thank God she's short. She starts gnawing on my arm, safely encased in Kevlar motorcycle armor. Even though the teeth aren't breaking skin, the pressure on my bicep is excruciatingly strong. I yelp.

Klein swipes her head with his tire iron and she folds, almost taking me down with her.

Falling is death. If you go down in a group of shamblers, you'll never get back up.

"Thanks." The little courtesies like that are what keep us from becoming like them. Well, that and not dying.

Fulcher, despite his earlier fear, holds quite well against a rather large basketball player of a zombie. He bats the zombie's arms away with his hammer, once, twice, steps in and swings at the teetering dead man's head, missing. Dap pops up, lashes out with a booted foot, and crumples the shambler's knee. The zed topples like a tree, and when he's down, Fulcher pounds his head to mush.

There's one more shambler, a charred corpse that could be man or woman. Its fingers are burned off, and it smells absolutely awful. At some point its jaw was knocked off or dislocated, chomping on someone.

Fantastic.

While it's palming and pawing at me, leaving streaks of char against my vest, I jab it in the face until it falls to the ground, then stomp on its head until it stops moving.

There's more moaning behind us. An extended damily, for sure. An extended nuclear damily. I hate to think how many more rads I can take before my body becomes one big walking cancer.

Dap's with the horses now, untying them. I run over. We left saddles on them just in case, and since the case is fucking affirmative . . . well, I'm glad we have Dap with us. Otherwise, we'd be ballast for zed.

When we mounted before, I had to have Klein hold my horse for me. Not now. I amaze myself by popping right up on the beast and whirl her around to look for Dap. Shadows move in the darkness and moans sound from all around.

There's times where you think you're gonna scream and you know you shouldn't and you do whatever you can not to scream, but it feels like it's gonna come out, like you're gonna lose control of your own body and let the terror out. That's how it is now, reins and shovel in my hands, not able to see shit, and the feeling doesn't subside even when a larger piece of darkness materializes in front of me, horse-shaped, an LED light flashing at the ground.

"Keep on my ass, boys."

For a second I think he's going to follow this with "or you'll wake up in a shambler's belly," or one of his other tidbits of zombie wisdom. He doesn't, thankfully.

The light moves away, and I spur my horse after him.

Things grab at me in the dark, rip at my legs. I swing the trencher like a demented polo player. Something grabs at me, I swing. Terrified, I have no clue, no sensation even, if I've hit anything, but I'm moving fast, trying to keep up with the swaying blue light ahead of me, rocking on the back of the horse, in the night, surrounded by unquiet dead.

The high-pitched horse scream, when it comes, is followed by bellows and cries for help. They stop within seconds.

Fulcher is fucked. As is the horse he rode in on.

We've gone into full gallop, that rocking, slow back and forth that feels liquid and effortless. Out of the night, I make out other bits of night that have more form. A tree line, a rock.

I hear too. Zombies don't have a corner on that racket.

There's a horse behind me. I just hope the horse has a rider.

Soon the light in front slows. Dap has dropped to a canter, and my horse, having more sense than I do, slows as well. The rear horse draws even with us, trotting now, and I see that Klein has made it.

"Well," Dap says, and the thickness in his voice tells me he's been hoarding chaw. How he popped it into his mouth at a gallop is anyone's guess. "We ain't camping no more tonight."

Dap doesn't bother mentioning Fulcher.

"Let's get a move on. We go steady and careful until sunrise, and then haul fucking ass."

Sounds good to me. I glance at Klein, and, from what I can tell in the dark, his usual implacable demeanor is a little frazzled. I can't even imagine what I look like.

Maybe my hair has turned as white as Mark Twain's.

I'd believe it.

* * *

Dap had been bitching when they came to tell us.

"This is a miserable damned detail, Broadsword, salvaging houses. What'd I do to deserve this?"

"You were born. And survived the Big Turnover. You rather be working the Wall?"

He hocked and spat.

Barker dumped an eight-foot two-by-four onto the wagon and walked back to the house. We'd already dismantled the roof into component parts—timber into one pile, the scrap roofing wheelbarrowed to the river to be dumped—and were working down to the studs. Klein was on guard detail, modeling sunglasses and hoisting a bludgeon instead of a shotgun, trying for all the world to look like a penitentiary guard from *Cool Hand Luke*. Even though we'd managed to ring Tulaville—twice—with chain-link, you can't be too wary. The zeds have ways of getting around anything. Climbing up from the river. Coming out of uncleared basements. Falling from the skies.

Who knows? But come they do.

When the house was down to its cinder blocks and studs, we drank water from a cooler, smoked grapevine, and sat on the concrete foundation and watched Bridge City.

"Damn, she's a pretty sight."

She is. We whitewashed the trusses in the first of summer to get rid of the verdigris, using the barrels of exterior paint found at Landry's Hardware. I guess whitewashed isn't the right phrase. We painted it, anyway, and that was a struggle, erecting the scaffolding and the rigging. The womenfolk planted clematis near the arches in spring, and now, late summer, it grows up the base of the trusses, over the women's quarter and northern section of the gardens, all of it making the bridge look like some forgotten Roman temple, multihued with a garland of purple. The clematis is stunted, but we don't get as much sunshine as we used to, before all that ash went into the sky. Joblo thinks the ash has settled in the Arctic, discoloring it. Causing the snow to melt. The oceans to rise. More water pushed into the air. Cooling the earth, maybe.

As far as growing seasons go, we haven't had a good one since the Big Turnover.

The shadows lengthened toward us from the west and Dap said, "Heads up, Broadsword. Here comes your boss."

"Hell could he want?"

Dap puffed on his grapevine and said, "Oh, I imagine quite a bit."

Most of Eureka Springs is long-dead cinders. It's surprisingly devoid of shamblers as we clop through the narrow, winding streets. Hard to tell if the fires were set or they occurred naturally, *postmortem mundi*. We had quite a dry summer last year, and Eureka is smack dab in the middle of a forest.

I haven't been inside a city in years. Eureka was never truly a town as you'd know it. Perched in the Ozark mountain forests, it was a Victorian holdout with small streets lined with dainty, embroidered houses and crammed with artisan shops staffed by hippies. Now the ruins look more European than American. Definitely not Arkansan. The charred skeletons of pines and deciduous trees scratch and scrabble at the sky, and we ride past black, jumbled timbers. Beyond the char of trees, the wind moans in the pines. Somewhere, in the little dead hamlet, a shambler answers.

I came here once with Julian, before the end. We stayed at a bed-and-breakfast and fucked ourselves silly, slept late, and ate thick toast with marmalade and drank wonderfully old scotch and walked hand in hand, unafraid, down the quaint little streets, peering in shop windows with their endless trinkets and homemade peanut brittle. Unafraid, even here in this little backwoods Victorian fantasy. The hippies smiled at us. Matrons scowled. And we laughed.

But that was a world ago. We never rode the train.

I pull the hand-drawn map from the interior pocket of my Kevlar jacket, unfold it, and lay it as flat as I can on the pommel of my saddle. Dap reins in next to me and leans over.

He jabs a finger at a nexus of connecting lines.

"We're there." He smells like sour sweat and chewing tobacco. Not all unpleasant. But not roses either. "And we're facing that way, I believe."

Makes sense.

"So we need to angle here, looks like, and descend. If I remember correctly, there's a gulley running through that part of the town."

"There's gullies everywhere around here, but yes, you're dead on."

Unfortunate turn of phrase, that.

We ride down the street, descending the hill, passing tight between buildings, some of them looking like they were built during the WPA-era works programs. Bathhouses, maybe. Libraries. But there are only a few, and they are sooty black on the outside.

The moaning grows louder, and it isn't the pines anymore. A shambler teeters from behind a building. This one actually has moss or something growing all over him. He looks like the Swamp Thing.

But there are more undead where he comes from. They shamble out from behind low-slung walls against hills or up from clusters of charred timbers.

It's the sound of hooves on pavement that draws them.

Dap curses, looking at Klein's and my horses' feet.

"You gotta wrap them in cloth! Goddamn it! If you don't, you've got a fucking procession."

He stops, wheels his horse around, cursing silently. His mount's feet aren't wrapped. I don't understand why he's yelling at us. Except maybe he looks like he's in dire need of a smoke, and I don't know why I think that but he's got the rangy build and wiry arms and chiseled face that would only look complete with a cigarette.

"Haul ass, boys!" Jesus, what a cowboy.

He canters down the incline, clopping on asphalt, weaving in and out between cars. My horse clops after him.

After a while, we break into a canter and pass beneath a canopy of dense, green trees. The branches hang low and whip past our heads. It smells good here, moist and leafy, fragrant with honeysuckle and the breathing of green things. When I was a boy, we'd walk past Gammee's fence, into the buckbrush, bucket in hand, and pick blackberries until our hands were bloody and blue. Happy. It smells like blood and buckbrush here.

Smells take you back.

I see a sign on our right. It has a train puffing billows of cartoonish white smoke into the air and reads: "Ride the E.S. & N.A. line! Parents and children, take your family on a *steam-powered adventure*! One mile ahead on the right!"

The locomotive on the sign looks like a simple boiler and turbine. Old school. Older school than I thought. Like this thing rode the rails in the Old West, or before. Shit. There are so many things that can go wrong here.

And there's the fact I've never driven a train.

On the bright side, there's only two ways it can go.

Backward and forward.

I can't hear any moaning. Despite the fact that this was a tourist attraction, we are still talking rural Arkansas. With luck, we won't have a throng of dead waiting for us or on our tails.

Yeah. Right.

Joblo and Gus rode bikes. Joblo did just fine on his, his long hair whipping around his head in a definite mad-scientist manner. Gus had a harder time of it, missing his hand. He held his stump in the center of the handlebars and his other one on the hand brake. He clenched his jaw as he rode. He didn't look like a child anymore.

Gus beckoned me away from the group. I pulled a shirt over my head, took one last sip of water from the ladle, and ambled over.

"You can say no, Broadsword. That's within your right."

That's how they started.

"Say no to what?"

"The mission."

I could've kept asking the obvious questions. But I didn't. I just waited for it.

"It's a train," Joblo said, his eyes bright. "And they won't let me go. So that leaves you and Richards and . . . well, that just leaves you, really."

"A train?"

"Yeah, an old wood-driven steam locomotive, maybe a hundred miles from here, north, in Eureka Springs. It was a tourist destination before the Big Turnover. They'd make little one-, two-mile runs down a stretch of railroad track. Carry the kiddies, their parents. Hot dogs, cotton candy, all that shit."

"Richards isn't up to it?"

"It's a *steam* train, Jim. Richards isn't qualified." Joblo grinned from ear to ear.

"And I am?"

"No," he said. Honest to a fault, that Joblo. But he didn't mean any harm in it. He was right. I'm not half the engineer he is. Which is why I break down houses and don't work on the water distillery. "But Doc Ingersol won't let me go. So that leaves you." He hopped a little and continued. "A steam train! We're gonna drive it right into the slaver camp!"

Shit. A train. What's this "we" stuff?

"So . . ." I led. I wanted the full story.

"Here's the deal, Broadsword." Gus looked as grave as

his fifteen-year-old face would let him, which, actually, was pretty grave. His eyes are older than his body. And he's got the same lack of tact that his mother has. When he looks at people, he always seems to be assessing, seeing how he can use them. The kid kinda creeps me out.

It's funny, but the older man acted like a kid and the kid acted like the elder statesman, now that I think of it. Fucked-up world, this.

"It's gonna be you, Dap, a couple of other men, to make a dash to Eureka Springs. Locate and restart the steam train, bring her south. We'll have scouts looking for you. From there, we'll get her as close to Bridge City as we can, load her up with men, put one of the Bradleys on her back, and get rid of this slaver camp once and for all."

I nodded my understanding. "Sounds pretty simple."

Maybe they heard something in my voice, I don't know.

"You don't think it will work?"

"I can think of a thousand reasons it'll fail." I began ticking off points. "First, the undead. Second, I'm unable to start the engine. Third, I start the engine and can't get the train where we want it to go—downed trees across the tracks, torn-up track, collapsed bridges. It's been three years now—almost four—with no maintenance, and I mean, I'm assuming you're sure the tracks go from there to here to the slaver place already. Fourth—oh, fuck it."

Joblo smiled and stared hard at me while Gus gave me this kind of predatory, unblinking look.

Finally, Gus said, "So you won't do it?"

"Of course I'll do it." I grinned. "It's a fucking *steam* train."

* * *

The gates are closed, but Dap is prepared. He pulls a miniature pair of bolt cutters from his saddlebag, hoists them, and grins at me. "What, you think I go around barbed-wire fences?"

He walks up and snips the padlocked chain and pushes open the gate. It clanks and creaks and swings wide. The moaning starts from inside the gate and on the road at our back. It seems we have a procession.

"Quick! To the locomotive, boys!" Dap pulls his head-knocker and spurs his horse forward, and Klein follows suit. I look around, spot a onesy coming from a portable toilet near the little station house and a damily of five shambling around the corner.

Gimping along behind us are fifteen or twenty more stragglers.

This is not good.

I kick my horse into a gallop.

Past the station house, the engine comes into view. You think of trains as black, puffing smoke, but this one looks red in the morning sun. It's streaked with rust. God help us if it has rusted solid.

We come around to the eastern side, in front of the engine, and Klein and I drop to the ground. I pull the saddlebags off my horse. They're heavy as rocks with extra ammunition, a helmet, water, kerosene and matches, and a portable winch. Klein follows suit.

Dap hops down, grabs our reins, and ties the horses together. Then he swings back into the saddle and thumbs the brim of his hat.

"Nice knowing you boys. If you make it back, I'll buy you a drink."

Klein starts cursing. Heavily.

"You can't just leave us here, Dap. We need your help."

"And you have it. I'm gonna try and lead these bastards away from here, give you a little time."

The look on his face tells me all I need to know. His concern is the horses. We're expendable. They aren't. Orders.

I nod.

"Thanks. Get back safe. And have that drink ready."

He chuckles. "Will do, pard." He looks to his right and chucks his head at the damily coming at us. "I ain't gonna be able to get rid of those, boys, so I suggest you put on your helmets and gloves and get busy."

When he rides off down the length of the train, past a dining car and a couple of cargo flats, I get this sinking sensation in my stomach. It's desperate now, and there's about to be bloodshed. Goo-shed, maybe.

Klein grabs the cast-iron railing and pulls himself up, up the metal rungs, ten feet into the air, to the half-door of the engine. That's a blessing. The locomotive is smaller than I imagined, but the cab is ten, twelve feet from the ground and defensible should an extended damily come calling. But still, it's an open cab.

After a few moments of jerking around and making me even more nervous, Klein manages to open the door. He bangs his helmet on the roof, knocking off its visor, and falls inward.

"Fuck! Broadsword, there a goddamned dead man in here."

292

I hoist myself up and peer in. It's darker in the cab, despite the open-air windows. Sure enough, a dead guy is sitting in the engineer's seat, slumped with a gun in hand and half his skull gone, yet somehow a hat remains perched on his desiccated head despite that loss of most of his left temple and a large amount of cranium. The hat is striped and spattered with blood, but it looks like an engineer's cap.

I glance down. The fastest of the damily has arrived, and it paws at my Kevlar leggings. I kick at its face, lose my balance, and almost fall, but Klein grabs the neck of my jacket-armor and pulls me backward, into the cab. The shambler grabbing my leg follows. It used to be a woman. Now it's just an ooey-gooey sac of stink climbing up my legs like a kitten on a tree.

Klein plants a boot in its face and kicks out, hard, and the shambler falls back and lands on top of the other zombies milling about below the stairs.

The cab is small. There's a dead man in the chair. While I'm trying to get my wits about me, Klein grabs the corpse—who knew Klein was so steady in a pinch?—lifts it up like he's dancing with it, and pitches the thing out the open door, after the one he kicked. Then he slams the door and flips the bolt.

"All right, boss. It's time to get busy." He grabs my arm and lifts me from the iron floor of the cab. Ringing the space are wooden benches, maybe for tourist passengers to ride with the engineer.

A bewildering mass of pipes and spigots and gauges decorate the curved ass-end of what looks like a boiler. Which is what it is.

"Get wood," I say. They're moaning now, from below. I peek out the locomotive window and see the damily pawing at the rusty iron sides of the engine. They haven't figured out how to climb it yet. I don't know if they'll be able to, but I imagine, luck being what it is, they will.

From my bag I remove two squeeze bottles. One has oil, the other regular old charcoal lighter fluid. It's important to get this party started quickly.

Setting the bottles down, I move to what I assume is the firebox and tug at the iron latch. It doesn't budge.

Putting my foot on the door frame, I yank as hard as I can. The latch gives, sending me flying backward. My hand is on fire. I've scraped all four knuckles bloody.

Klein begins chucking wood from the hopper into the firebox. Once there's a goodly pile, I squirt the lighter fluid into the box, soaking the timber. The smell of the dead cinders and fluid reminds me of barbecues, back when all the world was young. But the moaning and stench of the dead pull me out of that daydream.

"That wood is really dry. It's been in the elements since the Turnover."

"Great, it'll burn faster. And hotter. It's gonna take a while to heat the boiler enough for us to move. How much wood is there?"

"The hopper isn't full, but I'm guessing we've got enough to stoke the fire for hours."

"Okay. Keep it coming." I feel around on my jacket and pants. "Umm. Hey . . . you got a match? A lighter?"

The look on his face crumples and then gets desperate.

"No . . . don't tell me you don't have a—"

I smile. "Just kidding." I hold up the tinders for him to see.

He stares at me for a long while, not smiling.

"If we get out of this alive, I'm going to fucking kill you."

I laugh. It feels good to laugh. It's been too long.

"Yeah. Tell me about it. I hope you get the chance. What are our guests doing?"

He goes to the window, peers out. "Looks like they're at a concert."

I light the match and toss it into the firebox. There's a whoosh and I can feel the heat of the flames, even through my armor.

Not much to do now but wait.

There are numerous valves and handles and cranks and gauges. We're lucky that the gauges are marked with red paint at important demarcations. At some point, whoever ran the train tried to make it easier to understand.

I know it won't help anything, but I start tapping the gauges with my fingernail in the off chance they're frozen up.

Sprouting from the floor is a large handle with a release catch on the handgrip. I'm assuming this is the drive gear control. Forward and backward: the benefits of linear travel. But not until we've gotten a good head of steam. Looking at the blue gauge, which I'm guessing is our water reserves, I see we're near full up. The big red gauge is starting to flutter a bit but isn't rising. I have to assume this is steam pressure.

I dearly hope that the wheels haven't frozen solid. And that somewhere, deep in the workings of the engine, a valve hasn't rusted shut, dooming us to sitting dead in the boneyard.

Not something I want to think about, but it needs to be said.

"Klein, if the train won't move, we'll have to climb the roof, run down the length, and try to jump off and get away on foot."

"Bullshit." He shakes his head. "*Bullshit.* No fucking way, Broadsword. Don't even fucking talk like that, man. This bastard is going to *roll.*" He slaps his hand against the cast-iron wall and glares at me. "*Fucking* roll."

"Right. But just so you know the contingency plan."

"I'm not listening to any more of that shit. Pay attention to what's happening *here.*" He points at the cast iron at his feet.

Part of living past the end of the world is taking back talk from junior engineers. It's not like I can fire him.

There's not much for me to do but turn back to the steam pressure gauge. It's marked from one to two hundred, base ten. There's a red mark, woman's fingernail polish maybe, on the metal of the gauge at the 120 tick. It's been fifteen minutes now and the gauge is at ten.

At this rate, we're looking at three hours to get up to steam.

I go to the window and look down at the shamblers. There's about fifty of them now, pressing tight against the locomotive, and the ruckus coming from their dead gullets is enough to . . . well . . . wake the goddamned dead. The corpses in front, pawing at the sides of the engine, ripping off nails and breaking delicate phalanges, are beginning to rise from the pressure of the other undead behind them. They're being squeezed upward like toothpaste from a tube. And what do you know, one semifresh corpse seems to have a single marble left in his noggin. He's grasping at the rungs of the inset foot and handholds. I should shoot him now, but the sound would just triple their number.

But the smartie needs to be put down.

It's a toss-up if the pressure behind the front row of shamblers will build faster than the steam pressure.

Damn, I'm tired. Didn't get much sleep last night in that tree.

The gauge is at fifty after two hours, and there's a mosh pit of revenants moaning right outside the cab window.

We've got the headknockers at the ready when the first shambler manages to pull himself over the lip and his cranium comes into view.

Crack. Headknocked.

The blow sends percussive vibrations shooting up my arm. I should be used to this by now, all those hours spent on the Wall, in the murderhole. But the last few months clearing out Tulaville have left me out of shape. At least when it comes to headknocking zombies.

It's only a few minutes before another one is trying to pull itself over.

Klein bashes its skull in. He's very businesslike about it.

The problem with zombies, other than the fact that they're totally unnatural and want to eat you, is that they're very, very messy. They don't fall away from pain, or try to protect themselves, so when the mess comes, it's usually all over your shoes.

The one Klein just brained slumps on the edge of the window, the cast-iron casement digging into its stomach. Its body cavity—probably not too secure to begin with—ruptures, and liquefied guts dribble down the inner wall of the cab.

Then one of its damily members grabs its legs, trying to pull itself up, and the leaker rises, tilts backward, and falls back on top of the rest.

Unfortunately, not before its stomach contents release.

"Damn. I was hoping to keep the killing floor somewhat clean." Klein is surprisingly high-pitched for such a stout guy.

"I do appreciate tidiness in slaughter, but . . . they're zombies. And we've got a long way to go."

There's a couple this time, staggered, so he takes out one and I the other. They fall heavily, and the moaning gets louder. I look out the window on the other side of the train. Thirty or forty more shamblers.

On this side of the train, opposite where we entered, there are no steps or rungs or inset footholds for them to grab onto, and a large pipe running the length of the locomotive acts as a ledge they'd have to climb over if they were going to get in. They'd need hundreds of bodies to squeeze and lift themselves in here.

When the moans get this loud, no moan any more distinct than another, the noises blend together in your mind, and your brain does the magic trick of disregarding that information. The sound goes away. Things get easier then.

Like now.

Klein cracks another zombie's head, flipping it backward.

"You think we should be headknocking?" he asks. "Maybe

we should just push them back onto the others and not kill them."

"Huh? Why?"

"They aren't dragging their fallen away, that's for sure." He sets down his hammer, goes to the hopper, and gets an armful of logs and brings it near the furnace. It's really getting hot in here, and I'll need water soon before I pass out from dehydration. My back, ass crack, crotch, armpits, and chest are all sodden with sweat under my armor, which is about the same as wearing a bear suit, without the bear head, if not as bulky. I really should have on my helmet.

I'm becoming inured to death. Even the possibility of my own.

I peek again out the window at the ladder side. A shambler that had been working his way up senses me and reaches up a hand to grab my face. He falls back, on top of his compadres, and stays there. Other shamblers bat at him, and he floats off on a sea of arms until he hits a low-density area ten yards off and falls, finally, to the ground.

So they *are* dragging the fallen out of the way.

"No, let's keep braining the damned things. I just saw one surf the mosh pit. And it'd be a shame not to kill them when our position is so superior."

He snorts, most likely at *superior*.

I look at him, and he gives a terse nod. Then he pulls his canteen and drinks, shakes it, and hands it to me. I follow suit.

* * *

It's been close to three hours, and the gauge is at seventy now. I can see wisps of steam coming from loose solders in the pipes snaking toward the front of the locomotive. One blackish-red pipe leading to the roof and a string-activated whistle is positively bubbling.

"We've got some pressure." I rub my jaw. There's stubble there, and for a moment, I'd kill for a shot of Joblo's moonshine. Okay, maim. "A little more than half the pressure that's needed to roll."

Klein peers at the marker on the gauge.

"Those gauges are nearly two hundred years old. No manufacturer's marks for recommended level. Think the red mark could be for maximum pressure? I mean, it's in red, for chrissake. We could be sitting in the sweet spot."

"No way to know for sure."

"Other than crank the handle."

"If it's under pressure, cranking the handle could—"

"Not do shit."

"We'd lose pressure."

"I'm willing to risk it."

"It might blow a gasket. A solder. A seam. We'd be dead in the water."

Klein grimaces, turns, and lashes out with his hammer. With a loud crunch, another zombie skull distends, splits, and sends ichor flying. The zed slumps, hangs on the sill a moment, and then flops.

"If it's gonna bust a seam, won't that happen even if we get to recommended pressure? Which we don't even know?"

He's got a point.

I go to the drive handle, grip it, and pull.

The cab lurches, shifts, and then shudders to a stop. We both spread our feet, and our hands shoot toward the cab ceiling as if we were on the New York subway.

When I get to the gauge, it reads forty.

Klein curses. "Looks like the red mark is the recommended temperature."

"Yup. Looks like."

By my count, when the gauge reaches 120, I've brained 170 zeds. Klein says he's at 180, but there's not a lot of time for talking now. I'd be hard-pressed to say who's Legolas and who's Gimli. I'm taller and gay, so I'll take the elf.

The locomotive is making a loud hissing mingled with the dull roar of the fire burning in the chamber. It's starting to sound like a train.

With over a thousand shamblers struggling to climb into the cab with us—just a guesstimate—it looks a little hairy in here. Out there. Fuck, all around. We take turns stoking the fire while the other does his best to shove the bastards back on their brethren. They're coming over the sill three, four at a time. For the moment, we've still got the advantage.

The boom, when it comes, is deafening, rocking us back and giving the zeds on the ledge a boost. I see a rising plume of smoke and a fireball roiling on the ridge, back up the wooded slope, in Eureka. A gas station or building went kablooey. Big time.

What the hell?

The sound of the explosion confuses the zeds, sending them into some bizarre collective spasm. The three climbing cough up strange, oily sounds, gaining some bizarre strength to pull themselves up and over the ledge. Klein lunges, head-knocker out, and it glances of the shambler's cranium, knocking him to the floor. The other dead man falls to the floor and I flail at him, but somehow can't get a good shot at his head. He's moving about erratically and it's hard to give him a good braining. My arms feel like lead, heavy and dull. I've done this hundreds of times already in what feels like the last few moments. The shambler rises, half falling, half tottering, and smacks into me, jaws wide. I try to push him off, but he has the inexorable strength of the dead. He plants his face on my shoulder and begins to gnaw. Turns out zombie chompers work great on flesh, but not so much on Kevlar. He leaves behind a smear and a few black bits I have to assume are teeth.

I swing again and connect with his jaw, separating it from the rest of his skull, but not dislodging it from his face so that it hangs in the sack of skin that surrounds chin and cheek meat. Klein rushes at him, knocking him back. He hits the side of the engineering room and flips backward, back out into the general populace of dead.

Klein whirls and clobbers the zombie on the rail, crushing its skull. It slumps backward.

"We *cannot* let them start getting in here. Once they do, it's all over." He shifts, swings, crushing another noggin popping up over the railing.

"No shit," I say. "Tell me something I don't know. Like what the fuck was that explosion?"

He laughs. "Dap. A diversion—see?"

The mob shifts, moans, and begins to lose some cohesion. The zeds packed closest to the engine sink down, still scratching at the side of the locomotive.

"Dap!" I say. Never done this before, but I whoop and smack my thigh like I was a cowboy myself. "Dap did it!"

But Klein isn't looking at the zeds. He's staring at the engine. "She's ready, Broadsword. Look at the gauge! She's ready!" He's yelling now, too exhausted to act cool anymore. Klein is a machine, I must say. It's good having him with me.

"You want to do the honors?"

Klein grins and jumps at the drive handle. I move to the window and risk a look.

They're all back on ground level now. No moshing. But the zeds that turned away because of the explosion are coming back. With the sounds the engine is making, they'll be spilling through the windows again in no time.

"Let's do this," I say in my best tough-guy imitation, and I grab one of the window bars.

Klein grips the handle, depressing the latch, and slowly pulls it all the way to his chest.

The train shudders, chuffs a huge bellow of white smoke, and begins to move.

There are times and things you can never forget. Your first kiss from someone you love. The first time you have sex. Your first broken heart.

And then there's the first time you ride a steam locomotive through a horde of zombies.

I'd rank it up there with first kiss. Maybe even sex.

We ride north, swaying with the movement of the train, in order to get on the North Arkansas Line that runs west to Fayetteville. There, somehow, we'll turn south on the Arkansas Missouri Line until we hit Fort Smith, then east to Tulaville on the old Rock Island Line.

Klein turns the cab over to me, lies down on a bench, and begins snoring almost immediately.

The train takes the wide curve joining the NE Line before I know it. We're lucky—the train points west. It very easily could have gone east and we'd be screwed.

I stand at the window, ignoring the drying ichor crusting the sill and walls, and let the wind whip my hair and blow the stench of wood smoke and the dead away.

Gauges read steady, but the water supply is dipping and I have no idea how we'll resupply. In Westerns, there were always big wooden tanks by the stations, but I haven't seen one since we steamed out of Eureka.

It's hot. I drink water from the canteen and watch as deep pine forests, oak trees, and the rolling face of the Ozarks flow by, a stately procession.

I catch sight of a bear standing on its hind legs in the gloom of the wood, looking at me, watching the train, and I involuntarily raise my hand to wave, connected to the beast by some invisible thread, tenuous but distinct—the brotherhood of the living. The bear vanishes, and I have to wonder if the creature was a figment of my sleep-starved imagination.

I stoke the fire and keep watch.

I slow the train—moving the drive gear closer to the neutral position—when signs of the Fayetteville train yard become obvious.

Most of what I know of trains comes from living in Boston, riding the T when I was an undergraduate. And Westerns. Joblo, whose knowledge of everything mechanical is prodigious, would know exactly what to do as we approach the city.

I have to rely on my common sense.

As we come through the ruins of the city—burned shells of buildings, streets filled with derelict cars, tall grasses and saplings growing in the middle of streets—I become more conscious of the noise of the train. No use worrying. Nothing we can do about it anyway.

"When I was seventeen," Klein says, and I jump at the sound of his voice, "I got sick of watching my mom drink herself to death." He's got his arms crossed behind his head, and he's looking at the roof of the cab in a thousand-yard stare.

"So I ran away. We were living in these apartments . . . oh, pretty decent at the time, I guess. Not trying to paint it like I was living in the ghetto. Mom was pretty, but she drank and smoked, big time. And had a lot of boyfriends that kept us living pretty well.

"We argued one night. She caught me sneaking vodka out of her stash and went ballistic. I mean, yelling, screaming, and threatening to call the cops. Shithouse rat crazy, you know?"

Does he want me to respond?

A warehouse passes on the right, and suddenly there's another set of rails running parallel to the ones we're on. Ahead, I can see the maroon and blue boxes of shipping containers. There are fewer saplings here, and I see a few shamblers ambling around on the asphalt.

We're definitely coming to a train yard. Here's my plan, and it's the best I can do: head south, try and stay on the left-hand track, if I can. It's all I can do. I'm trained as a civil engineer, for chrissake, not an Amtrak engineer. Before the Big Turnover, my job consisted of checking the structural integrity of state bridges and the tensile strength of I beams. Monitoring construction sites and taking data back to the big brains. The closest I've been to a rail yard is my old electric train set.

From what I remember of that, there were switches, little toggles that made your choo-choo transfer from one track to another.

"I couldn't figure out if she was pissed at me for sneaking her vodka because she was running low or because it was wrong. She acted like it was wrong, but . . . she was a drunk. I was furious at her for being such a hypocrite. And told her. She slapped me."

He stops, breathes deep, and then sits up, hands on his knees. Looking ahead, I see a strange little abutment from the track that has a sign and a long-dead light on it. And beyond it, another double rail peels off to the left.

A switch.

I put the drive handle in the neutral position, and our train slows.

"We lived right across the highway from a spur of the old Little Rock Line, so . . . after I packed my bags, I just ran across the road, crouched in the bushes, and smoked cigarettes until a train pulled in. Hopping in a container and pulling the door shut was simple."

He sings a little snippet of song that sounds familiar but is hard to place.

"'Train, train, take me on out of this town.'"

Klein has a deep, rich voice, like a man who's spent years in a choir.

"That's what I was singing when the train pulled out. Blackfoot, you know. Fuckin' great band, Blackfoot. In my mind, I was gonna ride that bitch all the way to Memphis and visit my old girlfriend. Fuck, Broadsword, I was free. Free of my mother, free of everyone holding me back. Riding the rails."

He stands, checks his headknocker, and picks up his shotgun.

"When the train stopped fifteen minutes later in a depot and a security guard roused me, cuffed me, and delivered me to the police . . . let's just say I was a little disappointed."

He laughs, and I laugh with him. It feels good.

"Switch?"

"Sure." I turn the handle over to him. "But first I gotta—"

"Switch? I'll do it. You cover me and stoke the fire."

I nod, and he unbars the door, reverses, and climbs down.

"It's pretty slimy on this side of the train," he calls. "We really did a number on them."

The train chuffs big breaths. No shamblers in immediate sight, but that won't last long if we keep sitting here.

He trots over to the switch, goes to the far side, and then tugs at something I can't see very well. He braces himself with a boot and tugs again.

The rail shunts move, and the switch flips.

When he's back in the cab, I engage the gear and we roll.

"'Train, train, take me on out of this town,'" he sings.

When the tracks start taking us north, I slow the train, push the drive gear all the way opposite from me, and reverse her until we're back to where we started from, before the switch.

A few shamblers are stumbling over tracks and shuffling between derelict railcars.

"Take your gun. Don't bother with a headknocker," I say.

Klein grins like I've just given him a birthday present.

He runs back to the switch, waits until one crusty zed gets close enough, and blows its head off. Then he sets down the gun, tugs on the switch's handle, and the shunts slide away, disconnecting from the rails once more.

He doesn't sing this time.

Once the train angles south, it's my turn to sleep. If I dream, I have no recollection of it.

* * *

I wake, groggy and not at all refreshed, with the smell of river in my nose. Klein peers out the window.

"Come look at this, willya?"

I join him. The river passes underneath us, and the train sways on the tracks. Judging from the terrain and buildings peeking out on the far horizon, we're outside of Fort Smith, if my memory serves me, just this side of I-40. I must've slept for hours.

Our little steam train shadows the highway. Maybe a mile in front of us, the road levels and widens into four lanes. But there's a strange debris field covering it, skirting across the shoulder, onto our tracks, and into the buildings that kiss the railway.

"Holy mother of God," Klein says, and he cranks back on the gear, slowing us.

Zeds.

A damily so large that damily isn't even the word for it anymore.

A city of the dead. Thousands upon thousands of shamblers, on the hoof.

"Don't!" This whole mission can't be for nothing. "Put it in gear and help me stoke the fire."

He looks at me like I'm crazy.

"Klein, we're in a goddamned train. Let's just roll over the bastards. Stoke the fire, get up a full head of steam, and go right through them—"

"Like shit through a goose."

Colorful. "Exactly."

He nods and engages the gears.

"We're running low on water now," he says, tapping the blue gauge. "Don't know how that'll affect our speed, but our pressure is still good."

"Won't know until we're hauling ass, will we?"

We move wood, chuck it into the firebox. The flames roar behind cast-iron grates. The train chugs and hisses and bellows.

"I think I can, I think I can—"

I grimace. "Stop. You're pushing it."

The locomotive shudders and squeals on the tracks and shifting wind blows the smoke of woodfire into our faces. I tear up and wipe my face. Watching the horde of dead approach is like watching a wave come into in the gulf—so slow until it's truly upon you. My heart hitches and picks up its pace, as if it's keeping time with the steam engine.

When there are that many dead, you can't make out the faces. It's like an amoeba, inhuman and one thing. Not a collective of individual bodies anymore.

When we hit the outer edge of dead, the moaning becomes audible over the sounds of the engine. No slowing. I can't even feel it. Hitting a zed slows this train as much as a bug slows a speeding car.

The smell is horrible, though.

There are *way* too many shamblers.

"This is bad."

"What do you mean? We're doing fine."

"Not that. This fucking super . . . mega . . . monstrous damily."

He looks at me, cocks his head, glances out at the sea of reanimated corpses, then looks back at me. He blinks.

"If this . . . this . . . horde wanders over to Bridge City—"

"The chain-link will crumble, and they'll come pouring in."

"Right. I doubt they could break the new fortifications on the Wall, but the murderholes and men on the Wall will be going twenty-four-seven for months, and all travel will be by boat."

He rubs his chin. "This isn't good."

I peek outside. The wheels, their gears and drive arms, are lubricated with black liquid, the putrefaction of hundreds of dead. We're churning and cutting through the shamblers like a lawnmower over grass. The dead are beginning to get caught in the forward grille of the train and jammed in the gears, still waving arms. Still moaning.

It's hideous, if you think about it, that these blades of grass were once human. Why do I feel so ecstatic at their death?

The train doesn't slow, not one whit.

And it looks like the shamblers go on forever.

"You think we sound like a tornado to them?"

Klein throws back his head and laughs, a semimaniacal exultation brought on by exhaustion and stress. And, of course, the perverse joy in slaughtering the dead.

I'm watching his Adam's apple bobbing in his throat, like the pump action on a shotgun, when the train jars, shudders. I have no idea what we've hit, but we hit hard. Maybe it's the wreckage of a car, a downed telephone pole. We'll never know.

Klein flies into the boiler and gauges, and I'm thrown to the floor.

The train tilts horribly, and as the locomotive tips over, I see, through the window, upturned faces of the dead passing quickly by, then earth.

Darkness.

The burns cover most of my body. I'm thirsty. Pain permeates my awareness.

I hear moaning.

It's me.

Something is on top of my legs, crushing them. I can see a square of light above. A window of the cab is exposed to the air, and, right now, there are no zeds trying to climb in.

Another moan and I'm able to differentiate my moans from Klein's. Mine are the moans of the still living.

His are the moans of the dead.

I don't have much time.

But my pistol is still here, strapped to what's left of my leg.

I won't shamble. I won't. I'll take myself out before that can happen.

But first, I'll give Klein the release he deserves.

He was a good engineer.

7

THIS DARK EARTH

A burning light pierces the sky. It's happened before, in the few drills Wallis allowed, but there's nothing to compare it to now, with the slavers finally approaching.

Above the south ridge, in the dark of early morning, the signal flares arc hot phosphorescent blue, throwing multiple, long shadows from the men on the Wall.

Rector sounds the alarm, a steady series of bleats from a canned-air horn until the air gives out, like the end of some macabre football game, while Gus, with his one good hand, furiously yanks the cord to the alarm bell in the motor pool.

"To arms! To arms!" The call comes from many men and women along the length of the bridge.

They erupt from tents in the military quarter and farther away, from the inner span of Bridge City, all racing to preordained positions, slipping headknockers into belts and weapons into holsters. Many shrug on their motorcycle helmets and whatever piecemeal Kevlar they have left. The men from the G Unit clank and clatter in full battle rattle, Kevlar vests, M-16s, grenades, the full fucking monty.

Underneath the wavering light, the scouts, having discharged their flares, run through the open killing fields—the Dead Mile—toward the ramparts. Wallis stalks like a lion from his tent, cursing and looking as though he wants to throttle someone, a not-so-rare sight since the loss of Broadsword and the train. Gus dashes down the battlement steps to meet him.

"This is it, Lieutenant." Wallis doesn't balk at Gus's use of his former rank. "What we've been waiting for."

Wallis squints at the young man. "We knew they were coming." He turns and stomps up the steps to the battlements. "Howe, get those gates open and the Bradley into the open to maneuver. Take out the few zeds currently at the gate. What's the status at the north watch?"

Howe, a slight, studious man with glasses, barks, "No signal. All's well. A light crew accounted for." He spits a string of orders at a boy. The child nods and races off.

"What about the children? The women?"

"We're here!" This from Sarah. And at the edge of the Wall, Wendy waits, bristling with guns and headknockers.

"That information is coming, sir. They've drilled for this."

Wallis snags Rector by the arm, tugs him around.

"Get the doctor and Knock-Out. Make sure they board a boat. This is your sole duty. Understood? At gunpoint if you have to."

"Sir, yes, sir!" He salutes, even though he was never in the G Unit.

Gus stops him and says, quietly, "Make sure Barb is there too, will you, Rector?"

Rector nods once. Salutes.

When Gus turns around, Keb stands at his side, grinning.

"We here, then, Lil P? Huh?"

"Yeah." Gus pokes at Keb with his stump. An awkward pat. "We're here. Until it's over."

"It's cool, man. We gonna take care of this." Then, at the sky and clouds, he yelps, "Posted at the trap, motherfuckers!"

"Right," Gus says. He turns away and yells, "You! Smetana! Get the other snipers on the Wall ready. They'll be coming at first light."

"Or sooner." Keb looks up at the halogen lights, bright white and luminous, running from the ever-turning gennies below. "Sitting fucking ducks, P."

"Once everyone is in position and under cover, make sure their juice is cut."

Keb grins, his lip turning down in amusement. "Yassah, boss. I's do 'zactly what you say."

"*Jesus*, Keb. Do you have to pull that shit now?" Gus's one hand clenches tight and presses into the Kevlar armor on his leg.

The other man blinks and shakes his head. "No. Guess not, man."

Gus looks down at the space where his hand once was—a quizzical little pause, as if judging his body's weakness or testing his resolve—then up at the lights and then the Wall. "This might be the end of all things. I don't want to go out on a bad note with you."

Keb considers Gus, his height, his broad shoulders, his raw adolescent wildness in contrast with his gray, old man's face. He grabs Gus's stump, pulls it up between them—a reminder, a promise. "Lil P, you ain't going out here. My job is to keep you from shambling."

"And me you, Keb. And me you." Their eyes lock, man and half man, half boy, and in the moment each knows what the other is thinking. Then Keb releases the stump, smiles, and says, "I'll take care of the lights, P. Sho' 'nuff."

Gus takes the steps up to the battlements by threes, past the new brick and cement work, past heaps of sandbags, until he's at Wallis's side.

Wallis, staring into the half-light of dawn, flexes and unflexes his hands, as if in preparation for a fistfight. His hair has grayed at his ears and around the back, so that his head is laureled with white. He's dressed in fatigues and a green tee. Gus looks at him, and the way the men still look to him, and sees the rankless general before the battle.

"They'll come to the ridge but no farther. They want us, our people. They'll do what they can to convince us to surrender. Failing that, they'll kill as many of us as they need to convince the rest to give in. They've got to have at least a mega-damily on their tail. An army that size on the move will draw a lot of dead."

"We'll make them wait as long as we can. They'll be taking heat from the rear, most definitely."

"Need time to get the families and children out, down to the docks."

Gus nods, knowing all this, but it's important it's stated. There's a nervous energy to the man, understandably, and rehashing plans and repeating orders has become the litany of Bridge City and the remains of the old army unit. To bolster their courage, to keep the men focused. He can see scared expressions on the citizens of Bridge City, wide eyed and white knuckled, holding hunting rifles and shotguns, standing nervously. He looks over the fortified parapet, down to the cluster of zombies below at the gates, twenty or thirty strong.

"Yes. That's what we'll do. Keep them still, waiting at the gate."

Wallis nods. They watch as the scouts and ridge watchmen race through the Dead Mile toward the Wall.

"Howe!" Wallis's voice cuts through the clatter of weapons and armor. "Goddamn it, I said to take out the fucking zeds at the gate!"

Beneath them, a motor hums and the steel doors rattle back on greased rollers. The shamblers come through, into the murderhole, moaning. The waiting Bradley coughs and sputters and ratchets up to move after three years dormant with only maintenance checks every fortnight.

The gunfire, when it comes, sounds like rain on a galvanized barn roof, sporadic and tinny. The moaning stops, corpses drop, and the Bradley spews white smoke into the half-light, rolling over fallen shamblers into the Dead Mile. The smoke hugs the barren earth, floating east, downriver, and disappearing into the far trees.

"Wallis!" Rector trudges up the steps, breathing heavy. "They won't go. Refused and laughed when I pulled my gun."

Wallis curses under his breath.

Gus asks, "What about Ellie? The women? They at the docks?"

"Women's quarter is empty, and the north Wall secure. Barb has Ellie with Joblo and the engineers at the dock, awaiting the order to scuttle. But Knock-Out and Doc

Ingersol aren't leaving. They instructed me to alert you that they'll be here shortly, before the sun."

Gus jumps into the murderhole, among surprised men in Kevlar, and runs north.

Outside their tent, he stops, controls his breathing. Looking back the length of the bridge, past the new growth in the Garden, Gus sees the twin stars of halogens over the motor pool and murderhole, new flares arcing over the Dead Mile, the sky lightening, roseate, like fingers stretching themselves against the vault of heaven.

He stops, listening.

"No, I can't let you." She's crying, a sound so foreign to his ears that it takes him a while to identify it.

"I won't run. And this is something I can give to Gus. To Ellie. Give to everyone in Bridge City who will follow him," says Knock-Out. He coughs, and shadows shift in the small dome of tenting. "And they will follow him. This will *mean something*. For you. For Gus. It will make your position stronger."

The sound of her voice pulls at Gus. He's never heard her sound this way before, even after the Big Turnover.

"Will Wallis follow? If he . . . balks, no one else will. Does he know about this?"

"He knows. Or suspects."

"No . . . it's just a piece of metal. It doesn't mean anything."

"It *will* mean something. It already means something to the monster driving the slavers. But I will give it more meaning, *our meaning*, for *our* people. By what I do . . ."

She sobs. The tent rustles. "We can go downstream, baby, get more chemo and beat this. I can beat this."

He imagines her thumping Knock-Out's chest in desperation.

"It's won, Luce. I died in the fire. The fire where we met. And I'll never regret it."

He's kissing her now, Gus knows. There were years, years when he was ambivalent and even resentful of this brute, this bear that mated itself to his mother, supplanted his father. But now . . . now . . . his heart expands, like some unknown creature of the deep finally rising to the surface, expanding, growing warm, expanding.

"There's not much time, Luce. We've got to go. You won't take the boat?"

"No. I'll be there for Gus, at least, and the injured."

"The wounded will get treatment. From themselves or their company."

Suicide is mandatory. Take a bullet in the chest, you take yourself out or someone else will. Arm, leg, it's a drumhead court-martial. Head . . . then there's not much to worry about.

They remain quiet for a long time while Gus limits his breathing. He feels like a thief, stealing these moments from them.

"Luce, you've got to be there for Ellie. Go to the dock."

Her voice is bitter. "No. Goddamn me to hell for leaving her to Barb and Joblo, but—"

Wracking sobs, and for an instant, Gus wants to call out to her.

"It's not just about us. If you can wear that thing . . . and make that . . . I don't know . . . sacrifice—"

319

He shushes her like a baby. The sound travels in the air, loud, until a chatter of gunfire comes from the south.

"I've got to go."

Silence. The wind ruffles the fabric of the tent.

"I'll be there at the Wall, at least until—"

"The end."

The sky grows lighter, dawn coloring the dark blue of night. Gus, wiping his tears, reaches out to open the tent flap and realizes, for the thousandth time, that he's lost his hand.

"You never told me."

"What?"

"Knock-Out. You never told me how you got that absurd name."

Her tears are dry, if Gus is any judge of his mother, and she's back to business.

"It's a long story." His voice is thick and wounded. "We don't have time . . . and it's not a good one anyway."

"You can't . . . leave me with just that—"

Silence. Again. Silence so long Gus considers interrupting. "My father. He called me that after the first time he . . . knocked me unconscious."

She's breathing heavy, and he's quiet.

"I can't believe you kept it."

"A reminder. Of who he was. Of who I wasn't."

The bells ring again. Shadows in the tent join, part.

Gus clears his throat and scratches at the tent opening.

"The slavers. They're here. You've got to get to the docks. Mom. Knock-Out."

Lucy throws back the flap, steps into the dim morning light.

"We aren't going to do that."

Behind her, Knock-Out emerges.

"No, Gus," he says. "We're going to the Wall."

On his head, fashioned from blunt, black iron, is a circlet. A crown.

There's muttering and soft exclamations as Gus, Lucy, and Knock-Out approach the Wall. A smattering of applause, then silence, then a nervous laugh. One man curses.

Knock-Out walks slowly but shrugs off Gus when he tries to take his arm and steady him.

He's proud.

The cancer has withered him to a skeleton, and the chemo has denuded his skull of hair. But dressed in a white shirt and linen pants—surely a considered move, Gus thinks—he looks royal. He wears the crown well.

Slowly, the withered giant climbs the battlements above the Wall and turns to look out. He looks out not toward the Dead Mile but to the people of Bridge City, men ready to die in its defense. He holds up his arms.

"You all know me. You know me. In a moment, these slavers, this man, Konstantin . . . this man who took Gus's hand . . . this man and his followers, the slavers we've all been talking about for the last year . . . they are going to come over that ridge. Before they make war on us, they'll demand things."

His voice, at first weak, has gained power and now is rumbling, audible over the rattle and sputter of the Bradley in front of the gates, audible above the men, the gennies turning below, the hiss and pop of the halogens now fighting the dawn that has arrived.

"I'm no fool. I'm not your king, just someone who sat on councils and bounced a baby on his knee."

Wallis shakes his head. Gus says, "More than that." His voice catches in his throat. "So much more than that."

Knock-Out touches his shoulders but keeps his gaze fixed on the people at the Wall.

Gus glances at Wallis standing near, but not next to, Knock-Out. His face is tense, but no more than earlier.

In the distance, a sporadic chatter of rifles echoes over the Dead Mile. Then dies. There's a murmur from the gathered men.

Knock-Out says loud, so it carries, "They want us. This bridge. They don't want to kill us. They want to enslave us! How is that different from being one of them?" He jabs a finger down at the remaining shamblers at the gate. "He'll keep you alive, keep you breathing, but you'll be no better than those walkers. The dead! Slaves to hunger."

He paused and coughed hard into his sleeve. For a moment it seemed he'd topple over, the coughs wracked his body so violently, but with a great show of will, he stopped, and straightened, setting his shoulders and grinding his teeth. "Look, look there, at Wendy. You all know her. Her story. Look at her face and see what kind of *true* beasts those people are!"

All eyes go to the short, stout woman in mismatched men's garb with a .30-06 clutched in her hands. She looks embarrassed.

"They're coming, and they'll ask for the prince. The one he tortured before." He points a long thin arm directly at Gus's chest. "I plan to give them a king!"

The silence that follows is broken by a cough. Wallis.

He walks over to Knock-Out and smiles sadly. Then he kneels, bowing his head.

Knock-Out blushes and looks uncomfortable.

The men laugh, and Keb yells, "Long live the king, motherfuckers!"

Lucy sobs.

Knock-Out tugs at Wallis's arms. "Get up, man. No need for that."

Someone takes up the chant. "Long live the king!"

Others follow, pumping their fists.

"Long live the king!"

Beyond the Wall, past the Dead Mile, the black, thick silhouettes of war machines top the ridge.

It's full light now. A Humvee with a white banner ruffling from its passenger side rumbles over the ridge, down the hill, and across the Dead Mile. It approaches the Wall, keeping its distance from the waiting Bradley.

It stops equidistant from the slavers and the people of Bridge City. Two men get out, keeping the body of the vehicle between them and the Bridge's sharpshooters.

Wallis barks from his place on the Wall, "Smetana!"

Smetana and his men, crouching behind sandbags, take aim with deer rifles.

There's a squelch, and then one of the intruding men holds up a megaphone.

"Good morning. I am Captain Konstantin." The voice is calm, reasonable. "Please send out the little prince so that we might discuss your surrender."

The megaphone squelches again, an eerie sound that echoes off Bridge City and back across the expanse to where the man stands.

"You don't know it yet, but your city is already destroyed! Do not entertain ideas of fighting back. Look behind me."

Hundreds of men top the ridge, far beyond rifle range. They scurry about in clusters of three or four, setting up equipment.

There's another chatter of gunfire, longer this time.

Wallis yells, "They're taking heat from the zeds on their flank! Do not fire! Do not fire!"

The clusters of men on the ridge stop movement. Another burst of gunfire and then silence.

The man behind the Humvee, Konstantin, lifts the megaphone. "You have no hope of resistance. Send out the prince so that we might negotiate surrender. And just so you know we aren't playing, here's a little object lesson."

The second man pulls the flag from the Humvee and waves it in the air, and a corresponding puff of white shows from one of the groups of men on the ridge.

There comes a whistling in the air and then, thirty yards to the east of the Wall, an explosion.

Wallis blisters the air with curses. "Mortars."

The flag is replaced. The voice returns.

"You have ten minutes."

Knock-Out turns and descends from the Wall. At the bottom, Lucy clutches him, and they kiss. He disengages, turns, and looks up at Gus standing near Wallis on the Wall.

"Gus. I'm sorry you weren't my son. I tried to love you like you were. Lead these people."

He sighs and looks out at the men awaiting orders. "You could do worse than have him as a king." He looks at the gateman. "Open the doors."

The winch sounds, the doors roll back, and Knock-Out, dressed in white and wearing a crown, walks away from Bridge City, from the Wall, and into the Dead Mile.

All eyes follow him trudging up the slope, through the denuded land, small puffs of dust exploding from his footfalls and floating away.

He walks around the Humvee and is hidden from view.

Firearms sound again, this time for minutes at a time.

Howe looks over his glasses at Wallis. "They're going through shitloads of ammunition for their rearguard, sir."

Rector spits. "Good, the bastards."

"Idiots. Should've known they'd have a horde on their ass."

Gus frowns. "I don't think so. When Keb, Jazz, and I took it to them, we had to roll slow, so slow it was almost painful, in order to deliver the . . . payload. They didn't march up here. They've got fuel. All the military vehicles they could want. They could move fast. Fast enough to leave behind shamblers . . ."

"Maybe they're drawing them locally," Howe offers.

"Right," Rector says, his voice sarcastic. "And all the time I've spent on the Wall these last few years has been for nothing."

They fall silent, each in his own thoughts.

The skies darken with low, oppressive clouds tinged yellow. It is early October, a prelude to nuclear winter. The temperature drops, and men shift in their boots and rub their arms.

Hours pass, and the gunfire beyond the ridge grows almost constant.

It is afternoon when Knock-Out emerges from behind the Humvee, no longer wearing the crown.

The megaphone squelches again, and Konstantin says, "Sorry for the delay. We may now resume your surrender."

Crouching at a sandbag on top of the Wall, Lucy gasps, a little exclamation of joy, as Knock-Out begins to walk back to Bridge City.

Konstantin lowers the megaphone, extends his arm, and shoots Knock-Out in the back. He takes a long time to fall forward into the dust. They leave him where he lies.

The pistol's report reaches the Wall long after Knock-Out goes down.

"No!" Lucy screams and runs to the gates.

Wallis wheels. "Take him!"

Smetana gives the signal, and his men fire.

It's too late.

* * *

When the voice returns, it has an excited timbre. From the Wall, snipers search the Humvee for Konstantin's crowned head, looking for a shot. But he remains hidden.

"Once again, sorry for the delay." A chuckle. "Now, if you will all just look to the west, you'll see two very strong reasons for you to drop your weapons, put your hands on your heads, and exit your city."

All eyes turn west, to the river. Two barges, sitting low in the water from their cargo—one holds gravel, one shipping containers—float sideways down the river, toward Bridge City.

"The bridge might stand, but not for long." He laughs, a dry, humorless sound. "This is what we've been waiting on. Courtesy of your little prince and his big ideas for how to destroy things."

Gunfire sounds on the horizon, over the ridge. An armored Jeep races down the hill, brakes dramatically, and slews to a stop near the Humvee. A man seems to shout frantically as he points back over the ridge.

"If you get a clear shot of that motherfucker, take it," Wallis says in a harsh voice to Smetana. His shoulders are tight and there's a fury upon him that none in Bridge City had ever seen.

Gus leans in close to Smetana. "Keep Knock-Out down. Don't let him rise. Don't let him come back to the Wall as one of those."

His mother, listening, gasps and says, "No!" but then stands stock still, eyes streaming as Smetana sights, holds his

327

breath, and then squeezes his trigger. The sound of the shot echoes across the Dead Mile. Knock-Out's body twitches once with the impact and goes still once again.

"It's done." His voice hitches, and he bows his head before resighting his rifle.

Lucy wails, a high-pitched keening. Gus grabs binoculars from Howe and looks at the Humvee.

Konstantin's head bobs into view and then out again. He's wearing the iron crown.

Smetana and his men are too slow. The rifle fire riddles the vehicle but nothing more.

Gus turns to Wallis. "Something is wrong. Listen."

The gunfire beyond the ridge has grown wild, accompanied by the booms of grenades.

Wallis looks from the barges, caroming downriver, to the Dead Mile.

"This isn't good, Gus."

Then, over the far ridge, down the slope, come running men.

Konstantin yells into the megaphone. "Hold your positions! No! Hold your positions!"

The men ignore him. A Bradley trundles into view with men riding on its back, firing to the south, away from the Wall. Humvees and Jeeps roll over the hill. A running battle.

"Hold your positions!" Konstantin, his voice once calm and emotionless, sounds desperate now.

Hundreds of men run down the slope, some firing behind them, some firing at the Wall. Behind them, the ridgeline ripples and darkens, as if discolored by a spreading oil spill.

The dead. Thousands of them. Tens of thousands.

Bullets rip into sandbags and brick and the steel plates of the Wall gates.

Wallis falls, grasping his leg. Rector's head blossoms with gore, and he topples. One of Smetana's snipers groans, then screams.

"Open fire!" Gus bellows, taking cover behind a parapet.

From the Dead Mile, Konstantin screams in rage into the megaphone. "Hold your positions!"

Then there's a final squelch. Konstantin steps from behind the Humvee, hoisting a long black tube.

"RPG!" Howe's voice pitches toward the inaudible.

"Cover!"

Gus throws himself into the murderhole as the Wall explodes.

There's smoke pouring from the gates and fire and screaming, and as Gus levers himself up, he sees his mother, ever the doctor, bending over a man of the Wall, touching his head and coming away with blood. He has time to yell, "Mom! Behind you!" as a zed rises from rubble, blood caking its face. It's indistinct from all the other shamblers, the thousands coming down the hill, the ones among them. Slavers pour through the breach in the Wall, driving shackled men before them—the expendables, the slave shields—who are yelling "Don't fire! Don't fire!" but the desperate men and women of Bridge City are beyond caring and they fire wildly, indiscriminately at slave and slaver alike, only to meet the remaining defending force. And on their heels, more ravenous dead.

The zombie lurches at Lucy, and she twists, digging at her waist for the headknocker that isn't there.

Gus is up and running, his hatchet out in his one good hand, swinging at the zed coming for Lucy, when the bridge shudders once, shifts, and then stays still. The air fills with the sound of grinding metal, with gunfire and screams and the moans of revenants.

Bullets whistle by, and in the space where the Wall gate used to be, living, wild-eyed men pour in.

Gus, leaping, swipes the shambler across the temple, embedding the hatchet deep in its skull. He lets the headknocker fall with the body.

Keb appears from the motor pool holding an M-16 and opens fire on the men rushing into the gap. They twist and die undramatically.

Gus lifts his mother. "The zip-line. Now. We've got to join Joblo. Ellie. Before these go revenant."

At the sound of her daughter's name, Lucy blinks as if coming awake.

Keb motions them to run.

But Gus stops and yells, "Go. I'll catch up. I have to find Wallis."

Lucy pauses halfway to Keb.

"Come on, Doc. Ain't no time to waste."

"I'll be right there." Gus's voice is tight.

Gunfire sounds from outside what's left of the Wall. Through the opening, the Dead Mile turns black. With the army no longer focused on holding them back, the revenants have arrived.

Lucy chokes out a garbled sound, one of agony, and then Keb has her arm, dragging her away.

A shambler rises, lopsided and missing an arm, and Gus kicks out, knocking it backward. He picks up a cinder block and smashes it on the zombie's skull.

He moves. The gate fills with dead.

He finds Wallis half buried in rubble. Clearing the debris, he checks Wallis's pulse. Thready. Blood pumps sluggishly from the wound in Wallis's thigh.

Gus lifts Wallis onto his back and staggers away, hoping the old soldier doesn't die and turn revenant while he's carrying him.

Gus reaches the elevator when the second barge hits the bridge. The impact feels and sounds like the tolling of a gigantic bell.

The elevator batteries are dead.

The gunfire dies. Looking over the bridge wall, he sees his mother and Keb on the dock, looking up. When they see him, they wave frantically.

Wallis groans.

"You're not gonna make it with me. The bridge is crumbling."

"I can get you to the zip-line. We'll get you down from there."

The bridge shifts underneath them, and Gus puts his hand out to steady himself.

"No. You only have one hand." Wallis grins, and blood flecks his lips. "And look." He points down the length of the bridge. Beyond, in the garden, are the living dead shambling toward them. Hundreds. Moaning.

"Jump, boy. I can take care of myself." He pulls his pistol, puts it under his chin.

The bridge shifts.

"Go."

Gus touches the older man's cheek once in farewell and goes to the elevator platform. He stands, looking out over the river, gray in the half-light of dusk, snaking away from the devastation here, the remains of Bridge City.

Joblo, the women, and the engineers gesture wildly at Gus from the boats.

He thinks of Frazier.

The bridge tilts and shifts under him, and he leaps.

He doesn't hear the shot before the river rushes up to meet him.

Keb, rocking unsteadily in a johnboat, fishes Gus from the water a half mile before the dam.

Near them, other boats, carrying twenty-odd survivors, push against the current. Lucy weeps from the bow, and Joblo steers from the rear, one white-knuckled hand on the outboard's handle.

"Thought you were fish food there for a second, Lil P."

Gus coughs and lies on the boat's hull and stares at the sky, the indifferent heavens just beginning to prick with stars. Barb holds Ellie and looks at him, wild-eyed. The baby gurgles.

"That's a good baby," he says.

Barb inhales, sobbing.

"We'll make for the north cache. There's flares there, and maybe Dap's still in the area." Joblo, always practical.

They gain the north shore two miles south of the ruins of Tulaville and Bridge City and hike north, into the night.

Twin halogen lights from Bridge City pierce the dark, reflecting off the shimmering waters and the rows of chain-link. The workshop and distillery burn, casting yellow light against the trestles of the bridge.

"I thought I asked you to make sure the lights were out, Keb."

"Yeah. You did, P. But thangs got hairy. *Hairy.*"

From the overpass, they look out over the dark remaining roofs of Tulaville and the two bright sparks of halogen lights still standing, miraculously, on the south shore.

A moan sounds not far from them. A onesy.

Then there's rumbling, and the screams of twisting metal carry across the distance.

"This mean you our king now, Lil P?"

Gus doesn't answer. Barb puts her arm around his waist.

"That's nonsense." Her voice is terse, protective.

Hearing this, Lucy says from the front of the procession of hikers, "William Augustus Ingersol, do you swear to protect us, to never rest until mankind can hold its head high once more, to hold back the dark and the dead? To serve all of us here faithfully, until death?"

"Mom . . . I don't think that this is—"

She comes toward him, her face furious. She points to the bridge. "All those people—they died for this!"

She's holding Ellie tight to her chest. Her intensity is frightful.

"Do you swear?"

He stays silent for a long while, until the moan comes again, closer. Barb stays frozen, watching Lucy.

"Yes."

"Swear."

"I swear."

She wheels.

"Joblo, Keb. All of you. Do you swear to obey and protect Gus until he proves unable or unwilling to fulfill his duties?"

There's a general murmur of assent.

She screams the words. *"Do you swear?"*

Ellie wakes, squalling.

Joblo says, "I swear." Then Keb follows. Barb says nothing.

The rumbling and screaming of metal become deafening, rolling across the open space of Tulaville like thunder.

"Then, Gus, it's time for you to lead."

She turns and walks toward the rear, where Sunseri gathers men to brain the moaner.

"So, this mean you king now?" Keb pulls an old cigar from a wrapper, pops it into his mouth.

Gus shakes his head. "No. I'm just me, Keb. I'd swear those things anyway."

Keb pats him on the shoulder. Opens his mouth as if to say something and then goes quiet. In the dark, a zed moans again, a soft, urgent sound.

Then the thunder rolls across the ruins of Tulaville, across the river valley, cacophonous and raw. The bridge, at last, collapses into the black waters below, taking thousands of undead with it.

The lights on the bridge tilt, and then fall, and the earth goes dark.

Acknowledgments

Many thanks to my wife and children for understanding how important this whole writing thing is to me, for not questioning too closely my fascination with dead things, and for allowing me to take some nights and weekends to commit these strange little stories to paper.

As always, thanks to my father for (1) terrifying me with stories of nuclear annihilation when I was just a boy, and (2) allowing me to watch whatever I wanted to on television, including a midnight viewing of *Night of the Living Dead* back in 1980, and (3) buying me as many books as I wanted. In many ways, this book is the culmination of his parenting style.

Eternal thanks to my mother for living up to her name, Mary Sue.

I'd like to acknowledge my sister, Lisa Jacobs Moriconi, for her support and venison chili on those cold writing days out at Rob-Bell. She's very excited that I'm a published novelist now (though I think she's having a tough time coming to grips with the idea that my novels don't feature *her* as the star).

When I began writing *This Dark Earth,* the glut of zombie books currently on the market wasn't so prevalent. I'm grateful to my agent, Stacia Decker, for recognizing the merits of *This Dark Earth* beyond simply being another zombie novel. The same goes for Jen Heddle, who initially acquired *This Dark Earth.*

ACKNOWLEDGMENTS

I am especially grateful to fate for replacing Jen with an editor *nonpareil*. Enter Adam Wilson. Even though I've been published before, the path to publication sure as hell wasn't like *this*. Adam has given this book a second life (or third, depending on how you look at it). His fine eye and sure editorial hand have made the process of bringing *This Dark Earth* to print gratifying and fun and the end product something of which I'm very proud.

Many thanks go to Dr. Elizabeth Nestrud for her guidance and knowledge relating to the life of a pathologist and the medical details of cancer diagnosis. Any and all mistakes, boneheaded errors, are mine and mine alone.

I owe a huge debt of gratitude to my good friend Chris Cranford for continued and unwavering support, including donating a whole day to help me with a greenscreen shoot for the *This Dark Earth* book trailer. Also, *muchas gracias* to Duke Boyne and Allen Williams for donning their motorcycle gear in high summer temperatures and smacking around pillows—in lieu of zombie heads—with baseball bats.

Thanks to Knock-Out (real name unknown), the thick-forearmed handyman who used to repair our lakehouse when I was a boy. Rest in peace, KO.

A big ol' *danke schoen* goes to John Rector for actually reading this one and, on its strength, introducing me to my agent.

Huge ups to Lincoln Crisler for peeking at the sections regarding the G Unit and ensuring army verisimilitude.

I'm lucky to count Steve Weddle, Mark Devery, Erik Smetana, Kevin Wallis, John Miller, Joe Howe, Kate Horsely, and Mark Hickerson among my prereaders.

ACKNOWLEDGMENTS

Gratitude to Tom Waits for continued inspiration, including the title of this book.

Additional thanks go to Dan O'Shea, Weston Ochse, Lewis Dowell, Brian and Amanda Bailey, Joelle Charbonneau, Kent Gowran, Andrew Leonard, Stephen Blackmoore, Brian Keene, Elizabeth A. White, Ed Kurtz, S. G. Browne, Sabrina Ogden, Frank Bill, Owen Laukkenen, Matthew Funk, Tom Picirilli, Peter Farris, Bryan Smith, Dr. Terrell Tebbetts, and all my friends, both in real life and from the electric haze of the Internets.

And for my fans and readers, a big thank you. As long as you keep reading, I'll keep writing.

About the Author

John Hornor Jacobs is the author of *Southern Gods*, short-listed for the Bram Stoker Award for First Novel, and the forthcoming Incarcerado young adult trilogy. He lives with his family in Arkansas, where he is also a musician and graphic artist. Visit him at www.johnhornorjacobs.com.